TAKE ME FURTHERMORE

VENESSA KNIZLEY

WALK WITH ME SAGA BOOK IV

Selah Press PUBLISHING

Take Me Furthemore
By Venessa Knizley

Managing Editor: Loral Robben Pepoon, Selah Press
Prepared for Publication by: Kayla Fioravanti, Selah Press
Cover Design: Christine Dupre
Family Tree Illustration: Shweta Mahajan
Proverbs 37:7 Art: Alisa Taylor, Etsy.com/shop/AlisaTaylorDesign

Printed in the United States of America, Published by Selah Press, LLC
Copyright © 2020 Venessa Knizley

ISBN 978-1-7343016-1-8 Selah Press LLC

Scripture taken from the NEW AMERICAN STANDARD BIBLE®, Copyright© 1960, 1962, 1963, 1968, 1971, 1972, 1973, 1975, 1977, 1995 by The Lockman Foundation. Used by permission.

The definitions listed on the bottom of relevant pages and in the back of the book were compiled by the author from many online sources.

Dedication

To my children. I love you more.

Rest IN THE Lord
& Wait patiently FOR HIM
DO NOT FRET
because OF HIM WHO prospers IN HIS way;
BECAUSE OF A MAN WHO
carries OUT Wicked schemes
psalm 37:7

©Alisa Taylor 2020

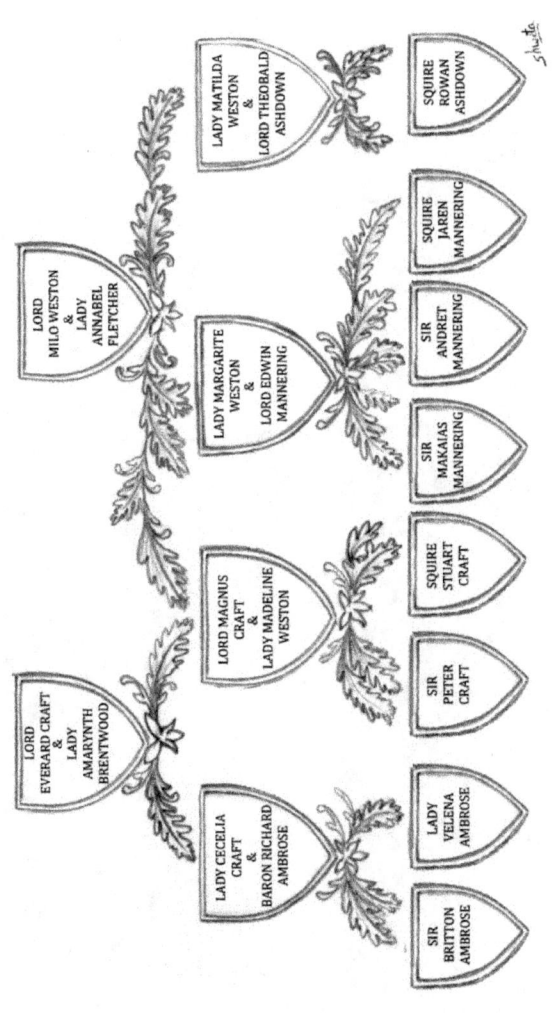

prologue

September 1351

Tristan was almost there, and he could feel the churning of an anxious heart deep in his gut. Would Sir Richard be angry he was back? Would his arrival cause more upheaval than good? *Surely not,* he concluded and shook his head. She was marrying Stuart—there could be no greater upheaval than that.

Back aching, he pulled Augustine up alongside the trail. There was a stream just ahead, and needing a good stretch, he dismounted to lead the horse the rest of the way. Augustine flicked his mane back and forth, as the reins were left to dangle about his neck. He drank greedily while his master moved upstream to satisfy his own thirst. Tristan finished with an icy splash of water to his face and then fell back upon his rear, relaxed by the burble of the stream. Unexpectedly, his thoughts turned to his mother. He didn't think of her as often as one might suppose a loving son would—the pain of her loss still something far too tender to visit with as heavy of footsteps as he came with. But every now and again, he allowed himself a tip toe into that place in his mind that he'd hallowed out as sacred. He'd draw near to her there. He'd talk with her—share his thoughts, his fears.

"I miss you," he spoke aloud, feeling a breeze curl in and around his unkempt hair—hair his mother would attempt to brush through with her fingers when he was small. But always she would laugh and give up, grabbing a tuft into her fist to complain about how wild and free it grew. He grabbed a handful of it now before pillowing his arms behind his head as he went onto his back.

"I miss Anne and Alice...and Mary." He gulped, feeling a deep ache for each of his sisters. "Velena has been the closest thing to family I've had since..." His voice turned inward. *Shall I bring her closer still? I love her, Mother, yet...I'm torn because I know in my heart there has to be a love far deeper than what exists between us now. And there is greater love welled up inside of me—I feel it—but I don't know how to reach it. Is time the bucket that draws it up? Or what if it never does?*

Drawing a ragged breath, he gave in to a sudden bout of coughing that bounced his chest up and down in a worrisome manner. Waiting for it to pass, he threw his arm across his forehead, fatigued. Despite the jolt back to reality, he stubbornly lingered at his mother's side, recalling, now, her ardent desire for him to choose his own wife someday—to marry for love. He'd been naught but a child at the time she'd told him, and he was having trouble remembering if there'd been any advice about how he should do that? His parents had loved each other, but he'd never thought to ask if it had started out that way.

Lingering in memories of his childhood, his thoughts drifted to Velena and the first time they'd met. Hocktide—just after a cock fight. She'd approached him with a boy—a boy he now assumed to have been Stuart. A sudden shudder of repulsion passed through him, and he wondered if it was right that he should so despise even the twelve-year-old version of the man. Convicted by the depth of his bitterness, he worked to blot Stuart's image out of his thinking until all that remained was the remembrance of the pretty little girl stopping to congratulate him on his win.

Velena had been on her way to finding her brother, who she said carried a stash of dried fruit and nuts in his pocket she was keen on obtaining. Kind to a fault, she appeared all too happy to share in the bounty and bid him come along and join them. But he was by nature shy around those of the feminine persuasion, and shyer still realizing she expected him to make an answer with actual words.

Tristan opened his eyes to the sky and smiled, the corners of his mouth being the only thing to reflect a twinge of his remorse. If he had it all to do over again, he would have said *yes*. He would have accepted her offer with as much enthusiasm as she'd expect from him today. Of course, then, he'd told her no—even after the cheerful way she'd asked him to walk with her... His breathing stilled.

Brow furrowed, he sat up. It couldn't be—could it? And yet he was sure it was. *Walk with me...* Had she said it for *real?* He was quite sure now but was still having trouble believing it. All this time...all those silly dreams he could never quite accept or dare to interpret—they belonged to a memory. An *actual* memory. His first memory of her.

Always in his dreams, he feared taking her hand, afraid she would lead him in the wrong direction...into a mistaken future. But he could see now that all his apprehension—all his fears—they but stemmed from the memory of a little boy who was simply too embarrassed to give reply when spoken to. It was a forgotten memory that had wheedled its way back into his dreams and had obliged him to walk away from her ever since—at least where romance was concerned.

He stood to his feet in wonder. He didn't have to be afraid anymore. All this time he'd spent searching out the will of the Lord, he'd been heeding the voice of his childhood instead. *Remarkable.* In and of itself, this revelation didn't bubble up any immediate feelings of a deeper or more tangible love for Velena, but it did shake free what had become a most troublesome burden, allowing him to truly believe that love *could* grow—with her as much as with anyone else.

With a much-lightened heart, he returned to Augustine, swinging back into the saddle. If God had already granted Velena deliverance from Stuart by the time he arrived, and she was no longer in need of rescuing, he could still see himself more than content to carry on as friends—with or without the miles of trail between them—though better without. *If,* on the other hand, she still needed him—for once— he could see himself taking her hand without fear. Thus decided, his lips pressed into a determined line, and he spurred Augustine forward.

1

confession

Craft Hall, August 1351

The dark was creeping in, much like his mood. Flames from the great hall's fireplace crackled and popped as it licked hungrily at logs now charred and hissing molten orange from every nook and cranny. The evening was almost spent, and soon all would be to bed. All, except Stuart, who'd lie awake, painstakingly aware of the fact that he now teetered along the edge of a knife.

It'd been three days since Daisy told him of the child. *His* child. He ran a hand over the stubble of his chin and felt the bite of two days' growth. How had it come to this?

Unable to keep focused, his attention parted from the game of chess he was playing with his father to the manor folk as they began trickling indoors after a long day's work. They chatted quietly amongst themselves and rolled out their mats. There was a yawn, a smile…an occasional laugh weighed down by nothing more than the next day's list of to-dos. Their life was disgustingly simple, yet for the first time in his life, Stuart envied them. His days had become a game of strategy, and he was growing weary of playing. One wrong move and…

"When are you going to tell me what's gnawing at you?" Lord Magnus drawled into his tankard. Taking a draught, he wiped his mouth with the back of his sleeve.

Stuart's eyes returned to the game, firelight hitting the rook as he held it aloft, casting a lengthy shadow across the floor. With a light tap, he set down the ivory piece and reached off to the side of the board for his own drink. He gripped the handle and melted into the back of his chair—or so he wished to, as paternal resentments rose to the surface. He'd sooner drink than answer, but the dwindling remains in his tankard forced him to do otherwise. He swirled the last bit of liquid and wished for something stronger than mead. "I'm just tired," he finally answered

Lord Magnus slid his pawn forward. "You never were a good liar."

Stuart drew upon his remaining bishop. "And if I told you I've improved?"

Magnus smiled. *Smug.* "Not with me you haven't." He dropped his knight into position. "Check."

Stuart removed his king from danger. "Let's say it's personal and leave it at that."

"*That*...was poor move," Magnus said, putting his son back in check.

Stuart leveled his gaze at his father.

"If I didn't know any better," Magnus continued, "I'd say you were looking to lose?"

Stuart bobbed his head, in a dark humor. "Perhaps I *would* do better to just get it over with."

Magnus hunched forward, voice low. "How can I help if I don't know what you're hiding?"

Stuart snatched up his king, the movement abrupt, toppling over several pieces as he pushed back his chair in his urgency to move. He planted himself, legs apart, before the oversized fireplace, grimacing at the intensity of heat that tightened his face and caused his clothing to warm until it seemed they would burn him. "There's nothing you can do," he said, squeezing his hand around the ivory king. He released a weary breath and balanced the piece atop the stone mantel above his head and stepped back, feeling no more significant than the object he left to sit mere feet above its own absolution.

No. That was wrong. Absolution was no threat to the soulless carvings of men. It was reserved for the soul-filled man. Men, like himself, who had a soul, despite what Daisy might say to the contrary. Would a man without a soul whither day by day as he did—he, whose sin was ever before him. Surely not, and thus it was a reminder to him now, as always, that his soul was in very real danger of devastation—not of earthly flames, but eternal ones.

Lord Magnus stared at his son's back until it became clear he would not turn around. With a shout that startled the castle folk to attention, he ordered everyone out. He shoved back his chair and went about the room delivering swift-booted kicks to those who'd not roused from their mats quickly enough.

Stuart crossed his arms. "Really, Father, we could have just excused ourselves to your solar."

"Excuse *myself?* I am the lord of this manor! If I want to talk here, then we'll talk here. Now, speak!" he demanded, sinking back into his seat. "What sort of mess are you in? And what will I have to do to get you out of it?"

What began as a sigh of annoyance became an unwelcome shudder that sent Stuart trembling to his core. He didn't want to talk to his father. He didn't want to admit that his life was one move away from checkmate. He cursed the hour Daisy disclosed to him her secret, leaving him with thoughts too deep to dive into—too turbulent to tred.

Secrets were better kept to oneself—and he could not see what gain would come of a confession. Yet…if he were to confess to anyone, his father would be the most likely choice. Hot tempered—yes. Quick to judge and unlikely to forgive—yes. But he was also proud and would never allow a son of *his* to be besmirched. He would take Stuart's sins to the grave before letting them damage his own reputation.

Stuart returned to his chair, steeling his nerves and ignoring the lesser voices that still warned him to reconsider. He breathed in and began. "I've committed a certain…*indiscretion.*"

"What sort of indiscretion?"

"One that involves a woman."

"What woman?"

Stuart lowered his voice. "Daisy." He waited but received only a blank look. "Velena's lady's maid. Hang it all, Father, don't you pay attention to anything?"

Magnus blinked, unsure if his son was serious. He began to chortle, low at first, then deep and throaty as Stuart looked on in confusion. "Is that all? A tryst?" He waved the confession aside. "I thought you were going to tell me you killed a man."

Stuart rubbed at his temple, irked that his father would think the worst of him. "No, Father, I didn't kill anyone."

"Well then, this is easily dismissed. Although," and he chuckled again, "it may take some time for you to return to your cousin's good graces should she become wise to it."

"Time?" He leaned his head back. "She'd never forgive me."

"Come now, you can hardly be held responsible for the seductive wiles of a poorly chosen lady's maid."

Stuart's mind drifted back to his ill-fated encounter with Daisy at Wineford Castle and ducked his head. "It wasn't *she* who approached me."

"Unimportant," Lord Magnus said, leaning back to rest his hands over his stomach. "It's what you'll say should anything surface." Again, he laughed, brushing off the severity of the sin to ramble on about the immoral and inconstant character of womankind.

Stuart interrupted. "If word of this comes to light, it will be that I...that I..."

"You what?"

"That I imposed myself on *her*," he said, taken aback by the genuine prick of guilt he felt upon admitting this out loud.

"Is she that handsome of a woman? I'll have to take better notice of her, eh?" he said, issuing one vulgarity after another, serving only to heighten Stuart's distaste for furthering their discussion.

"Father, stop it!"

"Sooo, you *imposed* on her first," he said, disregarding the greater meaning of the word. "It's a woman's way to say no when she means yes."

Stuart clenched his teeth. "It was more than that."

"What does it matter? No one is going to believe the word of a hired woman over a nobleman. Say she flaunted herself at you. It's easily done."

Stuart raised from his chair. "You're not listening to me!"

Lord Magnus stood as well. "I've heard every word. What else is there? Does Richard already know? Because if he thinks he can use this as an excuse to break the contract than—"

"Father—I forced her!"

Magnus froze, eyes wide, mouth agape.

Stuart collapsed back into his chair, the fight gone out of him. "I was drunk...and I forced her."

Clearing his throat, lord Magnus lowered himself, his movements stilted as his forearms came to rest atop his knees. "Were there any witnesses to this?"

Alert to the change, Stuart sat up. "No."

"Who else knows about it?"

"No one who would say anything—"

"Who else?"

"Jaren."

Magnus nodded but, like Stuart, dismissed this as inconsequential. "And this...woman? She's told no one?"

"I don't...I don't think so."

"Know so. Be sure."

Stuart nodded.

"I'm serious, Stuart. If you're to win at this game, we'll need to know all the players." He settled into a more comfortable position. "Now, when did this happen?"

"At Wineford Castle, the day before we—"

"Wineford?" His eyebrows rose. "That long? You *are* getting better at hiding things. And if that be so, what more aren't you telling me? Because the brooding face I've seen has only been around for days...not weeks. Better to tell me all of it."

Stuart bent over his knees, rubbing his hands back and forth over the top of his head as if the motion would help loosen his tongue. "Three days ago, I had a confrontation with Daisy at Landerhill. She told me..." He swallowed. "She told me she's...with child." His confession was met with silence. Growing anxious, Stuart spit out, "I offered her compensation. She'll be gone after the wedding."

"A good waste of money when she can't prove it's yours."

"She wouldn't have to. If she tells Velena—it's over. Her loyalties run deep...for those she loves."

"Her loyalty should be to you! You've been in love with that girl since before she could say your name."

Stuart's pulse quickened. "If you knew I loved her...why did you give her to Peter?" He wanted to mask his vulnerability but couldn't keep the pain from his voice.

"Whoever controls Velena, controls Richard. Peter would have done that for me. You, on the other hand, would have been wrapped around her little finger. Besides, Peter would have overlooked a tryst if you'd still wanted her."

Stuart's face contorted in disgust. His brother might have shared her with him, but he most certainly wouldn't have done the same. "Velena never would have accepted it. She's not like that."

Magnus smirked. "All women are like that," he said, relaxing his shoulders.

"Mother wasn't."

"I kept a close eye on what belonged to me. You'd do well to do the same. But as far as this maid business goes, I don't think you'll have to worry. No witness means no trial. And if she does tell anyone, the conception of a child is in your favor."

"I don't see how."

The corners of Magnus' beard lifted into a catlike grin. "Everyone knows a woman can't conceive unless she's enjoyed the encounter—in which case—it's not rape."

Stuart had never heard of anything so ludicrous. Even in his state of drunkenness, he'd been aware of how frightened Daisy had been. How he'd had to muffle her cries of pain… He swallowed as a wave of nausea took hold of him, surprised by his own feelings of revulsion as he relived the moment.

"And in either case," his father went on, "with or without a child, it's still your word against hers."

"What if Uncle Richard hears of it?"

"Doesn't matter. And for that, you can thank me for tying up any loose ends. Why do you think I wanted to partner with him for this sheep venture in the first place?"

Stuart stared.

"Surety. And now it's going to pay off. His pens aren't built yet. The sheep are on my land, which means they're under my control. If he attempts to cross me, I'll keep all profits in lieu of his breaking the contract. He'll not risk losing money over the word of a wench."

"You partnered with Uncle Richard in expectation of my future *blunders*?" He shook his head, resentment touching his voice. "Glad to know I'm in such good standing with you."

"Don't play the martyr. It's no secret Richard dislikes me," he said and laughed as if this amused him. "It was only a matter of time before one of us offended him. Simple as that."

Stuart turned his head towards the flames, glowing embers reminding him of just what kind of hell he'd gotten himself into. Standing, he felt less at peace now than before he'd confessed. Ready to excuse himself, he paused. "What about the child?"

"What about it?"

"It's livelihood. What do I…" his mouth went dry, "What of reparations? I told Daisy I'd—"

"Leave her to God."

"She won't survive on nothing."

"That *is* true," came his cool reply.

"If she dies, the child dies."

"Velena will give you legitimate heirs."

"It's still *my* child."

"It's Satan's child, born of her sin."

Her sin?

His father joined him by the hearth, but it was clear the

conversation was over, which was fine with Stuart because he didn't want to hear any more. It's not as if he wanted to lay claim to the child. Yet, the thought of it dying continued to be a disturbing one.

He glanced at his father's profile. Firelight pulsed in haphazard succession across calloused features, bathing him in an unearthly kind of glow that brought a chill to Stuart's body despite its warmth. A faint wrinkling of the skin about his father's eyes suggested a smile behind his whiskers and an inward delight at a thing yet to be shared.

"Thrilling…wasn't it?"

"What?"

"The struggle." Magnus' voice became husky. "There's nothing quite like bending a woman's will to your own."

Stuart blinked at the passive confession, allowing it to penetrate his thinking as far back as his childhood. Even in his page-hood years, at the impressionable age of seven, he could recall being well-aware of his father's philandering—never questioning it—even adopting the practice as his own the night he turned fourteen when his father entered his solar with a woman, paid and ready to make him into a man. But had he ever an inkling of his father taking a woman by force? He picked through his bank of memories only to find himself tripping over what might have been more obvious had he been old enough to understand. Muffled cries behind closed doors. Cowering eyes of the maids who attended him. Looks of disgust from his mother whenever she thought no one was looking.

"She didn't struggle," Stuart rasped.

"A pity."

Stuart felt bile rising high in his throat. He might not think much of Daisy as a woman, but he wasn't so reticent as to deny his behavior towards her had been obscene—not anymore. He wanted to blame her for being wanton. To blame Bowan for walking away—to blame Velena for rejecting him, the witch for tempting him, the bottle for offering up its strong drink. He could go on and on, but the blame for it all had become crystal clear, revealing him to be everything Daisy thought him to be and more. He *was* his father's son.

Stuart leaned his forearms against the mantel, hands clenched into fists beneath his forehead. Until now, he would have said it was his deceased brother, Peter, who'd been the one to exemplify their father in all mannerism and behavior. And this, he never envied, because deep down, he'd always despised his father. Now, he despised himself.

"What's the matter now?" his father reprimanded, the mere tone of his voice adding a dose of salt to his son's wounds. "If this is about the child, I beg you to think rationally. A gift of money would only be an admission of guilt. Anyone witnessing that little exchange, and it would be over. Your job, now, is to find out who else knows."

"I told you—"

"Be sure! I'll handle the rest…should there be a need."

Magnus' words were flat, but Stuart knew his mind was at work, and his heart sunk. Telling his father had been a mistake.

2

the game

Seated on a stump outside the barracks, Rowan ran a sharpening stone down the steel blade of his rondel dagger, the drag creating a *shhhinking* sound calming to his senses. Smiling, he lifted his head in acknowledgment of Velena as sashayed her way into his line of vision to lean up against the wall only a few feet away. To the untrained eye, she was the picture of contentment. But he knew better.

A fortnight had passed since Tristan left, and Rowan was finding it difficult not to lay blame on Sir Richard for what he perceived as a failure to act justly in response to Tristan's letter. It seemed out of character for Velena's father to do nothing. Yet nothing was all that was getting done as Stuart continued to parade himself thither and yon without consequence. What could explain it, but that Sir Richard had chosen not to read the letter in the first place. And this he could not reconcile with what he knew of the man.

"There, now," he said, lifting the narrow blade into the light and adjusting its position until it caught a bit of sun. Cheered by its brilliance, he danced the thin beam along the gravel at Velena's feet until he was able to maneuver it up the side of the building and across to her midsection. "Present for you."

She opened her hands to it, closing them just as he turned the blade away.

"Got it!" Her smile was lovely.

"What will you do with it?"

"I should like to save it for a rainy day," she answered without delay and made motion as if to put it in her pocket.

Accepting her answer with a satisfied grin, he held the dagger up to his face, one eye closed, examining the blade from hilt to tip. "I think this is sharp enough. If you will lend me but a single strand of your hair, we can test it."

Velena gave him a sideways look. "You can split your own hairs, Rowan."

He pressed a hand to his chest "You don't trust me? What ulterior motive might I have?"

"I don't know, but whatever it is, I imagine that one hair will not be enough, and you will suddenly be in need of two, then three, then four...until you have enough clippings to fill a locket so that you can go about telling Stuart how I gave it to you for a keepsake. This has been the sort of thing you do as of late."

Rowan laughed. "It wasn't my intention, actually, but it sounds like something I should have thought of. I'm disappointed in myself."

"For having had such thoughts, I hope."

"For not having had them. I'm getting slow."

Velena clucked her tongue before returning his smile. "Oh, Rowan. I really ought not to enjoy your company so much as I do."

"Is there anyone who doesn't?"

"I can think of one." Her tone was playful, but still Rowan's smile waned as he returned to the business of sharpening his blade though it no longer needed it.

"Yes, well...the feeling is mutual."

"As seen from your last poetry attempt—delivered to my hand but most certainly not meant to stay there." She quoted:

"Your manners are old,
My chivalry new,
My love is for Nenna,
And my notes not for you."

His grin returned. "Liked that one, did you?"

She pushed away from the wall. "It wasn't your best."

"You're saying I should give it more heart. I'll keep that in mind but tell me...what were Stuart's thoughts on it? Was he pleased? Because if he wasn't, I'd have to argue that my technique is just about where I want it."

Velena clasped her hands behind her and nodded her chin once for emphasis. "I shan't tell you what he said at all."

"I suppose you think Tristan could do better?" He watched as a small glimmer of joy evaporated from her eyes at the mention of their friend's name.

"No...I don't suppose he could. Though to be fair, he never tried."

Rowan dangled the blade of his knife between his knees, his smile missing some of its usual life.

"But that's neither here nor there, is it?" Velena continued, filling her lungs with air. "He's off doing what he needs to do."

"Think he's found his brother?"

"I pray so…along with his Iseult."

"Who?"

"His match."

"He never said anything to me about a betrothal."

"He's not betrothed. But there *was* a woman he left behind, and it's been my greatest hope she's still alive."

"Why Velena Ambrose, if I didn't know better, I'd say you didn't want him to come back."

A wisp of a smile flitted across her mouth. "I want him to be happy."

"That's very selfless of you, Nenna, but I believe he has other plans."

"Other than being happy?"

"Other than staying away."

"I think not." She held up her hand as if the matter was final. "I made myself quite clear that he wasn't to come back for me."

"You cannot order someone's concern away."

"Perhaps not, but neither is he a woman that he should be guided by it. Staying away is in all of our best interests."

"I feel a wager coming on." Rowan puckered his lips even as Velena's chin came up.

"Name your terms."

"Alright." Growing serious, he surveyed the area as if what he wanted should be right in front of him.

"What are you waiting for?" she pressed.

"An epiphany."

"Something big, eh?"

"Don't rush me now… Wait—I have it! When I am knighted, allow me to pledge my fealty to you and your household." Grinning, he listened to her falter.

"Rowan, I…I would…of course…I would, except—"

"Except Stuart doesn't want me anywhere near you—let alone as part of his own household."

She nodded.

"I know this, but I wish to pledge it all the same. So, here's my wager. If Tristan isn't present on that day to give witness to it, you can please our cousin by denying me my service to you in front of everyone.

Velena opened her mouth to argue.

"If, on the other hand, Tristan has returned to give witness…you accept it, Stuart be hanged."

"He's scarcely had time to arrive home, let alone to find his brother and return to us in time for the ceremony. By that wager, I'd have to deny you, and I couldn't possibly do that to you, especially not in front of everyone."

Rowan smiled. "I'm quite resilient if you hadn't noticed—though I won't have to be. Have you no faith in the man?"

"God's designs for us have come to an end. We had our moment, Rowan. Let it be."

"Soon." Rowan's eyes glittered with challenge. "Will you take the wager, or won't you?"

Velena stood closer. "Why is this so important to you?"

Rowan sobered. "Because you're worthy of my devotion." He reached for her hand. "And no one else will grant me land for doing next to nothing to earn it."

Catching the twinkle in his eye, she jerked it away. "That's what *you* think. But, fine. If you don't mind the embarrassment, then neither do I."

"Oh, I mind," he said, laughing as she stalked off to settle onto a patch of grass. "In fact," he added, settling himself before her, "I plan on securing my win with a shameless plea for help. Just as soon as I get off my lazy—"

"Rowan."

"Hind eeend…" His eyes chastised her for thinking he was going to say anything else. "I plan on writing him a letter, informing him of your dismal state of being without him and reminding that his loyalty to you as your friend obligates him to return, so as to secure your general happiness and well-being."

"Foul play! I forbid it."

He rocked his head side to side. "Very well. I'll plead both our cases equally."

"And say what?"

"That *I* want him to come back—and *you* want him to stay. His decision will be a test of who he likes better—me or you."

She coughed up a laugh despite herself.

"Perfect. Anything else you'd like me to add?"

"If anything, you can tell him that if I suffer, I do so at the hand of your altruistic attentions."

"Altru...what now?" Rowan grimaced. "You're using big words, Nenna. Do you want me to give him a message for you or not?"

"You should do as you always do—which is exactly as you like."

Rowan's look was pointed. "You used to do the same, you know."

"Yes, well, acting in one's own self-interest is not always a strength."

"Neither is bending to the will of others."

"Do not confuse meekness for weakness, Rowan. I still have a voice."

"It grows quieter by the moment."

"Then allow me to speak up," she quipped, "because Stuart isn't the only one drowning me out."

"I don't follow."

"How long am I to defend your silly romantic dribble to him?

"It's all in good fu—"

"But at *my* expense. You've put me in the middle of it, and *fun* has its costs. I feel as if I'm sitting beneath a burst of storm clouds. You and Stuart are crashing into one another, and it's all raining down on me. I know, to some degree or other, you've always been at odds— even as children it was there—but never like this."

He granted her a small nod, considering for the first time that he might be making a bigger mess of things than he intended. "He doesn't actually think I'm in love with you, does he?"

"Whether he does or doesn't, he holds me responsible for your actions."

"That's absurd."

"Nevertheless..."

Rowan frowned. "I'm sorry," he said with sincerity, "I'll fix it."

"No more poems," she pressed.

"Mmmmm..."

"No more."

"Alright. No more poems...for you."

"*Or* Stuart."

He rolled his eyes. "Or Stuart."

Satisfied, she leaned back on her hands.

"Speaking of the man, how has he been treating you?"

"His actions are as you observe them," she answered without much reflection.

"And how are they when they're *not* being observed?"

"What do you mean?"

"Daisy told me that Stuart has been forceful with you."

Velena met his gaze. "Since when does Daisy talk to you about such things?"

"Answer the question, please." Still toying with his knife, he slapped the face of the blade against the side of his shoe, waiting for an answer. But she sat silent for so long that he had to prompt her to speech a second time. Even then, she seemed more interested in a tuft of grass than in the question.

"He's more persistent than forceful. But you needn't be concerned. Tristan told me to make my lines, and so I have." A sardonic expression grew at the corners of her lips. "At least, I try."

"Does he stay on his side of said lines?"

Dismissive, Velena tossed the blades of grass aside. "As of late."

He persisted. "But he's had his way before?"

"At the banquet," she admitted with a nod, brushing back some wisps of hair tickling her cheek. "I thought..."

"What?" he pressed softly.

"I thought...if I let him show me how he really feels, I might feel that way too."

"Did it work?"

She shook her head. "Worse, I broke my promise to Tristan not to let him kiss me before the wedding. And I can't forgive myself for it."

Rowan's eyes rose to where the clouds had swallowed up their little patch of sun, his sympathies for her situation keen. "No spark in Stuart's kisses, eh?"

She shook her head, recalling the moment. "He kept trying to put his ton—" She stopped, embarrassed. When she raised her eyes, she could tell that his were laughing at her. "This is...normal?"

He might have encouraged her to give it a try had they been talking about anyone else but Stuart, but seeing as they were, he opted for a more matter-of-fact approach. "It's a more passionate way of kissing." Distaste for the idea brought her bottom lip between her teeth, and he couldn't help but laugh at her then. "It's not so bad as you think."

"I'll have to take your word for it, but a straightforward kiss was more than enough for me." Wiping her palms of earthly debris, she sat forward and wrapped her arms protectively across her body, provoking

Rowan's ire without meaning to.

He stood to his feet. Turning away from her, he flipped his dagger, blade over hilt, catching it by its tip. A deft flick of his wrist and the blade met its mark in the side of the stump some odd feet away. Facing her again, he spoke, "Hand me that twig by your knee."

Velena looked up but didn't move.

"Humor me. Tis but a game."

She sighed and reached to her left, handing over the twig. "What game is this?"

"It's called *Everywhere Stuart has touched you, I shall greet him the same with my fist.*"

"Rowan. You needn't take up an offense. I'm quite alright."

Rowan shook his head, lower lip protruding, "Worry not. It's all in fun."

"For whom?"

"For Stuart, most assuredly. He loves a good beating."

She smirked. "I doubt it."

"Nenna, it's time you faced the fact that you're marrying a man so self-proclaimedly strong, that I could inflict a goodly amount of damage and, to him, would be no more than a tickle. Just wait and see how he'll laugh and laugh. I'll do it in your sight if you wish.

"By my word, I wasn't trying to incite you to this. I only shared because you asked me." *And because Daisy doesn't know how to hold her tongue*, she thought.

"Tis true, and your words have been most gracious—but I would ask you not to use them anymore, as I am not looking for that particular character quality at just this moment. Your job is simply to nod."

She opened her mouth to protest, but the end of the twig was already resting atop her head. He looked so silly holding it there, with the stick bowed in the middle and drooping at one end, as if she were a great fish he'd just caught, that she giggled instead.

"Here?" he asked.

"Here, what?" She unhooked the tip from the top of her headdress.

"Here, he's touched you?"

She rolled her eyes. "On the top of my head?"

"We have to start somewhere," he reasoned, sliding the pointer down the left side of her neck before tapping her on each shoulder as if to knight her. "Here and—or—here?"

Velena giggled again.

15

"Nenna, you must *needs* only nod yay or nay."

"I believe it is now proper to call me, *Sir* Nenna—and, yay, my shoulders he has touched."

Rowan pumped his eyebrows as if he were very proud of himself for the knighting of his petite friend. Next, he attempted to point at her arm, but she yanked the twig from his fingers.

"*Sir* Nenna…give it back."

"*Squire* Rowan—no," she quipped, flinging it over her shoulder with a self-satisfied grin.

"When I suggested you need not always bend to the will of others, I was not, in fact, referring to that of myself. But you needn't apologize, as this game happens to be very versatile." Picking up a handful of small pebbles at his feet, he continued, "How about here?" and landed a well-placed shot to her right arm, the other to her left."

Velena flinched without pain. "Do I get to lead this game once you're through with me? For I would forgo the pebbles and play with stones and am quite certain of a few places *you've* been touched that I have not. Though, I would recompense the lady with words rather than fists, chastising her for her poor judgment in—"

He shushed her to silence. "I'm sorry, but only men can lead this game."

"I should have known."

"Shall we continue?"

"I dare not, lest you forget yourself with your next move."

"I would be giving Stuart the benefit of the doubt to stop here, though there is nowhere else his hands should go."

"Nowhere else *your* hands should go either…or sticks or stones or what have you."

Smile slipping, Rowan dropped to his haunches, voice soft. "I fear that the closer this wedding gets, the more he'll press you in this way. He is to be your husband…is to take you to his bed. But his future advantage should be no excuse for his present behavior. If his hands roam anywhere nature has not," he said, tossing aside the remainder of his pebbles, "you tell me. Look at me, Velena. You *tell* me—and I will see this game played out as it ought. Remember this, lest he become…*more* persistent."

Velena nodded, knowing if she did not, he may push her to promise, and she wasn't at all sure she'd be able to send Rowan to cause Stuart purposeful harm. "I hear you, Rowan, but I can't help thinking you should take your own advice."

He cocked an eyebrow.

"You have to admit it's an odd lesson coming from a man who's already known a woman to the fullest."

"I've slept with no one but you," he said, voice serious, but eyes twinkling.

"It would have been better for me if you *had* been sleeping."

He laughed. "How can you still be angry about that? I've *cuddled* with no one but you, then."

"*That* I don't believe."

Rowan relaxed his position, arm dangled over one knee, his other leg settled beneath him, his smile uncharacteristically shy. "I'll tell you a secret, Sir Nenna. My lines may have grown faint from treading so long upon them but if ever I do marry…I will be known fully to my wife alone—and she to me—Lord willing."

When her jaw went slack, a silly grin pulled at the corners of his mouth. "I'm not so big a knave as you think—and not for lack of opportunity, mind you. If you'd been here instead of Wineford those three years, you'd have seen it. I never received so many propositions in all my life."

"I suppose fear of death would chase a girl into just about anyone's arms."

"Listen to *you!*"

Velena laughed, then sighed pleasantly. "I can just hardly believe it."

"That a woman might want a go at a real man ere the Pestilence had its way with them?"

"No, the part about you turning them down.

"Ha!" He threw back his head. "Immoral behavior in the face of death you can understand, but my having self-control confuses you. Have I really made myself out to be such a heathen?"

Velena laid a hand across her mouth.

"Thank you for that vote of confidence. My faith may be weak, my lady, but I'm not entirely without it."

"I'm glad to hear it, but how much better to be filled to overflowing."

"Would that I had your kind of faith."

"Why not ask Him for it? It's faith in God that stays the course of our lives. If He grants you that, all else will be put to rights."

"Do you believe this for yourself?"

"I do."

He raised an eyebrow. "With nary a doubt?"

"Oh, I have plenty of doubts," she conceded, smiling, "most especially about my present future and if it'll be to my liking. But my earthly future wasn't exactly what I was referring to. What needs to be put right more than anything else, is the destination of our souls. That secured, all else can be endured."

"Even Stuart?"

She released a deep breath. "Even Stuart."

"So, I need not punish him?"

Velena lifted a finger to her mouth. "Hmmm…"

"Then I shall!" Rowan exclaimed, hopping to his feet to do the job, yet not a bit surprised when the sweetest knight to ever dawn a dress put herself in his way. Allowing her to subdue him, he grinned, feeling a certain sense of accomplishment for bringing back a laugh, such as he hadn't heard since Tristan's departure. Sad when it faded, he pulled her into a crushing embrace, rocking her from side to side until they threatened to topple. "Just remember I'm always here. I have a promise to keep, you know."

She withdrew to get a better look at him. "Tristan asked you to look after me?"

"Who do you think made it possible for me to come to Landerhill?"

Breaking into a smile, she held fast to his hands. "Then, if and when you really do write him, tell him thank you with all my heart, and that I'm forever in his debt for putting me under so good a care as yours—perilous as it may be. *Then* tell him to write to me, else I'll never forgive him."

Rowan ducked his head, taken off guard by her sudden praise of him. "So, letters from Tristan you'll accept, but not my poetry? Next, you'll tell me you've thrown them all away."

"Don't be silly. I collected an entire stack before Stuart started taking them away. From Tristan, I have nothing."

"I find that hard to believe."

"I have pages and pages of Scripture, but nothing in his own words."

"In that case, I'll impress upon him the importance of filling any future correspondence with nothing but sweet absurdities for you to remember him by." Smiling again as she laughed, he felt it a good time to ask a question he most wanted answered.

"So…" Rowan cleared his throat, "while we're on the topic of

Tristan and letters," he began, "he told me he left you with one to give to your father."

"He did, indeed."

"Well, what was his reaction to it?"

Her brow creased. "Why?"

"He mentioned their relationship was strained before he left…"

"Yes."

"And I think it would cheer him to know of your father's positive response to what he'd written…if you think he had one."

She nodded. "I'm sure it would. And if I'd handed it to him myself, I might be able to tell you. Unfortunately, I did not."

Disappointed at this lack of news, he forced a smile. "When did you get so spoilt as to be above such menial tasks as delivering letters? And why hasn't said behavior had you demanding to know just exactly what our noble friend said in his?"

Hands to her hips, she grunted. "Said behavior would be superfluous. He already told me it was naught but a goodbye, wherefore, I can surmise he wrote nothing of his return…which I'm sure is your reason for asking." Velena laughed at his expression. "You never give up. He's not coming back, Rowan. Leastwise, not soon. And even if he did…there'd be no reason to stay?"

Rowan laid a hand to her shoulder. "You were always his reason. Don't ever doubt it."

She reached up to squeeze his hand, the neigh of horses reaching their ears from around front of the manor.

"My lady…!" Daisy's voice hailed at distance. She stood at the back door of the kitchen, cupping her hands around her mouth. "Please come, my lady. Lady Margarite is within."

Velena raised an arm in acknowledgment, noting that Makaias' mother must not be their only visitor, as a whole passel of horses— Stuart and her uncle's at the forefront—began rounding the corner, led by various knights and squires, Jaren included.

Rowan found it difficult to tear his eyes away from Daisy as she disappeared within. More and more, the very sight of her was like a breath of fresh air he didn't want to do without, and he wished he had occasion to ask her to join them, as he'd not seen her all morning.

"What a blessing your aunt has been," Velena said, interrupting his thoughts. "Will you come say hello?"

"I'm meeting Makaias for practice."

"He'll want to see her too," she pointed out.

"I'll let him know, but as always, he'll be worked into a lather, so he might smell to high Heaven if he comes.

"No matter. Mothers always make allowances for their sons."

"The blessings of family, I suppose. Come. I'll walk you over," Rowan said, refusing to dwell on the loss of his own. "Auntie travels with quite the entourage for one who arrives only to help you stitch up your dress," he teased.

"Actually," she said, falling into step beside him. "I've asked her to tutor me."

"In what?"

"In anything she deems fit. I want to better myself. And the first thing in that direction is to admit my own incompetence when it comes to running a household. I'm simply not ready to be chatelaine."

"Your mother thought you ready three years ago."

She shook her head. "I've picked up too many bad habits since then."

"Like standing on chairs."

Velena extended him a sideways glance to see he was giving her the same. "I'm being serious."

He chuckled. "I know. But I'm sure you're doing better than you think you are."

"Not well enough—and others think so too."

"What others? Say the word, and I'll pluck their eyes out, myself."

Velena tried not to smile. "Stuart, for one."

"Trust me, Sir Nenna. You need never feel inferior to him."

"Makaias, for another."

"Why should you care what he thinks?"

She looked away. "Britton, then."

"It's a brother's job to find fault with his—"

"My father—and don't say I shouldn't care what he thinks. It's not right he should be embarrassed because of my failings."

"Failings? Pah! He said this to you?"

"No, but—"

"You're a bit impetuous is all."

"A bit?"

"Alright." They slowed to a stop between two fragrant rows of herbal beds just beyond the kitchen door. "You may need to rein it in a tad." He dropped a brotherly kiss to the top of her head. "In the meantime, don't be so hard on yourself and remember that faith of yours. What would Tristan say to all of this?"

She heaved a sigh. "Work for the Lord rather than for people."

"And in that area, I suspect God's incredibly pleased already. So, never mind anyone else's faces."

Velena swallowed. "Thank you, Rowan."

"Yes, well…" He gave her tippet a tug. "I can still pluck out their eyes, though, if you'd like. Better to be without them if they can't see that as far as God's creations go, you've turned out rather nicely." He pumped his eyebrows even as her lashes fluttered in something of an eye roll, but still she laughed.

"You certainly have a violent edge to your mood this day. And, no. I think any actual carnage might just ruin the moment."

Rowan's grin stretched across his face. "My dear girl, I create the moment."

3
pickled herring

A fortnight before the wedding

Now able to see only one of everything, Britton scanned the sitting room of his solar from the sheepskin covered bench he currently occupied, frowning at those who'd come to keep him company. Velena and Daisy sat beside him—the former reading silently, the latter embroidering on a section of wedding gown piled in a heap upon her lap and spilling over into Velena's. Stuart and Jaren occupied one of the benches at the wooden table, center of the room, and Rowan stood at the window with Makaias, both staring out at another rainy day and talking over plans for their next practice session should the sky clear on the morrow.

"You're all far too somber," Britton complained. "Have you always been this gloomy, only I just couldn't see it?"

"I'm not gloomy." Velena rested her book in her lap. "But if you are, I can read to you if you'd like."

"What are you reading?" He pulled her hand up so he could have a look at the cover. "Ugh. No offense, but I don't care for *Tristan and Iseult*."

"Here, here," Makaias echoed from his place at the window.

Velena's head swung around. "Well that was just a little too enthusiastic. What don't you like about it?"

Britton stretched his damaged leg out in front of him and flexed his ankle slowly, feeling the pull of his muscle run all the way up his calf and into his thigh. It'd been almost three weeks now, and although it was feeling worlds better, it was quite tender to walk on—and would be for some weeks more—causing him somewhat of a limp. "Same as what's not to like about King Arthur," he answered in place of Makaias.

23

"Which is?"

"He sums it up much better than I. You tell her, Kai."

"The short answer or the long one?"

Britton smiled. "By all means, the long one."

Makaias cleared his throat. "The problem with *said* books, and such bard tales as are similar, is that both sing the praises of men and women who've given themselves over to infidelity, showing more deference to *their* version of sacrificial love than to the long-suffering restraint of their spurned spouses, who are left to suffer under the weight of their beloved's sin, ultimately causing those who've remained faithful to be lost—not only to sadness—but also to the one-sighted purpose of revenge. Wherein, they also sin."

Velena's mouth unhinged, and Britton laughed. "I couldn't have said it better, myself."

"And didn't," Makaias reminded him.

Recovering, Velena marked her page with a sprig of dried lavender and tucked her book beneath her thigh. "In a word, you think it's garbage."

"Yes," they said in unison.

Daisy giggled, but Velena remained thoughtful, feeling the tug to acknowledge that her penchant for *Tristan and Iseult* had more to do with the hopes she carried for Tristan and *his* Iseult, than with the story's actual propensity towards moral behavior, or lack thereof.

"I was prepared to argue with anything you were going to say, Sir Makaias, but an answer that detailed, and previously thought out, demands some attention," she conceded. "I shall ponder what you've said."

Rowan coughed up a laugh. "No you won't."

"You don't knooow," she drawled, waggling her head at him. "I might."

Doubtful, Makaias turned back toward the window, securing Velena's pity despite his snub, as he appeared altogether unhappy to be stuck indoors.

"We ought to get up and get moving," Jaren suggested. "It'll be good for our dispositions."

"The rain is causing my leg to ache," Britton complained. "I don't much feel like moving around."

"It is rather dismal." Velena scooted out from beneath Daisy's project and crossed the room to peek out the window, having to come in between Rowan and Makaias to do it. "Normally, I like the rain," she said to no one in particular, "but when it keeps Rainydayas and the Baroness away, I'm forced to change my mind."

"They've come every day for nigh on a fortnight," Stuart reminded her.

"So have you," Rowan quipped, receiving his obligatory glare with satisfaction.

Sensing some mounting tension, Makaias brought the conversation back to Velena. "What do you like about it?" he asked, leaning into the wall.

She lifted her face to him. "The rain?"

He nodded.

"The smell."

Makaias' mouth pulled upward, and Velena thought, not for the first time, what a nice smile it was.

Jaren brightened with a new idea. "How about a game of hide and seek?"

Stuart perked at the mention of it and leaned over to say something into Jaren's ear.

"I don't think I'd make a very good seeker," Britton said.

"Perhaps, if Sir Makaias were to make you a second crutch," she suggested, making sure to use Makaias' title for Stuart's sake, "you wouldn't feel so bound to one spot. Leastwise, you could get around faster."

Makaias huffed. "He doesn't appreciate the one's he's got."

"Yes, I do," Britton said, looking wounded. He pulled the one crutch into his lap from where it leaned against the bench and began petting it. "It means the world to me because it's from you." He lifted it to his lips for a kiss.

Velena smiled at the banter. "Well, even with one you can play," she insisted.

Jaren slapped his hands against his knees. "We'll play fish in a barrel instead."

"Brilliant," Velena exclaimed, grabbing Britton's hand. "We'll hide *you*, and everyone *else* can do the seeking."

"Sounds good. Only, it's called pigs feet," Rowan argued.

Stuart rolled his eyes. "No, it's not."

"Then why don't *you* tell us what it's called. I'm sure this is your favorite game—for obvious reasons."

Stuart sneered. "You know, I rather liked it better when you weren't talking to me."

"Oooh?" Rowan's brows rose in derision. "Noticed that, did you?"

Britton shook his head. "What a bunch of children you are. You tell us what it's called, Velena. Surely, you remember."

"I thought it was called pickled herring…actually."

Laughter rippled through the room. "Up we go, then" Makaias said, crossing over to help Britton up by the arm. "Pickled herring, it is. I'll hide him—the rest of you count."

"You make me sound like buried treasure."

"If only," Stuart added.

"What do we count to?" Rowan asked.

"To whatever you're able," Britton said, giving him a wink.

"He'll have to count several times, then" Daisy said, making her voice heard for the first time. "Five isn't a very high number."

Shoulders shook while Rowan held his stomach in mock humor. "Well, listen to all you jesters. Ha ha ha, ho ho ho," he said with great exaggeration, targeting Daisy with his eyes. "I see you've gotten back your bite. I'm suddenly looking forward to being in a dark enclosed space with you. If you show me your teeth, I'll show you mine."

"That will *not* happen," Velena stated emphatically and began folding up the material Daisy had been working on into a nice, tidy pile. "Not with Daisy, and certainly not alone. Even if some of us do know that your bark is worse than your bite," and she gave him a pointed look. "As the only women present, we shall do our seeking together. Shan't we?"

A smile creeped onto Makaias' face at what he deemed to be Velena's first real show of propriety.

Daisy collected the material back into her arms. "Actually, I'd rather not play if it's all the same."

"I can't hide alone." Velena frowned. "Auntie would certainly disapprove. Please Daisy, it'll be fun."

Horrified she might somehow find herself hiding alongside Stuart—the man who'd taken her innocence, the man she'd dared to blackmail—her stomach began working itself into knots. Her gaze flickered in his direction, but if he had any thoughts bent on retaliation, he gave no indication of it. In fact, he didn't look at her at all.

"Alright," Daisy said, accepting Rowan's presence beside her as his show of protection.

At the door, Britton turned to face them. "That settled, instead of counting, recite three Hail Mary's."

Rowan crossed himself. "Why do I suddenly feel like I've done something naughty?"

The women giggled as Makaias disappeared with Britton into the corridor. Then together, "Hail Mary, full of grace, the Lord is with thee."

On the second go around, Velena began listening more intently to the words. *Hail Mary?* Why on earth had she never paid attention to this before? Stricken by her own blasphemy, her voice faded to nothing.

Finished, they proceeded towards the door. Stuart slipped out first, then Jaren. Velena counted to twenty.

Rowan leaned sideways towards Daisy's ear. "Deep breaths," he whispered, knowing nothing of her encounter with Stuart of more than a fortnight past in the corridor, nor of the secret nestled deep within her womb, but knowing plain as plain that she'd rather be doing anything besides this. This he knew, and he gave her his most reassuring smile, to which she reciprocated.

"Twenty," Velena said, grabbing Daisy by the hand. "Our turn."

"Don't follow me, Squire Rowan," Daisy threw over her shoulder.

Rowan's face displayed something of his surprise at the sudden coyness of her behavior. "I wouldn't dream of it. From now on I'll be waiting for you to come to me."

Daisy ducked her head, but not in time to hide her smile from Velena, who gave her an amused, if not quizzical, grin.

"Where should we look first?" Daisy asked.

Velena laughed. "Below stairs."

Daisy followed after her. "Is something funny?"

"You," she said, without looking back.

"Me?"

"When did you and Rowan become so friendly?" she asked, realizing she still needed to speak with her about what she'd told Rowan about Stuart.

Daisy frowned. "We're not that friendly."

Velena stopped mid-step, spinning around. "Oh, please."

Daisy's lips pressed together, then, "He's been different since coming to us at Landerhill. Kind."

"He's always been kind," Velena said, continuing their quest. "You're just coming to notice, is all."

"Does it bother you?"

Velena stopped at the bottom of the stairs, looking right, then left.

Only when it means sharing things you ought to keep to yourself, she wanted to say, but was unexpectedly convicted with the notion that perhaps Daisy really did need someone to confide in—Lord knows, she didn't confide in her anymore—and perhaps that was more important than Daisy's breach of her privacy. And since when did Velena know how to keep anything private anyway. One more thing to work on, she conceded.

"Actually, I'm rather pleased to see it. I know how much of a bother he was to you before."

Not knowing what else to say, Daisy glanced about the foyer. "I don't think Sir Makaias would bring your brother downstairs with his leg the way it is."

"That's exactly why I think he did." A sly smile slipped into place. "As you've gotten to know Rowan, I think I've gotten to know a little bit more about Sir Makaias. And he's more apt to do something unexpected than one might think." She held a finger to her lips. "Come on," she whispered.

Jovial sounds coming from the great hall let them know they weren't the only ones looking to escape the rain, and from the sheer volume of it, she guessed the room was filled to capacity. But Velena didn't think Sir Makaias had taken Britton in there, so they moved ahead, grateful for the noise masking their footsteps.

Their search led them from one room to another, landing them a lone shoe in the library but no people. She picked it up and carried it with her. A moment later, they entered the chapel to the sound of rain clattering against the stained glass. From back to front, there wasn't much in the way of furnishings where one could hide—only five rows of high-backed benches and a communion table. But the table, itself, was covered by a large white cloth, perhaps one inch from the floor on all sides, and with plenty of room for several grown men to hide beneath if they had a mind to.

Velena tapped Daisy on her shoulder and pointed. "There," she mouthed. Approaching as quietly as they could, Velena cocked back the shoe she was still holding, lifted the hem of the tablecloth—and chucked the item beneath.

"Ow!" Britton laid a hand to where the shoe bounced off his head. "What was that for?"

"For being sneaky."

"It was Kai's shoe. Next time hit him."

Makaias chuckled from his place behind him. "Come around," he said.

Finding not much room between the table and the wall, the women first worked to scoot the table farther out before lowering themselves onto their stomachs, Velena first, then Daisy beside her.

"I'll have to have a word with whoever's supposed to clean the floors," Velena grumbled.

Makaias' face peered out from beneath the back end of the tablecloth. "It's better on your back. Then you don't have to breath it in."

"I think I'll take that advice," Velena said, flipping herself over. She looked at Daisy who shook her head.

"No point in getting both sides of me dirty."

"Shh."

Velena couldn't see which of the men shushed them, but it was clear someone else had entered the chapel from the light scuffing of leather soles across the floor. Less than a minute later and Jaren was working to squeeze himself between Daisy and the wall. She scooted in tighter against Velena, who scooted further beneath the tablecloth and into Makaias' shoulder, so that the tablecloth was now hitting her dead center atop her nose. She turned her face to the side.

"We'll need to make room for at least one more," Jaren whispered.

Quick to comply, Britton rolled over to his left shoulder, giving himself a clear view of the floor beneath the tablecloth and pews. "Scoot closer, Kai, we can lay back to back."

Rolling to his right side, Makaias inched backward into Britton before reaching over to lift the tablecloth so that Velena could maneuver herself beneath.

She first glanced at Daisy to make sure she wasn't uncomfortable lying beside Jaren. "Are you alright?" she whispered.

Still on her stomach, Daisy rested her face on the backs of her hands and nodded.

Assured, Velena wriggled beneath the table, allowing the tablecloth to fall between them.

"This is one way to keep warm," Makaias whispered from his place beside her.

Turning to face him, she could only think, *Oh my!*

Propped up on one forearm to allow her more room, his face was little more than a handbreadth above her own. She tried averting her eyes, but there really wasn't a more comfortable place to land them.

There was either his face, his chest—or the underside of the table, which consequently, was still in the same direction as his face. She could turn her head back towards Daisy but looking away while he stared down at her seemed just as awkward. Thankfully, the scuffing of another pair of shoes drew his attention away from her, causing him to crane his neck in such a way that his face was now looking upward and his ear positioned to better hear the sounds coming from behind him.

Without forethought, Velena found herself studying his profile. Strong neck. Attractive cheek bones. Pleasant jaw line and just enough facial hair to form a goodly amount of stubble but not quite a full beard. Also, his hair had grown at least another half inch from when he and her brother had shaved it due to head lice, and she was having the most ridiculous urge to run her fingers across the top to see if it was as soft as it looked.

As the footsteps grew closer, Velena worked harder at keeping her breathing slow and shallow. She might have had better luck had the corners of his mouth not raised ever so slightly, piquing her interest, as he took on the look of a man both agreeable and dangerous at the same time.

For a brief moment, when it seemed likely the footsteps might retreat, they all began to let out their breath. But the man turned back again, and Makaias signaled for further quiet, even if to no one in particular, bringing all four fingers up to his lips—one behind the other—as if each finger was just waiting its turn to come into contact with his mouth. And for one unguarded moment, Velena contemplated what it might be like to take her place behind them.

Startled by the carnality of such musings, her pulse quickened, and she began reciting scripture to herself in a hasty attempt to put right her misplaced thoughts. *But put on the Lord, Jesus Christ, and make no provision for the flesh in regard to its lusts. But put on the Lord, Jesus Christ, and make no provision for the flesh in regard to its lusts. But put on the Lord, Jesus Christ, and make no provision for the flesh in regard to its...*

Finally, his hand fell away. But when his head swiveled back around, it was to reveal a full smile—and, again, Velena was struck with the nearness of him. Faces hovering mere inches apart, eyes mated, Velena couldn't help but wonder how many women he'd given such a look.

Whether his smile faded due to the transparency of her thoughts— a horrible consideration—or from his own discomfort, she grew so ill at ease that she eventually laughed for lack of knowing what else to do. It was nothing too loud or too long, rather the briefest of nervous titters, but in the space of that moment, Makaias' smile vanished into little more than a grim line.

No doubt, he was questioning her boldness, but where in King Edward's court did he expect her to look? She was practically in his arms.

"Well, isn't this cozy…"

Velena startled at Rowan's voice, realizing he'd lifted the outside edge of the tablecloth and was now crouched there, staring at them over top of Britton.

"You're a fortunate man, Cousin Makaias. I have it on good authority that Velena is an excellent cuddler." He winked. "Mine, actually. So, you're getting it straight from the horse's mouth."

Velena scowled. "It's rear end, you mean."

Britton pushed Rowan back at the shins, rolling out with a groan. "Was something going on behind my back I needed to know about?" he asked, wincing as Rowan helped him to his feet.

"Don't be silly," she said, allowing Makaias' to do the same. Unsettled, she brushed her hands over her surcoat, front and back, in an attempt to disperse the layer of dust. "It's your turn to hide, she said, shifting her eyes to Rowan."

Jaren assisted Daisy out from behind the table, looking around as he did so. "Actually, we may have ended the game a bit prematurely. Stuart's not here."

Velena glanced out into the corridor. "Then he's the new hider. Someone ought to let him know."

"I'll do it," Jaren volunteered. "I'll tell him to hide, and then the rest of us can count from here. Back in a wink."

Still laughing to himself over Velena's little embarrassment, Rowan sniffed the air before moaning in satisfaction. "Mmmm. Smell that? They're having fruit pies in the great hall."

"I could do with something to eat," Britton said, seeking a moment of respite for the leg that pained him by supporting some of his weight against the back of a pew.

Rowan grinned. "Are you ordering me to pilfer yonder room of its deliciousness?"

"Indeed, I am, Squire."

"Then I'm at your service." He gave an exaggerated bow, then turned his attention to Velena. "And might I borrow thy maid servant to help me return with said food?"

As Daisy appeared at ease with the request—even pleased—Velena nodded her consent before wandering over to one of the stained-glass windows lining the wall.

"I'm not sure you should trust Rowan with Daisy," Britton said once they were gone.

Pivoting on her toes, Velena did an about-face from where she'd been enjoying a whiff of rain-sweetened air filtering in through a crack in the mortar. "I've been watching them," she acknowledged.

"Be sure and use both eyes. Now, if you'll excuse me, I have need of the garderobe."

"Need any help?" Makaias offered.

Britton positioned his crutch beneath his armpit. "Velena needn't sit alone. I can manage."

Velena turned back to the sill, listening as he thumped his way out of the room. Motionless, she wasn't sure whether to sit or remain standing. Rain pelted the world outside, and the chill of the room was only amplified by the dwindling of its occupants. Peeking over her shoulder, she saw that Makaias had taken a seat in one of the pews. His back was towards her, and he was slouched down with his legs extended out over the pew in front, feet crossed at the ankles.

Stepping lightly down the aisle, she could see his eyes were closed, hands rested on his chest. Sharing the pew with his feet, she folded her legs, pulling them into her chest, so she could sit sideways. "Tired?" she asked.

He nodded in silent affirmation, cracking open one lid. "Rain is a good excuse to go to bed." He yawned and pulled his legs down in front of him, scooting up higher in his seat.

Finding herself the center of his attention, she felt the weight of his scrutiny—or perhaps it was just that he thought she had something more to say and was waiting for her to say it. It wasn't often Velena found herself alone with him—in fact, she couldn't recall ever having been so, except for the one time she'd approached him at the banquet with a glass of wine. Even then, they'd been surrounded by people.

"I suppose I should apologize for making you feel awkward."

Makaias eyebrows twitched. "I don't feel awkward."

"I mean before…under the table. I didn't mean to stare."

Confusion turned into amusement. "Were you staring?"

Now, *she* felt awkward. "There was nowhere else to look."

He chuckled. "Then you have naught to apologize for."

Velena watched as that same sweet half-smile she'd seen only inches from her face beneath the table came back to plant itself again, bringing a flutter of embarrassment to her belly. Self-conscious, she slid her arms around her middle, feeling ridiculous.

"Furthermore," he continued, "I don't know a man alive who'd choose to find fault with a woman who stared at him."

Her arms relaxed. "Britton has suggested that you don't like being stared at by women."

"Velena—"

"*Lady* Velena," she corrected, apology in her voice. "Stuart would rather you address me as lady."

Giving proper consideration to her statement, he continued without complaint. "Lady Velena," he repeated, "allow me to make things clear for you. While it's true that a man enjoys the attentions of such looks, as a friend—as I hope we are—I would counsel you against giving them. As learned from your encounter with Sir Harold, not all men can be trusted with such looks. They read into them what they wish and act on them without apology."

"Well, you needn't have read anything so untoward in mine. At least, nothing so wrong as to make you angry."

"I wasn't angry."

Her look was a reprimand. "You practically scowled at me."

"Hm." He rubbed his chin with the topsides of his fingers. "I'm not sure why you'd think—*oooh*, I remember. I was..." He stopped mid-sentence as if rethinking his willingness to share. Ducking his head, he failed to hold back his smile.

"You were what?"

"I was...displeased, you could say."

"But you said that—"

"If you hadn't laughed, Rowan might not have found us. That's all."

"You were angry...because I gave away our hiding spot?"

"Displeased," he corrected her.

"Really? *Actually* displeased—as in frustrated?"

He raised his eyebrows as if to say he'd already made his point. "You threw the game."

"Not on purpose."

He shrugged. "Still."

"Are you that competitive?"

"Has nothing to do with it. Staying quiet is an important skill—especially with enemies lurking about."

"What enemies? It was only a game."

"Games are practice—and holding one's tongue can be the

difference between life and death."

Velena gawked.

"Mock me if you like, but if I had a wife who couldn't hold her tongue in the midst of danger, I'd hate to think what evil could befall her." He adjusted his arms over his chest. "What if she were killed—or ravaged? I'd be left with a woman, bereft of innocence, and a house full of strange children. And all because she couldn't hold her tongue."

Velena blinked. "Just how many children are you supposing she'd have from such an encounter? And did you just refer to the offspring of such violence as *strange*?"

"Too harsh?"

"I would say so."

"Straaaangers to me, then. Better?"

Velena shook her head. "Sir Makaias, you may be far more serious an individual than ever I first imagined."

"You think I'm too serious?"

Britton thumped into the room just in time to hear the question. "She's mentioned it a time or two."

Makaias extended his arms overtop the back of the pew. "Reeeally..."

She was unrepentant. "I've never come across anyone so intent on making every facet of life, whether work or play, an object lesson for survival. If that's not serious, I don't know what is."

"What you intend as a criticism, I accept as a compliment."

Britton tore off a bothersome hangnail with his teeth, spitting it to the side. "Is there a purpose to this unpleasantness, Sister, or do you seek to ruffle his feathers purely for sport?"

Makaias shook his head. "I take no offense at her honesty," he said, keeping her earlier confession to himself. "She is a woman without secrets, and that I do admire."

She tilted her head. "I'm happy to know I meet with your approval, at least on some level. And here I assumed you thought me too bold."

Makaias' jaw shifted from side to side as an easy sort of smile slid into place. He didn't speak right away but held her gaze with those eyes—eyes still full of mirth and water, the same as she'd seen them the day he'd arrived at Landerhill.

Daisy's voice echoed in the corridor, followed by Rowan's over exuberant laughter, bringing their little tete-a-tete to an end, but not before Makaias would have the last word. He leaned forward, "You are *also* too bold."

Her brother's look was a clear *I told you so.*

"So, I was thinking…" Rowan began the moment he entered the room. "What if we end our little game a bit early and join the others back in the hall?"

Velena frowned. "Jaren isn't back yet, and Stuart will be angry if we just leave him to hide. Shouldn't we finish at least one more round?"

"Pish posh." Rowan opened up a napkin full of fruit tarts for her to select from. "He meant all along to find us last, and for obvious reasons."

"What reasons?" Makaias asked.

"Last to find Britton means the first to hide—potentially, making our Nenna the first to find him. And you know he'd like that," he said, looking over at her. "No doubt he's hunkered down in the darkest corner he can find."

"If you always think the worst of a person, don't be surprised when they measure up. Anyway," Velena continued, "he knows Daisy is searching with me, so your theory doesn't hold up. Now are we going to play or not?"

"Not," Britton said, rubbing his shin. "My leg is killing me."

"A little drink should dull that pain," Rowan said, gesturing with his thumb towards the great hall where a good many off-key voices were raised in song and doing their best to drown each other out. "Or a lot of it. They're having a merry time in there, I assure you."

Makaias tossed a grin at Britton. "I'm game if you are. My flute will keep Rowan in tune once he decides to start singing."

"Pfft." Rowan waved him off with a hand. "I'm always in tune."

"Not when you're snoggered."

Rowan shrugged. "There may be some truth to that, but snoggered or sober, I'm better than you."

Britton gave him a, "here-here," and then looked to Velena for the final word. "What say you, Sister?"

Faced with a room full of drink-thirsty men, save only for Makaias who never indulged in anything of any strength—and her maid, whose eyes begged her to say yes—she agreed.

4

opportunity

Stuart wasn't present to hear Rowan's suggestive remarks about him hiding in dark corners and why he might want Velena to find him in one, but it wouldn't have surprised him if he had. In fact, under different circumstances, it might have been the truth. But not today. The only dark corner he was looking for this time was one in which he could conceal the money he planned on giving Daisy—only he was having some trouble doing it.

Turning circles for what felt like the hundredth time, he reexamined the sitting room of Velena's solar, completely unsatisfied with his choices—fireplace, bench, table, and some sort of shroud hanging from the corner of the ceiling near the window seat—an oddity to be sure—and all places Velena could just as easily find a thing hidden as Daisy. Furthermore, nothing seemed to be Daisy's in particular, and if it was, he certainly wouldn't know it, nor would he chance getting it wrong.

Feeling the fool, he could just hear what his father would say if he knew where he was, doing exactly what he'd been warned against doing. But he had to do it. It wasn't right what he'd done to Daisy, nor would it be right to send her away without the means to care for his child. More than that—more than anything—he was desperate to do something that would set himself apart from his father. He just needed to be careful.

"Is it done?"

Catching his breath, Stuart spun around to see Jaren standing in the doorway. Breathing a sigh of relief, he spread his arms in frustration. "There's nowhere that Velena couldn't find it first." He ran his hand across his mouth. "How much time do I have?"

"Game's over. I told them I'd come tell you to hide. They'll count from the chapel as soon as I return." Silent for a moment, he asked,

"What are you going to do?"

"Hide, I suppose. I'll have to give her the money some other way."

"I wish you'd just give it to me. There'd be less suspicion if you did."

Stuart nodded. "But if my father finds out, I'd rather you not be involved."

Jaren looked as if he wanted to argue but held his tongue. He gripped Stuart's shoulder instead. "You're doing the right thing. I'm proud of you."

Watching him leave, Stuart doubted whether praise of any kind should be extended to him when the deed precipitating it was borne from such a sin as he'd committed. Turning away, he headed to the bed chamber portion of the solar for one last look around.

By the time Jaren found everyone in the great hall, Rowan was finishing his third helping of crumbly fruity tart. He had flakes of crust marking his lips, jerkin, and hose and was just at that moment pressing his thumb over the last smattering of crumbs he'd rounded up on the table. He looked up from where he sat wedged between Makaias and Daisy—Britton and Velena across from him—and grinned with a goodly amount of pleasure. "Games over, Jaren. Grab a tart."

"Well, that was short-lived."

Velena twisted around at the sound of his voice, a goblet half-full of wine still at her lips. "Forgive us. Is Stuart still hiding?"

"That was the plan."

"My fault," Britton said, setting down his empty tankard with a hollow thud. "I was hoping to drown out this ache in my leg with a drink or two. Hasn't helped yet."

Rowan chuckled. "Give it two more, and you'll be right as rain."

"I believe the rain is partly the problem," Daisy corrected rather offhandedly. Looking sleepy, she rested her chin in her palm, only for it to be knocked from its pedestal as a man stumbled into her from behind. Apologizing, he moved on with a helpful shove from Rowan.

Jaren reached between Britton and Velena for the empty tankard, an idea taking form. "Allow me to bring you another round."

Velena placed a hand on his wrist. "Will you tell Stuart where we are?"

He produced an ingratiating smile. "Next thing I do."

Thanking him, she faced forward, gripping her goblet with both hands. Tense, she stood, deciding to go, herself—and would have—if Rowan's voice hadn't stopped her.

"Sit down, Nenna. Jaren said he'd take care of it."

"He's going to be upset, waiting like this."

"He's a moody one, alright." Rowan's voice was light from across the table, but there was no mistaking the serious glint in his eyes. She'd known him too long to miss it. "And it's as I said before. He'd be only too happy it was you to find him. Better to stay."

Britton coaxed her back down with a pull of her tippet as Makaias looked up with something of a question in his eyes. Discomforted, her reply was terse. "You needn't paint him like that."

"He *is* like that."

"I could do without the constant reminder."

"I don't want you to forget."

"How could I possibly forget with you harping on him every chance you get? I know how he is, *Rowan!* Hope—give me that. I'm to be his wife; better to help me see what he can become."

Britton's groan interrupted his answer. "Velena, please. The two of you...let it be."

Embarrassed, her eyes fell to her lap. When she looked up, Makaias was staring at her with what she could only assume to be a pronounced look of disapproval pulling down at the corners of his mouth. Whether for her or for Rowan, she didn't know—but it was just the sort of look she'd expect from an elder brother—and perhaps that's what he was becoming.

She quaffed the last of her drink, happy for the interruption when Jaren appeared behind Daisy with the ale. "If you'll excuse me," she said, holding up the empty goblet, and headed for the dais table and the good wine.

Jaren nodded as she left. He had a tankard in each hand and was reaching across the table to hand one of them to Britton when his own drink bumped into Daisy's shoulder, splashing a goodly portion of its contents down the front of her chest.

Gasping, she rose to her feet as the cool rush of liquid colored the bodice portion of her cotehardie a darker shade of orange. It seemed an unlikely accident, but no one accused him of doing it on purpose.

"Forgive me..." Jaren looked every bit as apologetic as he sounded. "What a clod I am."

Swearing under his breath, Rowan leapt to action. "I'll get a towel."

"No. It's alright..." Daisy took a deep breath, collecting herself. Lord knew her first reactions were never the best. "It's alright. I'll...change clothes. Excuse me."

"I really am sorry," Jaren trailed her as far as the door.

Watching her leave, Rowan turned towards Makaias. "Now would be a good time to break out your flute, ere a foul mood captures us all."

"Agreed."

So, Makaias played and Rowan sang—and Velena learned his voice was every bit as good as those who knew claimed it to be. Feathers less ruffled, she accepted a dance from Jaren. Then another and another, until it seemed he had no intentions of fetching Stuart at all. Frustrated, she marched for the door. Rowan was correct when he said Stuart could be moody, but if he was allowed to stay in hiding with no one coming to find him for much longer, he'd have a right to be.

With naught but a backward glance in Rowan's direction, Velena slipped from the room.

Daisy had already unfastened the first five buttons of her cotehardie when she entered her solar. Latching the door behind her, she turned and nearly jumped out of her skin. Clutching the soaked material together at her chest, she fumbled behind her to open what had just been shut, filling her lungs to scream should he step out from behind the curtain.

Knowing he couldn't silence her in time, Stuart held up his hands in surrender, sinking to his knees to appear as non-threatening as possible. "Wait! Don't...don't. I was hiding. My turn to hide...remember? The game."

She remembered, but it didn't take away her fear. It was all she could do not to stammer. "They've stopped playing. Everyone...everyone's waiting for you in the great hall. Jaren was going to come find you."

He came to his feet...slowly. "Did he do that?" he asked, nodding towards the saturated material gripped within her small fist.

"It was an accident..." she started to say, but something in his expression told her different. "Or...maybe not."

"I need to talk to you."

Horribly self-conscious, she wanted to do up her buttons but dreaded bringing any more attention to her chest than was already there. And she would never—never—trust her back to him. What she needed was to get out. Panicking, she made a half-turn to unlatch the door, but Stuart was there before she could pull it open. Sidestepping him, she fled to the other side of the room. "What do you want?"

"I'm not here to hurt you—I'm not." Trepidation marked her face, but he was thankful she remained quiet. Satisfied, he took a step forward.

"What then?"

"I have your money—as promised." He took another step, realizing with some mixed emotion that he no longer thought of her as simply *some* woman he'd...

She took a step back.

He stopped his advance, trying to make sense of these new feelings, realizing that right now, he saw her also as the mother of his child—a fact he still didn't know what to do with. "It's in there." He pointed past her to the bed chamber. "Under your mattress."

Daisy's face blanched. Turning on her heel, she made a beeline for her trundle. Lifting the straw mattress, she heard a *chink* as a coin purse fell loose from its place between the mattress and one of the ropes that supported it.

With bated breath, she reached her hand farther beneath, searching for any sign of Tristan's letter. Her fingers brushed its edge, and she closed her eyes. It was still there, held in place, the same as the coin purse had been. But there was also something that wasn't.

"What are these?" Stuart had followed her to the doorway and was holding in his hand an open cloth, on which lay a small bundle of dried herbs.

Slowly, Daisy pushed in the trundle, picking up the purse as she stood up to face him. "They're for my stomach upset."

He looked down at the unfamiliar cuttings, too unskilled in such things to know if she was telling the truth. Doubtful, he saw that her breathing was becoming more labored, her eyes boring a hole into that which was out of her reach. "Then why were they hidden?"

"I wasn't hid—"

"What are they really for?"

Silence.

"Tell me." His voice was sharp, and she flinched. "What are these for? What have you done?"

"I've done nothing."

"But...you're going to."

Daisy stood taller, her face twisting in anger. "Why should you care? If I use them—and they work—you get to keep your secret. There will be no child, and you'll be able to take back your precious money."

There was truth to her words, and he thought for a moment that he ought to be happy. He ought to be ecstatic. Indeed, a part of him berated himself for not thinking to pressure her into it in the first place. But there was that other part—small but increasing in size—that sought to pay penance for his mistakes, not add to them. He already had enough on his conscience, and he knew in his heart of hearts he could bear no more.

"The money is inconsequential. I'll send you more if you need it. But this," he held up the bundle, "I cannot abide," and he crossed over to the fireplace, preparing to throw them in.

"I can get more!"

He paused, becoming deadly calm, despite the ache tightening the muscles in his throat. "I suppose you can. But I'm hoping you won't." He set the herbs atop the mantle before coming back around to face her. "Last time we spoke, you asked if I had a conscious that pitied you..."

"You have no conscience."

"I do—and it gives me no rest."

"Good."

"I need relief."

"Find a *confessor*." She spat the words, bitterly.

He shook his head. "It can only be you. I want to be done with this."

"Where was this remorse when there was naught but me to contend with? You had no compassion then. Only now that there's a child—"

"Who ought not to pay for my sins."

"Let it pay!" she shouted. Grieved by her own words, she couldn't help but say them, so much was her resolve to cause him injury. "I'm not interested in your redemption."

"What do you want, Daisy? A full accounting of my wrongs? A full pardon of yours? What will it take for you to let it live?"

She had no desire to kill her unborn but neither did she want Stuart to assume for one moment he had any say in the matter. "There's nothing. You are selfish. You are cruel—insincere in all your doings and incapable of sharing in any true blame."

"I'll take it all." He stood before her, and she seemed to shrink before him, draining of all color. "I blamed my drinking that night; but the drink didn't make me do it…"

Her chin began to tremble.

"I blamed Bowan for starting something he couldn't finish—"

"Stop."

"But it wasn't Bowan's fault."

"You can't make this better." She retreated a step into the bed.

"I blamed you for behaving wanton, but it wasn't your—"

"I don't want to hear!"

"I couldn't have Velena…" his voice caught with the truth of it, "so I…took you." Leaving the front of her bodice to hang open, she dropped the coin purse and covered her ears. He pulled them away, holding fast to her wrists though she fought him. "I was *angry* with Velena—so I took *you*," he repeated. She struggled, and he shook her, some part of him still at war with himself. "Listen to me. *Daisy*. Listen. Do you hear what I'm saying? The blame is mine. Mine—and mine alone. And if anyone is pitiable—anyone in danger of Hell fire, it's me."

Overcome, she dropped to the bed. But the fight had not gone out of her, and she refused to grant him tears. She—who'd been drowned many a night with a seemingly endless supply—had none for him.

So what of his remorse? A pox on his head! What did it change? Was she supposed to forgive him now—to express her elation over this miraculous change of heart? To rejoice in his marriage to Velena? To get on her knees in magnanimous praise of his monetary blessings? Must she sink beneath the weight of it in order that he should gain relief from his burdens? How does one simply give up one's fears—nightmares, self-loathing, and hate? She couldn't—and wouldn't.

"I *hate* you…" her voice came on a breath, a whisper. "I hate you!" She came at him then in a futile attempt that sent her sprawling back onto the bed.

He stood above her, body trembling. "And I you…but only because I've hated myself." He swallowed hard. "Our agreement of before still stands. You will leave after the wedding. Take the money and raise the babe how you will. I seek only to provide the means with which to keep you both alive. If you can't accept my penitence, so be it." He stepped away as if to leave. "You'll not hear it again."

Daisy sat up, watching his retreat until he stopped just short of the outer door. As if in afterthought, he spoke over his shoulder. "Now that you've been paid, I believe it's my turn to have the upper hand. No more threats regarding Velena. She's to be my wife…and if I want to kiss her, I shall."

"She won't let you."

He turned to look at her.

"She promised Tristan she'd not kiss you till the wedding."

"Then she broke that promise."

"And regrets it. As I was your mistake…you are hers." Saying her peace, she knew she'd wounded him. She'd drawn blood and had naught to do but await the outcome. He was not changed. He would retaliate. He would strike out at her. He would fuel the fire that burned within her and prove she'd been right not to forgive him.

But he walked out the door.

5

what eyes have seen

Velena was in no hurry to be accosted should Rowan be correct about Stuart's intentions for hiding, but she didn't share his concern. Stuart hadn't attempted an intimate moment in days, and even at his most persistent, he would never force himself upon her.

Believing this, she trotted up the stairs. The corridor was empty as she passed each of the spare bedrooms, running a hand across the one Tristan had last occupied. She passed her own solar, deciding to begin her search at the end of the corridor where Britton's door had been left open. Hands perched on her hips, she glanced around. It appeared empty. She peeked into the bedchamber. "Stuart. Are you in here? The game has ended."

No answer.

Retracing her steps, she paused in the sitting area to gather up the vibrant green velvet Daisy had been embroidering on earlier and set *Tristan and Iseult* on top. She would return the items on her way to search the other rooms, though perhaps a simple call down the corridor would be better. Determined to do so, she hadn't yet passed the threshold of Britton's door when the door to her own solar swung open. Eyes rounded in surprise, she stood rooted as Stuart emerged.

Had he turned his head even the slightest bit left, he would have seen her. Had he looked anything but completely distracted, she might have called out to him instead of watching as he headed straight for the stairs without looking back. Just as well. He would find his way to the great hall, and Rowan would have no reason to chastise her for searching him out alone. Recalling the rigid set to his shoulders, she hoped he wasn't too upset. A step forward and she startled as the door to her solar slammed shut.

She moved not a muscle save for her eyes, which shifted from her door to the end of the hall, to her door again. That's when her thoughts took off like a horse meant for the open fields—galloping down a road she wanted to avoid at all cost.

He was hiding…that's all. She pulled in her bottom lip, willing to accept it, but the closed door still begged the question. *Who was with him?* Wasn't everyone else below stairs? Had she paid enough attention, slipping out from the room as she had? Dropping her gaze to the book and velvet still in hand, she tried to recall if anyone had been missing. She ran a thumb over the golden threads of a small but intricately embroidered pattern exposed between the folds, and only one face came to mind, causing her heart to stumble.

This thought alone moved her forward, and the forward motion felt a lot like floating. The closer she came to her door, the greater her sense of urgency, so that when she finally arrived, she pushed down on the latch without hesitation.

No one.

Continuing past the sitting room, she thrust open the door to her bedchamber…and everything stopped. Her heart, her breathing, her thinking—time itself—it *all* stopped. Because there was Daisy, the closest thing she had to a sister, exposed and holding a money purse.

In an effort to close the flaps of her bodice, she lost hold of the purse, and the solid *chink* of it hitting the ground was like the last piece of a puzzle falling into place. *All this time…*

Struck by a wave of dizziness, Velena felt like she was out of herself, witnessing events that were too outlandish to prove true.

Daisy stepped forward, gushing out some sort of explanation about Jaren spilling his drink, but she didn't want to hear.

"I was just bringing these back," Velena interjected, and pushed her bundle into Daisy's arms with such impetus that her book flew to the floor, leaving the room as abruptly as she'd entered.

"My lady…"

"I have to go." And that was the truth. She couldn't stand it, not one more minute of it—not if she wanted to make it out the door before falling to pieces—not that there was anything to hold her together once she did. But she tried. Heading for the stairs at a fast clip, she pressed the palm of her hand across her mouth, swallowing against the ache in her throat and the prick of tears behind her eyes.

Halfway to the great hall, she realized she couldn't go in. Stuart was most certainly there by now, and besides that, she was about to break. Whirling around in the opposite direction, she ran for the front doors of the manor. She threw them back and was hit by icy blasts of air and water-spray as gusts of wind brought the rain in past the protective overhang. One look at the sky showed there was no sign of it letting up, as great sheets continued to pour down, soaking the earth to capacity. And now, the puddles that had first spotted the dips and low areas of the gravel yard had gravitated towards each other, forming what appeared to be one unified lake of water, albeit only inches deep. Her heart sunk.

She could go to her father's cabinet or the library, but she needed to scream, to sob—to pray with words spoken aloud. Standing there, the front of her cotehardie grew damp, and the fur trimming the end of her sleeves drooped. She raised her face to the sky. It wasn't yet noon, but the expanse above her was dark and ominous, like an angry, suffocating blanket stretched over them as far as she could see. Gone were any feelings of delight over the sweet odor of rain rushing in to cocoon itself around her. It was changed now, sending her to places that felt dank and musty like a mildew-ridden closet.

Tristan. He'd been right about Stuart. He'd been right about him all along. Had he known of Stuart's tryst with Daisy? Had he known and not told her? Is that why he said he'd come back? Is that why he had Rowan brought to the manor—to keep his eye on them—to put a stop to what they were doing? If it had ever been about protecting her from Stuart's less than honorable intentions, it now seemed only a small part of a much bigger picture. What he'd really been protecting her from was the truth.

She shook her head, letting fly the dust that had always muddled her thinking, exposing at long last what should have been visible and plain. This was why Tristan had offered Daisy his home—not to provide her a haven, but to get her away. And though her many nights of tears upon their return from the castle suggested she regretted her actions or, at the very least, carried guilt over them, it mattered naught. Her betrayal was of the acutest measure—as was Tristan's. He should have told her.

Velena's eyes lit up as bolts of lightning flashed deep within thick layers of clouds, brightening the sky in patches. Claps of thunder echoed her unrest, and the steady drone of the downpour washed away all thoughts but one. *Faithful are the wounds of a friend but deceitful are the kisses of an enemy.* Velena buried her face in her hands, recalling the last bit of Scripture Tristan had penned for her. He'd said it was what she needed to remember. He *had* to have known the truth. He'd known—

and he left knowing, fully aware that his silence would someday wound her. How could he?

How could you?! The ache in her heart demanded she scream it, but what came were fierce whispers lost on the wind. "You told me you'd always be honest with me…but you weren't. You weren't honest; you were a *coward*." She cried then. "You said you had no words, but for my sake you should have found them. Even a coward's letter is better than…"

Her father's letter…

Might Tristan have said more in his letter to her father than he admitted? Had he tried to spare her from Daisy's deception while still warning her father of Stuart's unfaithfulness? She had to know. Spinning around, she flew headlong into something tall—and quite solid.

Rowan took in Velena's rain-sopped appearance—top to bottom—from the loose hairs, wet, and clinging to her temples to the discoloration of her rose-colored cotehardie and fir trim clumped lifelessly at her wrists and hem. "Nenna. What on earth are you doing? Close the doors," he said, not waiting but moving past her to do so. By the time he turned around, she was already rushing off in the opposite direction.

Bewildered, he caught up to her in her father's cabinet. Standing in the doorway, he watched as she skirted behind Sir Richard's desk, testing the drawers to see if any would open. Her purpose was singular, and her effort to see it accomplished completely unaffected by his presence or his moment of earlier concern upon finding her absent the great hall. He'd kept his tone light when he'd asked her not to go after Stuart, but she'd known good and well he meant it. Frustrated with himself for not sooner noticing she was no longer about the room dancing, a quick look to Makaias had told him all he needed to know, as the knight pointed his flute in the direction of the door. He hadn't expected to find her in the rain—or nearly so—nor attempting to break into her father's desk.

"You need a key," he pointed out.

She exhaled in frustration. "I know it needs a key," she said, moving to a bookshelf where she began peeking beneath and behind items two at a time.

"What are you doing? Nenna, stop! Talk to me."

Closing her eyes, she gripped the shelves, laying her head against the backs of her hands.

"What's wrong?"

She rolled her head to face him, indecision wrestling her insides. "I need to find Tristan's letter."

He came up beside her. "The one he gave to your father? Why?"

He asked the question, but Velena could swear from the look in his eyes that he already knew. It brought her up straight and her voice down to a whisper. "I think he told him…something he wanted to keep from me."

"Is this about Stuart?" His gaze became steely and his tone reprimanding. "I told you not to go after him."

"I'm sorry, but I…I dare not say, lest I speak it into existence." Tears pooled in her eyes. "I just need to find the letter. Will you help me?"

Rowan sighed, wishing for the hundredth time Tristan would walk through the front doors and set things right. He hated that he already knew what the letter said. He could tell her but believed it was more complicated than simply giving her the truth. Tristan had felt that it was better for her not to know what Stuart had done if he couldn't free her from him—and Rowan agreed.

But if she found the letter, herself, choosing to confront her father with it, he'd not stop her. Furthermore, he felt very strongly that the next best thing to hearing the truth from Tristan's own mouth, was to read it penned in his own hand. So, he nodded and took up the search on the shelves above her reach. In quick time, he discovered a key hidden within a plaster bust of St. Peter. He opened the desk but dare not riffle through his lord's belongings. This, he left up to Velena, who was guaranteed her father's forgiveness should they be discovered. Meanwhile, her movements were that of a mad woman, piling the entire contents of each drawer atop the desk, spreading them out to look over each one.

"It's not here…" Her shoulders sagged, and she began slowly gathering everything back into its proper place. Locking the drawers, she handed the key back to Rowan.

"Nenna, talk with your father. If he won't let you read it, he might at least tell you what it says."

Velena rubbed her hands over her cheeks. So far, they were steady, but inside, she was trembling. Looking towards the open door, she asked, "Is Stuart in there?"

"The great hall? Not when I came out." He shifted his feet, his movements becoming agitated. "Did he touch you?"

"Not me..." Her voice broke, and the flood she'd held back made tracks down her cheeks.

He went to her, lowering her into a chair, crouching at her knees. "It's alright," he spoke softly, taking her chilled hands into his warm ones. "Shhh...tell me what happened."

She held tight, every word a struggle. "I went above stairs looking for him—to Britton's solar—but he wasn't there. He was in mine—with Daisy."

Rowan's muscles grew taught, and too late, Velena thought of what he might do when she revealed the rest. "When I saw him come out, I thought he'd just been hiding. But when I went in, Daisy was in the bed chamber. Her buttons were undone..." She had to stop and take a breath. "She made some sort of excuse about Jaren spilling his drink, but—"

Rowan exhaled, relief flooding his features. "That's true. I was there when it happened. She left to change clothes."

"She would never undress while he was there."

"Perhaps he *was* hiding. Who knows? He may have seen her come in and left as soon as she went in to change."

"I wish that with every fiber of my being. But she looked guilty, Rowan—really and truly guilty. You know I would never disparage her character without—"

"Then don't. Stuart had reason for hiding, and Daisy to undress. That they got caught together is not out of the question, as unlikely as it seems. None of us knew where he was."

Velena pulled back. "Why are you defending him?"

"I'm not."

"*Yes*, you are. You hate him."

"Him, yes. Daisy, no... And I'll defend her to my last breath and so should you. Remember who she is. More than a maid—she's your friend. She would never—"

"*Lie* to me? *Deceive* me? They've been keeping secrets ever since we came back from Wineford. Clearer to me, now, is that they've been keeping them together."

Recapturing her hands, he brought them to his lips; breathing hard, he pressed them there, stroking her knuckles as if wanting to offer her a level of comfort which could not be spoken, as if having some understanding of her pain. "I know it seems that way. But speak with your father first, lest you rest your judgements falsely."

"I make no light judgements and would never accuse her falsely. Hear me...please," she begged. "She was holding a money purse. It was full. It wasn't mine, and it wasn't hers. What's left to think but that he paid her."

He shook his head, lips rolled in, considering her words. "There has to be another explanation. I say again, speak with your father; then, we'll talk." Glad when she remained silent, he stood, escorting her to the great hall in hopes that she would do so without delay—praying her faith would hold strong when she found the answers she was looking for.

"Where will you be?" she asked before entering.

"Over there," he said, nodding towards the foyer, "mopping up your mess." He meant to soften his words with a smile, but it was something he couldn't seem to muster.

Squaring her shoulders, she left him standing there, stricken and alone, still trusting that Daisy was innocent, but unable to explain how. Closing his eyes, he turned aside, opening them just in time to see Daisy descending the last of the stairs. Drawn to her, he followed her into the foyer, her gait that of a tortured soul—and Rowan knowing why.

6

not how the game is played

Daisy stood in front of one of the tall, paned windows to the left of the double doors. Her reflection in the glass, as Rowan came up behind her, was of a woman despondent and lost. He knew she was fighting a losing battle. What was hidden would soon come to light, and even if it didn't, she had to know what Velena thought of her now, having seen her in her state of disarray—having seen her…with the money.

Rowan took a deep breath but asked none of the questions he wanted to. Instead, he came closer, so close the fronts of his shoes disappeared beneath the hem of her tunic. He half expected her to grow stiff—or walk away. When she didn't, he reached for her hand, and to his amazement, she leaned into him.

Darker outside than inside, the window was as good as any mirror. He stared into it, examining himself alongside this woman he was growing more in love with by the hour—at least closer to love than anything he'd felt before. Her eyelids had fallen closed, and he was glad of it. He wanted to study her without making her self-conscious. Wheat colored hair, dimpled cheeks, a full set of curves to draw a man's attention—there was no denying he wanted her. She *had* to know he wanted her. But would she have him? *Truly* have him. Or had Stuart taken the desire for a man's touch from her altogether?

Out of the stillness of the reflection erupted movement along the outer edge of the windowpane. Behind them, Velena had re-emerged from the great hall. She walked towards him, then stopped. What must she be thinking, catching them like this—and right after what she'd witnessed in her solar? Head down, she veered into the chapel rather than approach him with Daisy.

He suppressed a groan, knowing she'd come to speak with him about the letter but was, as yet, not ready to release her maid. Tightening his hold of Daisy's hand, he stroked her wrist with his thumb, fighting with his conscience. He'd have to answer for it but told himself he could make it no worse if he lingered.

He was wrong.

Betrayed on every side...or so it felt, as Velena entered the chapel ready to scream. She had need of Rowan, but there he was consorting with the enemy. It was a strong word, she knew. And it pained her to feel this way, for never in her whole life did she ever think to feel this way about Daisy, having always loved her and thought the best of her. But the sound of those coins hitting the floor...

She wanted to believe as Rowan did that there was some other explanation for what she'd seen, but she couldn't fathom what it could be. And it wasn't until she finally closed her eyes to take deep calming breaths that she began to recognize the niggling in her heart to pray. Yes. The Lord was who she needed. She must go straight to her knees and—

"Velena..."

Oh, Lord, not now, she begged, barely having to turn her head to see that Stuart was sitting in the back most pew, watching her. Quickly, she turned to leave.

"Velena, wait. Stop."

She paused.

"Come. Please..." He motioned for her to sit beside him. "Join me."

Closed in on both sides, she realized she had just as much reason not to want to leave as she did not to stay. Going to him, she exhaled all that she could from the tempest of her emotions so as to hold her tongue.

"Join me," he said again, taking her hand to draw her down to his side.

She was rigid.

"It's so strange that you're here," he confessed. "I was just thinking about you. I was praying—leastwise, I tried—believe it or not. And now, like a fool, I've been sitting here awaiting my answer."

She dared look him in the face and thought then that he looked about as unsure of himself as she could ever remember seeing him. Yet she felt so little pity for it.

"You spend far more time at this than I. Do you suppose He heard me?"

She pulled in her bottom lip and nodded, seeing naught but him coming out of her solar...and Daisy, with her buttons undone.

He turned his attention to the crucifix hanging high on the wall above the communion table. "I wonder sometimes if He does...or if He's really stone cold like that scrap of metal over there. Unseeing eyes staring back at me." He leaned down over his knees. "Sometimes, I wonder if there's really a God at all. Do you ever think that?"

"I used to."

"If there is, it's no wonder we need a woman to intercede for us. Only a mother could turn a heart that hard."

She shook her head, longing for silence but unable to keep quiet in the face of such blasphemy. "He's a loving God," she corrected, hands fidgeting in her lap as she spoke softly. "Kind. Merciful. Long-suffering. It's Christ, Himself, who atones for our sins. It's why we need Him so." She looked at him then. "Mary's only a woman...same as me."

"Then you're the answer to my prayers."

"What?" She looked away.

"You're who I need," he said, startling her as he took her face in both hands, pulling her towards him. "You're my *Mary*—the only good in my life. Left to myself, I see only flames, but you—you'll bring God's favor to our home."

"Weren't you listening? It doesn't work like that."

"It has to!" His voice rang of desperation. "It has to—else I'm lost. No one understand me as you do. No one knows the person I could have been if it weren't for my father—the person you always saw, despite him."

She pushed back on his wrists until he let go. "You make me an idol."

"So be it. I'll worship you the rest of my days. No woman in all of history will be so loved as you."

"Don't say that."

"It's true. I wish we were married tonight. I wish it were already done. Then I could tell you—"

"What? Tell me what?" she asked, her voice now just as desperate as his, wanting answers and dreading them all the same. "What would you tell me?" she asked again, watching in misery as his eyes clouded over.

He tried to smile, but it was a sad attempt—a weak flicker that faded to nothing. "Things that weigh down on a man. Things he hopes a wife will accept...and forgive. Oh, Velena!" He made no further attempt to disguise his anguish. "I need you near me. I need you near me so *badly*," he said, leaning in and kissing her before she could object.

Taken by surprise, she managed to twist free, nearly tumbling from the pew in order to do so. "No!" she exclaimed, gasping for breath. "No more. I...I can't be here."

"Don't leave!" He gave chase, capturing her by her arm.

"Don't ever leave me. If you did, I'd..." he shook his head. "Better to kill myself than—"

"Enough!" Her mind reeled with what he was saying. "How could you saddle me with such a burden?"

He hung his head. "I don't mean to. I'm just...I'm just so alone." He ran his hands up her arms and neck—cupping her face beneath her jaw—caressing the height of her cheek bone with the tip of his nose. "Stay with me...please."

Wanting to run, she froze. Wanting to rail against him, she pressed her lips firmly together just as he brushed over them, claiming them with his own. She came to life then. Pushing against him with elbows and forearms, he would not be moved, except to snake his arms about her waist in a crushing embrace.

"Stu—" Wriggling and squirming, she wasn't able to get her breath until he moved his attention from her mouth to her ear. She cringed, crowding him out with her shoulder. "Stop."

"Kiss me, Velena. Just *once*, I want you to kiss me as a wife should." Heady and breathless, he muffled her protests—taking first advantage of her open mouth.

God, help me!

Then there was Rowan. Out of nowhere, he was upon them, pulling her free—flinging Stuart across the floor as if he weighed no more than a child. "Did you want that?" he asked, pointing to their cousin sprawled awkwardly against the wall.

"How can you ask?"

"Because I think he needs to hear the answer."

"Rowan...I'm alright. It's over."

"Did you want that?" he repeated.

She took a step back as Stuart came to his feet, bells of alarm ringing free in her ears. "Please...let's just leave." She laid a hand to his arm, but he jerked it free.

"Answer my question!"

"No!" she shouted back at him, making fists at her sides. "No, I didn't want it. But it's over now...please," she begged. "Rowan, please..."

"I'm sorry, Sir Nenna. But that's not how the game is played."

Wary, Stuart approached them. "What game?"

"This game." Rowan spun around and planted a fist square to his mouth, knocking him sideways and into a pew. A squeal at the door announced Daisy's presence, but Rowan sighed as if he hadn't heard, relief rocking his head back and pulling at his arms as if he'd been waiting for that moment a long, long time. Breathing heavy through the mouth, he watched Stuart scramble back to his feet.

Rowan shook off the pain in his fist and smiled. "It's called *Everywhere you touch her I'll meet you the same with my fist.* What do you think of it?"

Stuart touched his fingers to his lip where he was bleeding. "I think you're insane."

"I think you have three seconds to be on your way before I take another guess at where you touched her."

"I kissed her only," he insisted, looking from Velena to Daisy, then back again. "Velena, tell them."

Visibly shaken, she nodded but without a great deal of certainty.

His excuses faded to nothing. "Oh, Velena. I don't know what came over me. Please forg—"

"Three, two, one—leave," Rowan pronounced abruptly, intercepting him before he could touch her.

Stumbling backward, Daisy pressed herself against the doorjamb as Rowan took him up by his jerkin and shoved him from the room.

"Leave, else I call Sir Richard." he demanded, almost surprised when he did. Returning to Velena, he stood before her. "Are you alright?" he asked softly, watching the wide range of emotions play out across her face.

Confused, disgusted, angered, embarrassed—she said the only thing she could think of before giving into a sudden sob. "It was the other kind of kiss."

Incensed, he simply held her, hating that with one foul stroke, Stuart had ruined something which should have been pleasurable—and taken from her something she should have discovered with someone else. And there *would* be a someone else. Whether or not Tristan made it back in time, Velena would not marry Stuart. Of this, he would make certain.

"I'm putting an end to this," he said, putting her away from him.

She grabbed hold of his sleeves. "No more fighting...please."

"We're *just* going to talk."

"You're too upset for talking."

He gave her hand a squeeze. "You're trembling."

"I don't want you to get hurt."

"Me?" He hugged her again. "We've grappled before. Never fear, Sir Nenna; he hasn't bested me yet."

"I don't want you to hurt him either," she mumbled into his chest. "He's lost. He's *so* desperately lost."

Rowan shook his head, stroking her back as if to warm her. "You're quite a woman, Velena Ambrose," he whispered, smiling at how long it'd been since he'd called her by her given name. "Merciful in ways I can't comprehend. But mercy isn't the only heavenly attribute, and there will come a time when you'll understand the absolute need for justice." He gave her another squeeze. "Now, go up to your solar and wait for me."

"I'll wait here."

"I promise to come and—"

"I'll wait, *here*."

He let go a deep breath and looked to Daisy, who'd all but faded into the background. "Did you see which way he went?"

She pointed towards the front doors. "Outside."

"Thank you." He gave her a reassuring smile, but when he passed beneath the threshold, her voice stopped him.

"What are you going to do?"

He looked past her to Velena, but she turned away from them, giving no indication whether she approved or disapproved of them having the conversation. Seizing the moment, he drew Daisy into the hallway, keeping his voice low. "He thinks the two of you are the only ones who know what he did. It's time he learned different."

"I already threatened him with going to Sir Richard, and it did no good."

"Even I know you'd never follow through on that."

"I still don't think that—"

"Don't think. Trust. A threat coming from me will play out differently. You'll see. He'll think twice about acting out again if he knows there's someone else to expose what he did."

Fear gripped her chest. "But you *won't*."

A grim line split his face. He wasn't going to argue with her now.

"You'll be safer if he thinks it. You both will."

Left standing there, Daisy stared aimlessly at the tapestry on the wall. The image was a depiction of Tristan and Iseult, set amid a sea of thorns. Their eyes were downcast and their expressions bleak. And for the first time since he left, Daisy found herself wishing for the real Tristan to come back. Oh, that he might take her away from here and the secrets she'd hedged round about herself. He'd offered her a home once. Now that she had Stuart's money, she would go to him. She just wasn't sure how.

7

blood and water

Faced with the elements, Rowan paused beneath the manor's few inches of overhang, the wind and rain muffling the sound of the doors coming together behind him. Cold, his breath materialized into large clouds of vapor as he rubbed his hands together and squinted against the spray of water, wondering whether his cousin would have actually ridden home in all this weather. As he scanned the shallow ocean of water before him, he didn't have long to contemplate the matter.

"Something you want?" Stuart asked, turning a dull eye towards Rowan from beneath the selfsame overhang, a mere few yards away.

Undeterred by Stuart's puzzling attitude, he got right to the point. "I want you to stay away from Velena—and from Daisy."

Stuart rolled his head so that he again faced the rain, a humorless grin rising as wet clumps of bangs blew across his vision. "Why would I come near her?"

"I've wondered that myself."

Stuart combed his hair aside with his fingers. "I can tell you like her, but jealousy is really more my thing."

Rowan narrowed his eyes. "I mean it."

"Oh, I believe you," he said, giving half a laugh. "And fully expected there to be another round of discipline—in regard to *Velena*. How Daisy's a part of this, I surely don't know."

"Then allow me to enlighten you," he said, hiding from his voice none of the impending violence, they both knew was coming. "You see, I know what you did to Daisy at Wineford. And I think it's time for *you* to know that I do—just in case buying her silence isn't good enough for you. Because if you hurt even one hair on her head, I'll have yours on a stake."

Dumbfounded, Stuart stood silent, until quite unexpectedly he began to laugh. Half-crazed, at first, it took on a bitter twist, as one who knows he's about to meet his end. Finishing with a prolonged sigh, he pushed away from the wall and into the downpour. There, he raised his face to the sky, closed his eyes, and stilled himself for the streams of judgement about to rain down on him.

Slicking his hair back with one smooth motion, he turned around to face his hangman. "Well, now. I wager you're glad to get that off your chest."

Rowan sloshed through the inches of water until they were nose to nose. "Aren't you even going to try and deny it?"

"Do you want me to?"

"I want it to be a lie!"

Stuart scoffed. "Now there's the lie. You've never had any trouble thinking the worst of me."

"You've always made it easy to. Yet, never did I expect you to—"

"What, Rowan—to what? Say it! To do anything so heinous—so evil? Underhanded? Unforgivable?"

"Exactly that."

"It wasn't something I planned, if that's what you're thinking."

Lightening flashed, illuminating Rowan's growing contempt. "I suppose you're going to say the devil made you do it."

"Would you settle for heredity?"

"This isn't a joke."

"On that we agree. There's nothing funny about it."

"*Truth*, Stuart. How could you do it?"

"You weren't there!" he shouted, striking out like a cornered animal, slamming his palm into Rowan's chest. "You didn't see. She'd have given herself to Bowan if he'd been man enough. She...." He stopped abruptly, catching himself as he relapsed right back into passing the blame. Weary, he ran a hand over his lids, clearing his vision of water. "I wouldn't have touched her, except...I was angry with Velena...and drunk."

"It's no excuse."

"No, it's not. But it's what happened."

Rowan shook his head. "I feel sorry for you, Stuart. I really do. You've pined over Velena since we were children. Did finally having what you've always wanted mean so little? Are you so conditioned from all your *mucking* around that you couldn't have waited the time it'd take to wed her before bedding someone else?"

"I won't justify myself to you."

Rowan swore. "Then help me understand."

"You don't want to understand me any more than you'd extend a hand to save me. I know you. And what you want is for Velena to see me as some poor wretch who doesn't know how to deny his baser instincts—like some sort of animal—attacking women in the night."

"Which *is* what you did."

Stuart grabbed him by the front of his jerkin. "I know what I did!" he growled, forcing the words through clenched teeth. "I live with it *every day*." He released Rowan with a shake. "I live beneath the shadow of losing Velena *every day*. Do you think I'm without regret?"

Rowan shoved him away. "You think of no one but yourself."

"And you're different? Declaring courtly love to Velena, all the while following Daisy around behind her back like some buck in rut." He sneered. "I see the way you look at her. I'm not the only one with baser instincts."

"At least I know better than to act on them."

"As God is my witness, I'd undo it if I could—but I can't. Mine is to be a life of penance—beginning with Daisy. That's what the money was for. Not silence—penance!"

"You're telling me you were in her solar to apologize?"

"It matters naught that you believe me."

"Then believe this. You took Daisy from Bowan—and now I'm going to do everything in my power to see Velena taken from you."

Fuming, Stuart threw the first punch but missed. "As if you cared anything about Bowan," he said, stumbling past him. "If it'd been you she wanted, you'd have taken her in a heartbeat."

Rowan stretched his neck from side to side, oblivious to the cold and feeling a bloodlust he didn't know was in him.

Widening his stance, Stuart readied himself, water running down every limb. "I'm going to rip you open."

Rowan's lips curled into a catlike grin. "You have one try…"

Makaias handed his flute off to Jaren and sank down on the bench across from Britton. Their table was empty now that the majority of castle folk were up and rollicking about. Thus, he sat quietly, observing the gaiety of those around him, wondering—and not for the first time—if they were truly enjoying themselves, or if it was just the drink that told them so.

Letting go an inward sigh, he thumped the meaty side of his fist against the table. Time was wasted enjoying such frivolities. Was he the only man who wished he could be outside swinging a sword? He thought of Velena and what she'd said in the chapel. Perhaps he *was* too serious. Then, he recalled her little confession and felt himself smiling.

Britton swallowed the last bit of ale he'd been swishing around in his mouth, only now feeling some mild relief in his leg. "Where's Rowan gone off to?"

Makaias shrugged. "To find your sister."

Britton's smile was half-cocked. "He certainly takes this courtly love thing seriously."

"His concern for her is admirable."

"I suppose."

Makaias, drummed his fingers against the edge of the table in time with the music but continued to feel uneasy. "Did he mean what he said about Stuart?"

"When?"

"Before—in the chapel. And here. He said he was only playing the game to get your sister alone."

Britton laughed. "Stealing kisses behind closed doors is exactly why games like these were invented in the first place."

Makaias frowned. "If you thought that, you shouldn't have let her play."

"Come off it." He readjusted his crutch from where he'd wedged it between his legs. "They're engaged. Are you going to tell me you never stole a kiss from the fair Johanna? Never tried to touch her..." Britton cupped his hands in front of his chest.

"Careful..." Makaias warned.

"As I recall, she was fairly—"

"*Britton.*"

"Ample."

"I'll not give answer to that."

Britton laughed. "You don't have to, but who'd blame you if you did? Large-breasted women *are* difficult to resist."

Makaias stifled a smile. Beyond Britton's shoulder Velena's slim figure re-appeared in the room, absent either Rowan or Stuart. Curious, he found his gaze lingering as she approached the dais to speak with her father. Less buxom than most, he had to admit she still held a certain appeal. Disturbed by his sudden train of thought, he looked away.

"I think Joanna's chest must have ruined you for all other women," Britton continued, twisting round to see what had captured his friend's attention. "It's why you find it so easy to resist my sister."

"Your sister is *engaged*."

"And if she weren't?"

Incredulous, Makaias laughed. "This is ridiculous…"

"Humor me," Britton insisted. "What is it about her that doesn't meet with your approval?"

"If I tell you, will you stop?"

"I can't swear to it."

Grumbling, Makaias took a swig from his tankard, but gave in. "For starters, she's still more girl than woman."

Britton's jaw went slack. "You insult her. Four years past marrying age, she's every bit a woman. Be honest and tell me you haven't noticed."

"Not as you have," he said, laughing.

"If you bring that up even one more time, so help me…" He began to chuckle despite himself. "I'll beat you senseless with the very crutch you took ever so long to fashion. And anyway," he continued, "it's not fair to judge her as less than a woman because of the size of her—"

"I judge her by her impetuous and careless nature. I've not taken note of her chest," Makaias said, realizing he was now being less than honest about that second part. "Really Britton, no one could ever accuse you of being protective of your sister—not from me and certainly not from Stuart."

"It's not that I'm not protective; it's more that there hasn't been a need for it. We both know you're too chivalrous for me to worry about, and when has Velena ever needed protecting from Stuart? That whiner. He tried kissing her when they were young, and she gave him a decent sized handprint for it. I've no doubt she'd do it again if she had a mind to."

"And what if she doesn't have a mind to?" Makaias watched as she retraced her steps, leaving the room at a brisk walk. Gone was the easy manner he'd come to expect from her. In its place, there was an anxiousness, and it didn't bode well. "She's an innocent. She has no idea where a kiss can lead."

Britton chuckled. "Neither do you—or so you claim."

"Granted," he said, raising his hands, "but if gossip proves true, Stuart does. Women are easily seduced, and you shouldn't be dismissing Rowan's concerns. If he's pressuring her, you should be the one doing something about it."

"She doesn't even want him, Kai—or haven't you noticed? The likelihood of Velena succumbing to Stuart before her wedding night is infinitesimal." He leaned in. "This wedding is taking place for one reason and one reason only. My father seeks to honor what he thinks our mother would have wanted. No more and no less—a sweet gesture, but all in all, utterly ridiculous. In fact, I can barely stomach the thought of it," he said, planting a finger topside down on the table as if to emphasize his point. "Do you think I want Stuart for a brother-in-law? Or Uncle Magnus playing the role of father to my sister? God, help her." He crossed himself and looked up. "I hound you about her because I keep hoping I'll bore through that thick skull of yours and find the person who was once willing to do his part for our family."

"I do my part."

"You were willing to marry her once. If you'd be willing again, I know I could change my father's mind about Stuart. He's not right for her. Never has been, never will be. Is there nothing I can do to bring you around?"

Makaias ran his hands over his face, reminded of his need to shave as something bearing the grim likeness of both a groan and a sigh escaped his mouth. "I...can't. I'm sorry, Britton...but I just can't. And it's not just that I have no intimate feelings for your sister—which I don't—but how could I, in good conscience, purposefully thwart..." Words fell away as he considered the consequences of such an action. "No matter what you think of Stuart, he's still family—and I could *never* do him the dishonor of placing myself between him and—"

A woman cleared her throat from the end of the table, and two sets of eyes turned to see the head cook's grown daughter. She had blond hair, brown eyes, and enough curves to satisfy the most insatiable of men, as evidenced by the ones not two feet in front of their faces.

"Begging your pardon, but..."

Makaias had the inkling that she might be the woman he'd seen eyeing him from behind the curtain wall—not just today, but for weeks now. Not given to flirtations or leading women on, he'd been dead set on ignoring her. Now, wondering what courage had drawn her out without so much as an ail pitcher in hand, he sat politely, waiting for her to speak.

"What?" Britton asked brusquely, when she seemed too tongue-tied to continue.

"I…um…I was just wondering if this knight would like to join me for a dance."

Britton laughed. "Sorry, miss, but this man has sworn off women."

"Only engaged ones," Makaias quipped. Then—as if to prove his point—he stood to his feet. Leaving Britton naught but a self-satisfied grin, took the girl's hand into the crook of his arm. "I'd be happy for a dance, miss…"

"Juliana, my lord."

Makaias smiled. "A beautiful name to be sure. Shall we?"

Britton swung his legs around so he could lean against the table and watch. If a fair smile and a flushed complexion were any indication of joy, the wench was clearly the happiest she'd ever been in her life—leastwise, since the last man who'd taken her up on her offer. And she *had* made offers.

Grinning, Britton crossed his arms. Makaias thought to teach him a lesson, but he'd soon find out he'd have his hands full with that one. Three dances later, he foresaw Makaias having to fend her off with a stick.

"FATHER!"

The scream rang through the corridor at a fever pitch, bringing up the hair on the back of his neck. Realizing he was too slow to reach whatever trouble had come to Velena in time, Britton looked to Makaias, but he'd already sprinted across the room to be the first one out the door, unlike himself, who was left to hobble after nearly every other able-bodied man in the room—including his father, who had to circle around the dais. "Fool leg," he muttered.

In the corridor, Makaias had no sooner made eye contact with Velena's drenched exterior, then she whirled around, dashing back through the manor doors and into sheets of rain. Girding himself for the unknown, he chased after her, along with an entire host of men following closely at his heels.

When Velena and Daisy had first burst upon the scene outside, it was a spectacle ripe with blood and violence. The rain was coming down hard, but it did nothing to hide the two combatants bogged down in the midst of it.

Though Rowan's height was less pronounced with him on all fours, Daisy recognized him by his pale blond hair—afore in a top knot, it was now limp and dangling over one ear. For him, she felt a great trembling. For Stuart, not the slightest thread of sympathy. Velena cried out for them to stop. She begged and pleaded, but to no avail. She shouted for Daisy to get help—but she didn't want help. She wanted to see him suffer. Transfixed, she was unaware that Velena had left her there, or that she'd fled inside screaming her father's name.

Under the pouring rain, the grunts and groans continued as both men wrestled for the upper hand. With a mighty heave and a warlike cry, Rowan finally pinned Stuart to the ground between his legs. Watching him slam his fists into his face, one after another, Daisy could see Stuart's nose was broken, as streams of red flowed freely and without end, washing away with every raindrop and returning with every blow. It was a single moment lasting forever; an image of blood and water seared into her brain.

"Rowan, NO!"

Startled from her stupor, time returned, leaving Daisy to gape in horror, hands pressed to her mouth, as Velena lunged past her, attempting to stop one man from pummeling the other. It was the same as she'd done when they were children, only this time, her uncle wasn't able to hold her back from harm's way. Not even Makaias' desperate efforts to do so would be fast enough to stop Velena as she flung herself into the fray, using her body to shield Stuart's face.

Rowan tried to stop himself but was unable to do much more than slow the force of impact before his fist connected with her ribs in a sickening *thwak*. Before he could utter a sound—let alone an apology—Makaias was upon him, hauling him back.

Daisy rushed to Velena's side, dragging her away, thus revealing the extent of Stuart's damage. The rain did its best to wash away any outward evidence, but Makaias could see plain as plain that his cousin's face was a sorry mess.

"What's happened?" Sir Richard demanded, pushing through the crowd of knights and manor folk, all soaked through and speechless."

"She's hurt…" Daisy whimpered, calling attention back to Velena.

Makaias joined Sir Richard as he knelt beside his daughter, his gruff release of Rowan sending him off balance and back to his knees.

Wrapped tightly within Daisy's embrace, Velena held her side, fighting for breath.

Rowan choked, "Nenna...I'm so sorry! I didn't mean to—"

"Silence!" Sir Richard barked.

"It was an accident, my lord."

Jaren pushed through the onlookers, going immediately to Stuart. "Heaven and Earth, look what he's done," he proclaimed, going to work immediately with Lord Magnus to get him up from the mud.

Sir Richard got up to see for himself and was immediately set back on his heels. "Take him to my solar," he ordered, coming back down to help Makaias coax Velena from Daisy's arms. She'd had the wind knocked out of her and was only now able to get a full breath.

Blinking against the rain that pelted her eyelids, she cringed, catching a glimpse of Stuart as he passed by. It was a most pitiful sight.

Seeing her lying there, he would've moved in her direction, if it weren't for his father and Jaren still holding him firmly in place. "Velena..." he rasped. Doubling over, he stopped to choke out a throat full of blood.

Tears mingled with the streams of water making tracks down her face, and it seemed like every man stood silent waiting for her to speak, but her efforts resulted in little, as each draw of air served only to take her breath away.

"Don't talk," Makaias said, lifting her to her feet.

Sir Richard laid a hand to his shoulder. "Take her to her solar for me. Stay with her, and I'll be there as soon as I can." He kissed her forehead, lingering, with his hand tangled amid the matted hair at the back of her head.

What he turned on Rowan was a look far removed from the loving expression he'd bestowed upon his daughter. "Follow Britton to my cabinet," he ordered and then nodded to his son, who had thus far remained framed in the doorway.

Rowan flexed his bloodied knuckles, rooted in place at the sight of Velena still unable to stand upright.

"Now," Sir Richard demanded.

"Yes, my lord," he said, casting one last fleeting look towards the women as Daisy tried to get a grip of Velena's waist.

Her fingers were numb, but she did her best to get a grip of the wet material while Makaias steadied her on her feet.

"Slowly..." he spoke alongside her ear. "That's it...nice and slow." She took a few steps, but when she raised her face to him, he could see her teeth were chattering. Time was suddenly of the essence, so with as gentle a touch as he could manage, he took her up into his arms and carried her the rest of the way.

Under the overhang, Sir Richard slicked back his hair before running a hand down the full length of his beard. Water splattered at his feet, but it mattered naught, as he was already soaked through to the skin. Steeling himself for the hours ahead, he left orders for Sir Tarek to dismiss the crowd, as well as discipline the gatekeeper, who'd surely used the rain as an excuse to sleep rather than remain alert in the gatehouse, as was his orders. Having done so, he might have put an end to the fight before it began.

Sir Richard took a deep breath, letting it out slowly. The true blame of it seemed to be on Rowan, though, and he was dreading the conversation he was about to have with Magnus over his actions. Certainly, he'd demand nothing less than his nephew's head on a silver platter.

8

insult to injury

"Lady Velena…" It was the first Makaias had spoken since delivering her to her bed chamber. "I'm going to set you on your feet now."

"Uuuuh," she groaned, gripping her side.

"She'll need help with her clothes," he said, looking to Daisy. "Get dry—the both of you. Call me when you're done."

Daisy nodded and shut the door behind him.

Makaias took a survey of his surroundings—from the mess he was making on the floor to the dwindling fire in the hearth. A shiver coursed through his body as he began feeling the effects of his wet clothes.

With an experienced hand, he got a proper blaze going and stripped off his jerkin. There wasn't much he could do about his tunic or hose in front of the women, so he continued stoking the flames, standing as close as he dared in hopes of a good steam. He rubbed his hands together, then held them palms out as an image of Stuart's bloodied face came to mind. *What on Earth was Rowan thinking?* In all honesty, he was worried for his cousin. Barring any acceptable explanation of his actions, he could be facing a severe penalty for what he'd done.

Inside the bedchamber, Daisy pulled back the blankets so Velena could settled in. She moved gingerly, letting go small gasps as Daisy helped lower her to her pillow. The transition was agony, but once down, she was able to find a modicum of comfort.

"What else can I do?" Daisy asked, pulling Velena's wet hair out from beneath her shoulders and over the pillow so it wouldn't give her a chill.

"I'm fine," she answered, not really looking at her.

Daisy nodded, feeling plainly the wall between them. She was anything but fine—neither of them was—even so, she tucked the blankets high over Velena's chest, as she was wearing naught but a shift, and called Makaias back into the room.

Pulling up a chair, he gave her a sympathetic smile. For once, she didn't look him in the eyes.

"You don't have to stay," she assured him.

"I do, actually."

She tried shifting to a more comfortable position. "It hurts to breathe."

"You might have broken a rib. With your permission, I'd like to check."

"You?"

"I need only probe the area with my fingers—above your shift, of course."

She looked skeptical.

"You received a hefty blow. The sight of it, alone, nearly brought me to my knees."

Velena's eyes flitted to Daisy, then back again. She didn't need her permission. "Alright."

Adjusting his position to better slide his hand beneath the blankets, Makaias' expression remaining impersonal until he felt the cool grip of her hand slip over his. He looked up in surprise.

"In case you miss," she stated simply. "I'd hate not to be able to look you in the face again."

Eyes glinting in good humor, he allowed her to lead his hand across the soft part of her stomach and up to her left ribcage. He applied pressure—gently at first and then more by increments, keeping a close watch of her face. She winced but didn't cry out, so he probed a bit more before asking, "Is the pain minimal, or are you just being brave?"

"I'm being brave," she admitted.

"Take a deep breath for me."

She tried, but filling her lungs didn't quite happen, as sharp pains stabbed at her side. She gasped.

He withdrew his hand. "Nothing feels out of place, but with as much pain as you're in, I'd wager they may be cracked."

"I'm sure they're just bruised."

He looked doubtful. "Better to error on the side of caution."

"What's done for such things?" Daisy interrupted.

His expression turned grave. "Surgery."

"Oh, my lady..." She clutched her hands to her breast.

Makaias chuckled. "I'm sorry. Forgive me—I'm only teasing. I'm sure Sir Richard will call for the healer, and she'll decide whether she needs to be wrapped or not." He spoke again to Velena. "The bone heals on its own; the wrapping serves to hinder your range of motion, which helps a bit with the pain. It'll just be a long stretch of cloth wrapped around your midsection, here." He used his own body as reference.

Taking a better look at him, Velena realized the pitiable state of his tunic. Soaked through and pressed flat against his body, it did nothing to hide the swell of his broad chest and shoulders. Realizing he must be cold, she sent Daisy to Britton's room for a dry tunic, knowing he took seriously his orders to stay by her side.

Alone with him for the second time, she muttered, "*Surgery…*" and narrowed her eyes. "You deserve a good punch in the arm."

"It'd hurt you more than it'd hurt me I'm afraid."

Her gaze landed on the bulge his bicep was making beneath his wet sleeve. "I believe it," she admitted, hoping she'd properly suppressed any looks of appreciation she had for such things.

His lips quirked in amusement. Not quite a direct compliment to his physique, he took inner pleasure at her notice. Strength training was something he paid careful attention to, not only pushing *himself* to be ready and able to defeat any opponent, but the knights he trained as well. All in all, he found himself having to resist the urge to flex when the thump of Britton's crutch sounded behind him. Quickly, he vacated his chair so he could sit.

"How's she doing?" Britton asked.

"She may have cracked some ribs. Most likely, she'll need to be bound."

Britton nodded. "We've sent for the healer."

"So, what news of Rowan and Stuart?" Makaias asked, crossing his arms.

"Not a whole lot. Rowan wanted to speak with Father alone, but Uncle insisted Stuart be heard first, so…" He shrugged. "Rowan didn't need a baby-sitter, so I left. What started this?" he asked Velena.

She looked upwards at the ceiling.

He leaned in. "You were there before any of us. What did you see?"

"Nothing. I was in the chapel when it happened."

"Then…how was it you came upon them?"

"It was Daisy. She was in the corridor…and heard them shouting. She called to me, and I followed her outside. They were already fighting when we got there."

"And no guesses as to why?"

Velena was still deciding how to answer when Daisy walked in with the clean tunic for Makaias. Grateful, he left the room to change, leaving Daisy empty-handed at the end of the bed, where she stood quietly, adding not a syllable to the awkward silence.

To Britton, she appeared anxious over the state of her mistress, yet Velena refused to even look at her. It was out of character for his sister, and he began feeling a growing sense of agitation over it. He decided to pay heed to his instincts and dismissed Daisy, sending her below stairs with the wet laundry and further instructions to take her time.

"What's going on?" he asked directly.

Velena pulled her arms out from beneath the covers but remained silent.

Aware that an injury to the ribs could make it painful to breathe, Britton watched the rise and fall of her hands above her chest as her inhalations increased, sure it was bringing her an added degree of discomfort. "You must know something."

"It's...hard to begin."

"For Rowan's sake, you'd better. Or don't you think Uncle is going to ask for his head in a basket after seeing what he's done to his son?"

"Alright," she whispered, "I'll tell you," then paused to catch her nerve. "I was in the chapel alone...with Stuart. He, um...kissed me. Then, Rowan came in and..."

Britton looked confused. "You're telling me he nearly took his face off for kissing you?"

Velena swallowed "For kissing me...when I didn't want him to."

Britton stared, unwilling to fully accept what she'd said. Thus, began a war of words and half phrases, the one speaking over the other in an attempt to be heard. "As in...he talked you into it, but you—"

"That's not what I'm s—"

"But you let him, anyway?"

"Persuasion had nothing to do with—"

"Did you tell him to st—"

"Of course, I told him to—"

"Then why did Rowan have to get involved."

"It became neces—"

"You should have just slapped him and saved Rowan the trouble of—"

"I *would have* if I could have moved. You're not listening."

Britton could have sworn the temperature of the room changed as a wave of cold heat swept over his body. Helpless, he watched as tears gathered in his sister's eyes, making tracks over the bridge of her nose and onto her pillow. *It couldn't be.* "He held you down?"

She ran a hand beneath her nose. "We were standing. I tried to push him away, but...he wouldn't let go." Her last words were a whisper, but both men heard—Britton, from where he sat beside her, and Makaias, from where he stood at the door.

Britton fell into the back of his chair. "I'm going to kill him. So help me, he dies tonight! Why, on God's green earth, did he think he could get away with such a thing?"

A sob escaped her throat, and she rolled into her pillow, trying with much effort to stem her emotion to a series of shallow breaths. Anything else hurt too badly.

"Has he forced himself on you before?"

She shook her head. "No. But..."

"But what?"

"He's kissed me before."

"Which you allowed?"

Chin quivering, she nodded. "Only once." She looked away. "I didn't actually want to kiss him then either. I just..." She wiped her palms over her cheeks. "I think I made excuses for him."

Britton began massaging the back of his neck.

"He only wants me to love him."

"But you don't," he said, looking over his shoulder at Makaias.

"Not for a while—and certainly not the way he wants me to," she admitted, knowing he already knew as much.

"Why didn't you tell me?"

"I thought I could handle it. Plus, Rowan knew. He knew about the once, and also about..." her fingers played with the top edge of the blanket, "the other times he'd tried—which is probably why he was so upset when he found us." She could have also said that his feelings for Daisy might have had something to do with it but was, as of yet, unwilling to expose her involvement in the matter.

"Are you afraid of him?" Makaias questioned, stepping farther into the room.

Embarrassed he'd been listening, she began wiping away the last of her tears. "I'm angry more than anything else. Still, I...I didn't want Rowan to hurt him like that. He should have stopped."

74

Makaias nodded. "It did seem excessive."

Britton agreed. "Not that he didn't deserve what he got," he assured her, "but it makes one wonder if there was something else."

"May I come in?"

Britton turned around to see Rowan coming up behind Makaias. "Speak of the devil."

"At least one of them," he admitted. "May I see her?"

Velena nodded, and Britton motioned for Makaias to let him pass.

He lowered himself to the edge of the mattress, grinning through his concern. "Anything broken?" he teased.

"Sir Makaias thinks I might have some cracked ribs. Hurts to breathe."

Rowan's smile faded. "Really?"

Makaias nodded.

"Oh, Nenna." His shoulders sagged. "What a lousy protector I turned out to be. I'm so sorry." Her smile was forgiving, but her eyes told him she wanted to say more. All in good time.

Britton gave him a light kick to the foot to gain his attention. "You still have a lot to answer for. But I owe you a brother's debt. You defended her when I didn't think she needed defending." He felt Makaias' hand upon his shoulder. "I was wrong, and I thank you."

Rowan nodded, unsure how to respond. "Well, Stuart's probably said his peace by now, which means Sir Richard will be looking for me, so…" He gave Velena's hand a squeeze. "If I happen to have a few stripes down my back the next time you see me, just know I don't regret a one of them.

"I'll talk to my father," she assured him.

His turn to say thank you, though he wasn't sure it would help.

Daisy was at the bottom of the stairs, holding a handful of folded cloth when Rowan arrived at the bottom. She took a step towards him, close enough that he could have reached out and touched her. Instead, he waited for her to speak.

"Have you spoken to Sir Richard?" she asked.

"Not yet."

She looked down. "People are already talking."

"Well…I garner quite the audience."

"They're wondering what provoked you."

"They won't be wondering for long, I guess."

"When you tell Sir Richard what happened, you won't…" She took a breath. "You won't tell him anything else, will you?"

He kept quiet, not knowing how to tell her that he probably already knew but didn't care enough to do anything about it.

She pressed the fabric to her chest. "You'll be on your own if you do. Don't think that just because you've been…kind to me that…I'll confess to anything. I've not changed my mind."

"I didn't think you had."

"So, you won't say anything, then…about what he did to me?"

"I think Stuart's imposition on Velena will be saying enough."

Her shoulders relaxed just as Sir Richard's valet emerged from his cabinet down the corridor. He didn't have to approach for Rowan to know he was being summoned. "If you'll excuse me, my hangman awaits." He moved past her, but she called him back.

"Rowan…"

"Yes."

Daisy held her breath, growing warm, as he appeared to be studying her. Was she being too presumptuous? "I suppose I was just assuming before, but…was any…any of what you did to him…also for me?"

"And if it was?"

Withdrawing her gaze, she lowered her chin. "I'm grateful, is all."

"You can rest well now, Daisy. He'll not hurt anyone again."

Daisy waited until the door closed to Sir Richard's cabinet before turning back towards the stairs. A part of her felt as if she should have gone in to defend him, but she shook it off. His chivalry didn't obligate her away from her secret.

Half-way up the stairs, she passed Britton, who acknowledged her with a strained face, explaining that he'd asked Makaias to stay with them in the room until his father arrived. Nodding, she watched him brace himself for the next step down, hoping he'd soon be able to give his leg the rest it needed.

Once in the solar, she laid the material out upon the table and began making long strips of the material, as per Makaias' instructions. It was quick work, and she soon found herself restless for news of Rowan to return to them. Excusing herself, she went in to check on Velena, leaving Makaias to stoke the fire.

He warmed his hands briefly, then turned around to face the room. He felt out of place sitting in a woman's quarters alone, in comfort, as if he were merely a guest instead of a man on orders. Meandering across the room, he arrived at the window seat, hoping to look out onto whatever he could see below, except the rain made visibility nigh impossible.

Seating himself in the alcove, he propped one leg up and allowed the other to dangle, careful not to disturb the sheets, hanging from ceiling to floor. Strung up to conceal a small corner of the room, along with half the alcove he was seated in, he eyed them with curiosity, allowing his mind to conjure up the many different reasons Velena might have had for hanging them. In the end, it became far too tempting a thing not to switch sides and experience what it felt like to sit behind the shroud.

Discretely hidden, he looked down at the triangular bit of floor beneath him, realizing it was actually a fairly decent sized area to sit if he had a mind to sit on the floor, which he didn't. The sheet was thick enough that anyone on the outside would have a reasonably difficult time seeing who was within, yet thin enough he could make out the shadows of the room from the glow of the fire. It was a cozy feeling, the tapping of rain behind him and the flicker of light just beyond. Relaxed, he contemplated the whole of the situation thus far.

On the one hand, he commiserated with Velena a great deal. He felt brotherly towards her, and the ill-treatment she'd received at the hands of his cousin was unsettling, to say the least. On the other hand, he couldn't help but see her as foolish, allowing Stuart's advances over the course of however many previously unwanted encounters without engaging someone's help for it. Then again, she had told Rowan. He shook his head. Whether Velena had shown true discretion or not really wasn't the problem.

A man ought never to take advantage of a woman. This was his firm belief—and should have been Stuart's—*especially* as a squire about to obtain his knighthood. He knew the codes of chivalry, and for this reason alone, he felt no pity over Stuart's beating. What he did pity, however, was his future plight as an unloved husband. Once he wed

Velena—when physical advances would then be appropriate—they might still go unwanted. His problem of patience would be solved, but her resentment of him would not.

Makaias flexed his hands, comparing their unhappiness to his own. What if he'd married Joanna, thinking she loved him, only to find out down the road—and he would have—that he'd married into a lifetime of unfaithful behavior? He wouldn't compare Velena's lack of feelings for Stuart with Joanna's deceit—but her relationship with Tristan certainly had given Stuart reason to doubt. And doubts could eat away at a man. They certainly would him.

9

a matter of authority

Having heard Rowan's side of things, Sir Richard began to pace. He'd seen the damage done to his nephew's face—and the proof of it written across Rowan's bloodied knuckles. That his daughter had been kissed against her will was certainly upsetting, but Stuart had readily admitted to this as his mistake, and the reason for Rowan's actions against him. The fact that they'd had a physical altercation over the matter was understandable, but what unsettled Sir Richard, now, was why Rowan had chosen to dispense such retribution so absolutely and without mercy.

"Anything else?" he questioned.

Getting down on one knee, Rowan took a moment to clear his throat. "Yes, my lord. Sir Makaias has assessed Lady Velena's injuries and concludes that my actions have quite likely cracked...at least one of her ribs."

Though outwardly composed, Sir Richard's heart sank. If he didn't feel the absolute necessity for this blasted interrogation, he'd be upstairs with her this very moment. He gestured for Rowan to stand. "On this account, I forgive you. Velena's decision to intervene in the fight—though noble—was also incredibly foolhardy. I'm bereaved to hear of her injuries, but under the circumstance, she could expect no different. Let us pray she has better sense in the future than to throw herself between two men looking to kill each other. As to that..."

"Am I to expect to be disciplined?"

Sir Richard sunk into his chair. "I'm not sure what to do with you, actually. Stuart has already admitted to kissing Velena. Consequently, he's taken full responsibility for his beating and her injuries."

"Against her will," Rowan added firmly. "He kissed her *against* her will."

"Yes. He admits to that as well and will provide her with a formal apology on the morrow."

Rowan blinked back his surprise, as Sir Richard continued.

"And, if she's so inclined as to accept it—"

"Which she will," Rowan interrupted.

"Excuse me?"

"Which she will," he said again. "She's all mercy—we know this. It's…it's what she does. For that reason, alone, any extension of forgiveness on her part should hold no bearing over the severity or leniency of your judgements on a man who would take advantage of such. For Stuart, I can only hope there is the strictest of punishments, for he deserves the worst you could prescribe."

 Patient with his squire's outburst, Sir Richard rocked back on his heels. "Worse than what you already dealt him?"

"Care you nothing for the molestation of your daughter?"

Sir Richard's voice lowered in warning. "I care a great deal, as a matter of fact. But what if I still told you that your punishment of him went well beyond what was necessary? And what if I told you that you owed Stuart an apology?"

"I'd sooner rot in hell," he spat.

"I see." Sir Richard took a moment and pursed his lips. "Instead of that…how about you tell me what's really going on between the two of you?"

"He *attacked* Velena!"

"Attacked or took advantage of?"

Rowan threw up his arms. "Took advantage of then—but does it really matter which?"

"It matters to me," he stated calmly. "In fact, all truth matters to me. And the truth I want now is why you went so far as you did. What more drove you to it?"

"May I speak freely, my lord?"

Sir Richard laughed coolly. "As freely as you've been doing."

"Then my apologies, my lord, but you know what more."

He raised his eyebrows. "Do I?"

"I speak of Tristan's accusation against Stuart. My respect for you is of the utmost, but I don't understand your inaction."

 "So, you took action in my stead. Is that it?" Sir Richard frowned. "This is the problem with taking up the offenses of another. Tristan did wrong to involve you," he said, recalling their conversation the day he announced his intention to leave Landerhill.

"He asked me to protect Velena."

"And so, you have. I'm not an unreasonable man, Squire Rowan, nor am I an unfeeling father. His accusation *was* worthy of consideration, but without proof—without an accuser—I cannot and *will not* act as judge."

"So, you'll go on as if nothing happened?" he asked, dropping his tone of respect.

"Neither will you act as my judge," Sir Richard cautioned. "There was no proof—and a wise man doesn't make decisions on conjecture."

"Do I still have permission to speak freely?"

"N—you do not," Sir Richard said, coming around his desk. "I understand you well enough. Now, all that's left is for you to understand me. For your service towards my daughter, I owe you my thanks. For the excessive amount of damage done my nephew, I'll take into consideration the concerns you had regarding an unsubstantiated accusation brought against him and limit your punishment to night watch for the next seven days. As to this topic of conversation, it *is* over. Anything left to discuss remains between myself and Tristan. On this, we must have an understanding, else I'll need to release you from service. I won't have a man I can't trust."

Rowan took a moment to breathe, muscles twitching along his neck and jaw line. "My fealty is yours, my lord. I will drop the matter, as you say, asking only that when my punishment is over, I might return to my duties as Lady Velena's protector."

"A duty I never gave you."

"Nonetheless, I request it on the merit that I've proven myself useful to act as such, with a future promise to temper my actions and reflect your good will towards anyone you deem worthy. Leastwise, I wish to remain useful in whatever capacity you'll keep me."

"You may start by replacing the front gateman. No food or water until morning."

Grateful to have already filled his belly with three fruity tarts, he asked, "Will you deny me the rain, my lord?"

"You are a bold one, Squire Rowan. I'll give you that. The rain is God's mercy, not mine. If the Almighty has a mind to quench your thirst, far be it for me to stop you from opening your mouth. You *are* excused."

"Thank you, my lord."

Sir Richard followed him out, only to find his son leaning against the wall opposite his door, eyes pinched, teeth clenched. "Were you waiting for me?" he asked.

"I was," he said, opening one eye.

"Accompany me above stairs. I want to see your sister."

Groaning, Britton's head fell back against the wall. "I can't go another step."

"What's wrong?"

"My leg is what's wrong. I'd rather cut it off than go up those stairs one more time." He started to lower himself to the ground, but Sir Richard caught him beneath the arm.

"Where is better for you? The great hall?"

"No, not there."

"Why not?"

"Because, I'm about to cry like a woman, and I don't want anyone to see."

Sir Richard chuckled, assisting him the shortest distance back into his cabinet instead. Ten minutes later, Britton was laying on a bed mat before the fire, leg elevated. "After the healer examines your sister, I'll have her take another look at your leg."

"Father," Britton said, before he could leave.

"Yes."

"She doesn't want to marry him."

Sir Richard let out a deep breath. "I'll speak with her."

"No…you don't understand. She doesn't ever want it."

"She told you this?"

"Not in so many words."

Sir Richard crossed his arms. "It was never in my mind to force her."

"You wouldn't have to," he assured him. "She trusts your decision as a sign from God."

"What?"

"God's placed you as her authority, therefore, she's accepted your decision as God's will. For this reason alone, she's determined to see it through. But love has long since flown, and right now, she's just trying her best not to resent him. Father have pity on her. Please. We both know he'll only be a blight on her future."

Britton's words pierced straight through Sir Richard's heart, sending his thoughts hurtling back to a time when he could seek the council of his dear wife—a time too long gone to help him now. His insides groaned. *Oh, Cecelia—what must I do?*

Feeling much too overwhelmed, he cleared his throat. "I don't make hasty decisions."

"I know."

"But I'll think on it," he assured him.

Nodding his gratitude, Britton took a contented breath and closed his eyes to the throbbing in his leg.

Above stairs, Sir Richard sat by his daughter's side until the healer arrived, and even then, he left only once when she was to be examined. At no point did he require anything of her in the way of an explanation for Stuart's poor behavior. As was best, he expressed his assurance of her innocence in the matter and his sorrow for her suffering. Tonight, he would have much to think about. Tomorrow, he would address her future.

10

choose

The following day, the clouds rolled back, exposing clear skies. The air was crisp and carried with it the smell of a well washed earth, drawing people out of doors to do their work, restless from having been shut in.

Velena stood by her window, clothed only in her shift and a robe. She wanted to crawl into her prayer closet but thought it would hurt too much to lower herself to the floor. Already dressed, Daisy stoked the fire until a knock at the door had her welcoming in Sir Richard.

In the sitting room, Velena settled across from him at the table—settling quite a bit more slowly than he. "Hwoooo," she let out her breath slowly, rewarding her father with a simple smile as Daisy tucked a blanket over her legs before disappearing back into the bedchamber.

"How do you feel this morning?" he asked.

"Worse in some ways, better in others. I can get my breath, but my side is far more tender. If you've come to cheer me up, I pray you do nothing to make me laugh."

Her father's smile was grim. "I want to talk about Stuart."

"Alright," she said softly, rubbing her stockinged feet against one another. "I don't know if I expressed this last night, but I wanted you to know he was forthright with me about what he did—and repentant. You may or may not know this, but he is much the same as any man awaiting the day of his wedding. He's anxious to be married—and excited for the physical intimacies that go along with it."

Velena curled her hands into the blanket and stared at her lap.

"But you're not…are you?"

She looked up.

"Britton has asked me to release you from your engagement to Stuart. He says it's what you want."

"I didn't tell him that."

"I think he saw it plainly enough. I, on the other hand, did not. I mistook your melancholy for missing your friend rather than an expression of an arrangement you didn't want."

Velena's eyes glassed over, but she didn't cry. "What I want is to be obedient—to trust that God is working through you for my future and His good pleasure."

"I'm just a man, Velena."

"I know," she whispered.

Sir Richard smiled. "You're a good daughter, the best a father could hope for, and it was never my intention to force you into something you didn't want."

"You didn't."

"Nor will I," he assured her. "I want you to know there are alternatives to marrying Stuart."

"But the contract—"

"I'll worry about that. What you need to think about is who you'll be wedding if you don't marry him."

"Is that really something that needs to be decided right away?"

"Soon," he said, nodding. "Now, I want you to know that I've had some time to think about this—not as long as I'd like—but enough. So, I want you to listen carefully before making any decisions of your own, because I'm going to give you a choice, as limiting as it may seem."

He readjusted his legs beneath the table. "If you decide that you wish to marry someone other than Stuart, the easiest way for me to break the contract—without financial liability—will be for me to speak to King Edward and petition for its removal. But in doing so, I'd be making you available for a marriage of the king's choosing—and choose he would. Since the Pestilence, there's much land lying fallow and unmanned, and Edward will be granting it to those he wants in power and to those he thinks will form the most advantageous alliances.

For instance, there's a piece of land in Devonshire I've had my eye on. He knows this, but instead of granting it to me directly, he may give you in marriage to the one he intends on giving it to, as an assurance of peace between us. He knows I'd never seek to take that which belongs to one of my own. Do you understand what I'm saying? Betrothed now, you remain beneath his notice. Without that, you become a pawn for a much larger game."

Velena nodded slowly. "If I don't marry Stuart, I could be given to…"

"Anyone. Not only would the choice be out of your hands—it'd be out of mine."

Velena's mind began to race. "And there's no other way for it to be done privately? This is…this doesn't seem fair. I mean, I'd rather marry Sir Tarek than a stranger."

"I know," he said, considering his loyal steward—scarred and much too old for Velena—and frowned. "I would do everything in my power to influence Edward toward a good match. But whoever it is, he must be someone who can secure added protection for me, as your uncle will surely seek retribution—financial or with blood."

She felt numb.

"Don't choose now," he counseled. "There's wisdom in waiting."

"How long do I have to decide?"

He stroked his fingers through his beard, thinking out loud. "Your injury works to our advantage. We can delay the wedding until you're healed, three weeks at least. Magnus will throw a fit, but after Stuart's behavior, he's in no position to bargain. Still…it's no good waiting until the last minute. I received word only this very morning that King Edward will be attending the tournament. My guess, he'll be arriving early, in the next ten days or so. This makes it the perfect time to address him, so I'd like your answer by then. If I waited, I'd have to travel to see him, and I don't want to leave you alone."

She nodded.

"In the meantime—you're to carry on as before. I know you have your confidants but use your discretion. It won't due for Magnus to catch wind of this before you've made up your mind. For myself, I will include Lady Margarite into the matter. A woman sees things that a man does not, and I trust her, as a valuable source of sensible and sound advice. Would that I had your mother's opinion." Smiling sadly, he stood to leave. "Before I forget, Stuart is to come up and make his apology. I know you're in pain, but you'll need to get dressed."

Velena groaned. "I'm not ready to see him."

"I understand, but it's best not to delay it. Sir Makaias will attend you."

"Must he?"

"You're not to be alone with Stuart anymore."

"Still, it's embarrassing."

"You'll get through it. I'd send your brother, except his leg needs rest. As for me, I have important business in town. This sheep venture with your uncle could quickly turn into a sheep debacle if I'm not careful."

"Oh no, the sheep… Would you lose a great deal of money on account of me?"

"Nothing I would regret." He rounded the table to kiss her goodbye, but she held fast to his arm.

"What of Rowan? What did Uncle demand as punishment? I know he went too far, but—"

"He's not said a word."

Her eyes rounded. "Not anything?"

Sir Richard raised a conspiratorial brow. "My thoughts exactly."

11

apology accepted

In the library, Velena sat perched on the edge of one of the armed chairs, gingerly holding her side and trying to bring her breathing back to something more tolerable after what felt like an eternal descent down the staircase.

"It'd have been easier if you'd stayed in your solar. I'd be present the whole time," Makaias reminded her. "Your father's given me no other duty this morning but to oversee this meeting."

"Thank you for your concern, but I have my reasons for not wanting to see him there." She needn't explain that having him in her solar would just be a reminder of his being there with Daisy. "Here is better," she finished simply.

Makaias rocked his head up and down, but still, she could see there was a glint of disapproval in his eyes.

"You have something to say?"

He looked surprised she asked. "It's not for me to say it."

"I wish you would." Tristan would have told her exactly what he was thinking—or so she used to believe. Still, she missed him, and the unexpected wave of sadness she'd been suppressing since his absence left her feeling lost and empty, and the emptiness was a deep ache, rivaling the pain in her side.

Makaias took a seat across from her. "I was thinking that you're not going to be able to keep him from your bedroom forever."

She blinked, having not expected him to be thinking anything near that.

"What he did was deplorable," he continued, "but you're to be married. And if you're ever going to succeed in this, you're going to have to forgive him."

"*Succeed?* What is success to you regarding a marriage? Something else to be mastered, I suppose—like the art of silence, to keep oneself from being ravaged and the bearer of strange children?"

His look was tolerant. "Success, itself, is not mastered but is the product of gaining mastery over our own sinful flesh. Scripture says that a man without control over his spirit is like a city broken into without walls. I know that you're unhappy, but happiness, itself, is not a worthy goal. It's the art of being sanctified—becoming holy. Love is not found, Velena—it's put into practice. It 'bears all things, believes all things, hopes all things, endures all things...' And doesn't keep an account of wrongs. The first step in loving Stuart, if you so choose, is to forgive him."

She knew this to be true, but still she argued. "And what of his part? The same passage also says that love isn't supposed to be jealous or to act unbecoming."

"When you take him to husband, you must take him with both hands open, accepting that he is a sinful man—and devoting yourself to prayer on his behalf."

"And what if I find that his sins are...more than I can bear?"

"What do you mean?"

Velena looked away. "Just...what if?"

"I won't ask you to say your mind, but what I can tell you is that while God doesn't change, the people He saves do. Stuart may not always be as he is. Is that not a reason to hope?"

She nodded, wondering if his thoughts on the matter would be different if she told him of Stuart's tryst with Daisy. "I know this," she said. "I've hoped it all before. Hoped beyond hope to get back the friend I once had in him. But what he's done—"

"You mean something else?"

"No," she corrected, chastising herself for the slip. "*Did*. What he *did*—to me—it's opened up a floodgate of emotions I knew were there but haven't allowed myself to feel. And right now, I don't know if I want to forgive him?"

He stared her straight in the eyes. "We don't forgive because we want to; we forgive because we've been forgiven."

Frustrated, she looked away. She'd said the same thing to Tristan. How she hated her words being used against her. Worse yet, it was doctrine to which submission was the only proper response. She turned back to him. "May I ask you a personal question?"

Wary, he nodded. "Aye..."

"Did you forgive your someone?"

His head jerked back in surprise, his mouth opening, then closing again, before eventually laughing at himself for being caught unawares. "I suppose advice is more easily dispensed than followed. Britton told you about her?"

"Pure conjecture," she admitted. "You stayed in London, while Britton continued on. What else but a woman could keep you from coming home to your family and friends during such uncertain times as these?"

"Hm." A corner of his mouth lifted.

"What was her name?"

Taking a deep breath, he crossed his arms, settling back in his chair as he exhaled. "Joanna."

"And…"

He chuckled. "And…we were engaged before I left for Calais— before the Pestilence."

"What happened?"

"Well…" He looked down, taking a sudden interest in his own forearms. "When we returned from war, I sought her out but discovered…she was unfaithful. I caught her in the act, actually."

Velena pulled in her lower lip, not really knowing what to say. "Did you love her a great deal?"

"I suppose I did. Leastwise, I thought I did. She was a fishmonger's daughter, but well-mannered and pleasant—a beautiful woman, really. She'd found someone who taught her to read and—I don't know— somehow, she seemed ill-fit for her life. I thought if I married her, I could give her more."

"What did she look like?" she asked, curious to know what kind of woman could turn the head of this knight.

Makaias was looking at Velena but ceased to see her, as he retreated into his mind's eye, recalling Joanna's features, one by one. "She was a bit tall for a woman but shorter than I—blond hair, blue eyes…" He thought of her figure. "Very feminine." Coming back to himself he patted his thighs. "I'm not sure what else to tell you."

"Did you kiss her?"

Makaias coughed a smile into his fist. "You're very direct."

She gave a slight shrug, smiling herself. "I think you already know that about me."

"Yes, I do," he said, bringing his arms back across his chest, a glint of humor reflected behind his eyes. "Let's see," he spoke out loud as if trying to recall. "Did I kiss her…?"

Suddenly, embarrassed, Velena ducked her head. "Never mind.

Don't answer. I...I was only thinking of my own situation...and Stuart. Whatever you did, I'm sure there was nothing untoward about it. In all your seriousness-*ness*," she said smiling. "I can't imagine you taking advantage of anyone."

"I thought we decided I was intense."

Velena giggled, stopping abruptly as sharp pains traced a path through her rib cage.

He smiled sympathetically. "*Actually*, in all seriousness-*ness*, as you put it," clearly poking fun, "there were times I ought to have mastered my spirit better. But—no—I never forced my attentions on Joanna. As to whether I've forgiven her for her unfaithfulness, I don't know. In fact, I've done most everything I can think of not to think of her at all."

Velena's lips pressed together. "Was she sorry for what she'd done?"

Makaias huffed. "Sorry she got caught, I think."

"If she'd been truly sorry—would you have accepted her back? Would you have forgiven her unfaithfulness and tried for your own...*success?*"

Makaias rubbed at his jaw.

She continued. "You see, if Stuart were already my husband, I'd be more inclined to do as you say. To find love where it isn't. To work for it. To put it into practice. To *succeed* at one of God's greatest sacraments. But we're not married. Not yet. You're right that I have to forgive him, but after..." Her voice trailed off. "What I'd really like to do is walk away...as you did."

Makaias considered the seriousness of her statement. "I can't imagine you'd defy your father."

"No, I wouldn't," she agreed, folding her hands in her lap. "But he's given me a choice." Makaias raised his eyebrows, and she found herself squirming to get comfortable in her chair. "Not that I've made one yet."

He looked doubtful. "It sounds like you have."

She shook her head. "Father says there's *wisdom in waiting*. That, and I don't know if I'm brave enough."

"For what?"

"The alternative." Her finger traced the embroidery of her surcoat pocket. "Do you know what my option will be if I don't marry Stuart?"

He didn't answer.

"Due to the nature of the contract my father has with my uncle, he's decided that the best way to have it annulled will be to speak with King Edward when he's here for the tournament. This done, he expects he'll choose someone for me…because my marriage must be to advantage."

Makaias leaned forward. "You want away from Stuart so badly you'd really consider that?"

"Has it not been his own behavior that's brought me to this? I have to consider it," she said, raising her chin.

"Even with Stuart's failings, it seems an awfully big roll of the dice to think you'd find something better with a complete stranger." He pointed his finger. "I say this not to hurt you, so please weigh the truth of it, but it suddenly occurs to me that your tendency towards bold behavior—your tenacity and aptitude for speaking your mind—might actually be what Stuart needs to smooth out his rougher edges. And while you remain in Totnes, you have family to keep him in line—a father who loves you and would keep you from harm. If you marry the king's man, who knows where you'll end up. As close as Devonshire—as far as London? Would you allow yourself to be isolated from those who could help you?"

The truth of his words sent her sinking into her chair, until pain from the movement brought her up again.

"I don't mean to upset you," he apologized.

"Those are most sobering thoughts," she admitted, feeling the pendulum swing back in Stuart's favor, despite the possibility of his having lain with Daisy. "What would you do, Sir Makaias?"

"In your place?"

"Yes."

"My duty."

"Just like that? No qualms or hesitations?"

"On the contrary, the very subject causes me to hesitate. I've no desire to marry—not anytime soon, anyway."

She softened. "I think you ought to forgive Joanna… It'd be a shame for her to be the ruin of a potentially *successful* future marriage."

His lips lifted into a half-smile. "That it would."

"Lord Stuart has just arrived, my lady," Daisy said, appearing at the door. "As has Baroness LaDawn and Lady Rainydays. Were you expecting them?"

"No, they're welcome. Please have them wait in my solar."

Daisy curtsied and Velena looked away, wondering when she'd have the mental and emotional fortitude to speak with her about what needed to be said. She raised her eyes to Makaias, who was now back on his feet. "I hadn't intended on confiding in you. None of this is common knowledge, you understand."

"It's still not."

Preparing herself to face Stuart, Velena took a rather deep and painful breath. "I wish you didn't have to be here."

"Pardon?" he asked.

"You know too much now. Whatever I say to him now, you're going to judge me."

He chuckled. "I'm not going to judge you, Velena."

"I feel like you are." She suppressed a smile, while he grinned broadly. "And remember to address me as *my lady* in front of Stuart." Anxious, she adjusted the folds of her surcoat while Makaias stood relaxed on the sidelines, legs hip-width apart, right hand resting on the hilt of his dagger. Velena wished she could be so calm.

When Stuart entered the room, he did so without a sound. He simply seated himself where Makaias had been and waited for her to raise her eyes to him. "Velena," he said, speaking softly.

"Stuart." She fought the urge to look away—and not just because of the damage done to his face—but because he appeared truly miserable, and she hated herself for still wanting to leave him.

He looked to Makaias. "I'd like to speak with her alone."

He shook his head. "As of today, she is to be attended at all times."

Stuart stared at his feet and grunted. "All times with me, you mean."

"I believe you're hear for a reason, Cousin," Makaias prodded, allowing his eyes to drift back towards Velena, who now appeared quite calm despite the disquiet he knew was there.

He nodded. "How's your...side?" he asked, gesturing towards her injury.

"It hurts. And your face?"

He smiled with as good a smile as he could manage without re-opening his scabbed over lip. "I suppose I repulse you,"

"No. I'm just sorry to see it."

"I'm the one who's sorry, Velena. For this...and the other."

She looked down at her hands.

"My behavior was deplorable—worse than that. Truly, I...I don't know why I took it so far." He waited for her to speak, but there was only silence. "Please, say something."

"What do you want me to say?"

"That you forgive me."

Velena wrestled with her conscience. Still steeped in resentment, it helped to tell herself that forgiving him didn't imply she was making him her choice. *Lord, help me do this.*

"Velena…please," he tried again.

She could sense Makaias watching her from the corner of her eye, waiting—like Stuart—for her to answer. "I forgive you," she finally said.

"Truly?"

"Yes. But I no longer trust you."

Undaunted, he appeared relieved. "You will again. Another sennight, and we'll be man and wife, and what happened yesterday won't matter at all."

She cleared her throat. "The wedding date has been extended."

"Extended? What—"

"Father feels it's in my best interest to heal properly before—"

"I should have been consulted in this. How long will it be delayed?"

"Three weeks."

"*Three weeks?*"

"For me to heal."

"I know for you to heal, but…" he dug his fist into his thigh and closed his eyes, fighting to control his temper. He began again. "I understand you need time to heal. But a wedding isn't exactly a display of acrobatics."

"Then let it be a display of patience—waiting before you touch me again, as is proper."

"Your father puts my patience to the test. I want you for my wife, Velena! That I desire you, it's natural."

Embarrassed, as she knew she would be, in front of Makaias, she did her best to appear impassive. "It wasn't my decision. If you don't like it, take it up with him."

"I will."

Shaken, her temper flared. "If you do, you'll ruin all that's left between us. Three weeks is nothing compared to a lifetime of marriage. Must you come against it?"

"Yes." He rose to his feet. "Because this isn't about your injury. This is about you getting even with me."

Before she could respond, Makaias stepped forward.

Reluctantly, Stuart sat back down, leaning on his elbow, hand over his mouth as if to staunch the flow of words that would bring Makaias any closer. "Three more weeks..."

He wasn't sure Rowan would stay quiet for three more weeks, yet it seemed he had no choice. Grudgingly, he nodded. "I can wait. Three weeks—but no more. Promise me."

"I cannot."

"I see." His expression darkened. "You only give promises to Tristan. Is that it?" Always at the mention of his name, there arose a great jealousy in him, otherwise contained for most anyone else—including Rowan.

Velena's guard went up. "I don't know what you're talking about."

"You promised him you wouldn't kiss me." He smirked. "Or was it not to let me kiss you?"

Her heart stopped. "Where did you hear that?" she asked, knowing exactly the answer.

Dejected, he leaned over his knees. "I thought once he left, I'd have you back again—all of you. But all I've ever gotten is bits and pieces. Then again, perhaps I shouldn't be jealous of your promise to another man. After all, you didn't exactly keep it."

Eyes pooling with tears, she forced herself to stand. "None of this has anything to do with him." She turned away, but he came up behind her.

"Tell me the truth. If it'd been him holding you instead of me—if it'd been his attentions you were receiving instead of mine...would you still have perceived them as such an affront to your precious honor?" He turned her around, and she gasped. "Would you be asking him to wait?"

"That's enough," Makaias said, coming between them. "You've said your piece; now, go."

Stuart retreated a step. "She can deny it if she wants, but we both know she doesn't need three weeks to—"

"I'm happy for the delay," she blurted. "Happy for it! I'll need each and *every* hour just to convince myself to take vows—let alone enter your bed of my own volition."

Stuart winced, and Makaias along with him.

She looked away, unwilling to let either of them judge her for her words, though perhaps it was only Makaias she was truly sorry to offend. "We're ill fit for one another."

"What are you saying?"

"I don't know," she whispered.

"You told me you trusted your father's decisions. He gave you to me. He's forgiven my actions; the contract stands! Would you disobey him?"

"No. I would not." Velena focused on the cinnamon brown of his eyes. She recognized the color but not the man she used to hold so dear. She knew too much about him now—had experienced more of his father's flaws than she would have ever admitted existed. If she were to choose him above a stranger, they'd have to begin anew, and she wasn't sure she knew how to do that. "If you'll excuse me, I have friends waiting for me."

Stuart watched as she fled the room. If the look on Makaias' face told him anything, it told him not to follow her. Just as well. It was time to leave. Fleshing out such a conversation in front of his cousin had stripped him bare. She didn't love him. She'd said as much before but having her affirm this in front of Makaias... He could no longer deny its truth. Obligation would be the only thing bringing her to him now, and the realization of it broke him.

12

solace

Velena had gone to her friends and explained the obvious—her injured side, Stuart's face, and the incident that had prompted both. As expected, they were both sympathetic and offended for her sake. Entrusting them with the rest, she entreated them not to offer any advice.

How many times since Tristan had left had she gone to people instead of the Lord? Disappointed in the answer, she determined to do differently and bid her friends an early farewell. Embracing, she asked them to pray for her. But prayer, itself, was an act of patience, and there were many times in the days that followed she might have been tempted to seek out Rowan's advice, except he was kept busy. With the tournament so close, her father had Makaias working his knights and squires hard. All day they trained, and at night, Rowan took the evening shift at the gatehouse. She wanted to tell him about Tristan's letter—that it'd never made it to her father—but it no longer seemed significant in comparison to her current state of affairs. So, she remained on her knees.

If she wasn't eating, she was praying. She had almost no interaction with Daisy except for mornings and evenings. During the day, she dismissed her from service, caring not what she did or where she went but was fairly certain she was working with Auntie to finish her wedding gown. The time would come when she would talk with Daisy about what she'd seen of her and Stuart in the solar. But not yet.

In an effort to maintain complete privacy during her times of prayer, she chose a spare bedroom—Tristan's room, the one he'd stayed in for those last days before leaving them—and it began from her habit of touching his door every time she passed by. She missed him, and it was her way of saying hello and goodnight to a friend she still held most dear.

After Stuart's apology, she'd leaned into it, pressed her cheek to the wood and wished beyond all hope that she'd find him on the other side. What she did find was a modest room, its only furnishings a table, chair, and bed mat. Bolting herself inside, she'd crawled atop the mat and cried until she fell asleep. When she woke, she prayed. The next time she came, she came with her father's ornamented Bible to consider the decision she had looming before her, abandoning all other duties, with her father's blessing. For three days, she read, prayed, cried, and slept—receiving a measure of peace from her time with the Lord—but no solution.

Alone with her thoughts, she'd replayed her conversation with Stuart in her mind over and over again. In her imaginings, she allowed herself to shout out everything she hadn't said before but wanted to, very near hating him for the situation she was in now. She knew it was wrong—that in God's eyes it was murder—but it wasn't until the morning of the fourth day she could bring herself to repent of it.

It was good she hadn't told him she knew about his being with Daisy, especially in front of Makaias. No one need know, as she was treating her horribly enough on her own. This particular burden was especially troubling, and so it was the final sin she laid before the Lord.

With tears and trembling, she begged His forgiveness, recounting every wrong Daisy had done against her and acknowledging the same done in her own heart as many times over. Could she, herself, claim not to have lied, or deceived…or lusted? She didn't know why Daisy had chosen to act on these things or to stray so far from Christ's teachings but concluded it was because she must not know Him as she should. If she loved Him, she would obey Him. Wherein Daisy didn't love, she was most in need of it—and Velena would no longer withhold.

Coming up from her knees, she exited Tristan's room for her own solar, placing her palm against the door as she left. She washed her face from her water basin and re-plaited her hair over one shoulder. Lastly, she donned a sheer headrail and secured it atop her head with pins and a ruby encrusted circlet.

King Edward would be in Totnes in five days. Her father would have only two days to speak with him, followed by two days of tourney and what should have been her wedding to immediately follow, only now delayed. She needed to make a decision, and she needed to make it soon. Taking a last look in her mirror, she prayed, *Lord, I trust your decisions for my life better than I trust my own. Please guide me to your will.* After hours upon hours of prayer over the last few days, this one—her briefest—gave her the most peace.

Augustine quickened his pace as Totnes finally came into view. Tristan pulled back on the reins and received a restless snort in return.

"I know, boy." He patted his horse's neck before coughing into the crook of his arm. "I see it too. We're almost home."

Home. Funny how Totnes felt more like home than Oxfordshire did, even with his brother there. After all he and Velena had lost and gained over the years at Wineford, was it any wonder she'd become home to him? And the closer he came to it, the surer he felt about why he'd come back. Mostly.

"Lord, stop me if I'm wrong," he mused aloud. Homes were now clearly in view as he turned down the main road that would lead him through the center of town. To the east of High Street was Craft Hall. He'd not have to go that way, thank goodness. He just hoped Stuart was there and not in town—even with Velena at Landerhill would be fine, for he wasn't going there straight away either.

In fact, because he figured there was a good chance Stuart *would* be with Velena, he decided to stay at an inn and send word to Sir Richard from there. In the meantime, he veered toward Market Square where vendors were gathered aplenty. He dismounted Augustine and lead him by the reins through the milling crowd. Walking always helped him clear his head, and perhaps the noise would help as well. Thus far, his ride had been far too quiet—and he needed to shut out a few of his more apprehensive thoughts.

Counting himself fortunate, he spotted a man selling firewood out of a run-down cart, a small crate of books at his feet. He could use something to read while he waited to see if Sir Richard would accept him back to the manor.

"You're an answer to prayer," Tristan said, approaching the man. "I was in dire need of a distraction just now."

The man had a crooked smile. "Never been no one's answer to prayer before."

"Well, there's a first time for everything. How did you come by these?"

"Didn't steal them, if that's your meaning." The man cleared his throat in a most unpleasant way before turning his head to expectorate. "Lots of homes gone empty since the Pestilence come and gone. Ain't no one claimed 'em, so I figured they was free for the taking. Hardly worth it though," he said, placing a fist atop the side of his cart. "Don't sell much of these as I do the fagots, but their pages come in right handy if you're in need of a good squat—if you know what I mean."

He did but held back his smile.

"Been working my way through this one," the man said with a wink, pulling out a copy of Meister Eckhart's *The Book of Divine Comfort* he had wedged beneath one of the fagots.

Tristan did have a good chuckle then, finding it amusing that he'd been using a copy of the German heretic's work to take care of his less than pleasant business.

"I suppose you can read," the man continued, as he nudged the bucket towards Tristan with his foot.

Tristan crouched to the ground. It occurred to him that Velena might appreciate a good work of fiction, but it was a rather meager selection, and there didn't appear to be any at present. Pulling the books out, one by one, he raised his eyebrows at the title *Le Livre des Merveilles*. What a find! It'd do nicely on two accounts. First, it was something he could read now, and second, it was something they'd enjoy discussing together should they…if they…if it came to that.

The possibility still brought on a series of mixed emotions. He knew Velena would be just as happy to see him as he was to see her. But coming the way he was—prepared as he was to do what he must—made everything different. Not that it was a bad different. *Why shouldn't we be married to each other?* He reasoned. *I mean…aside from the fact that we've never wanted to be.*

Happy with his selection, he fumbled around in his purse for some coins. *Or maybe it's that we never really thought to be,* he reasoned again. And if this was so, he knew why. "Here." He emptied the contents of his hand into the seller's palm. It was double the worth of the book.

The man licked his lips in appreciation. "Awfully generous of you, I must say."

Generous, he mused, and smiled at what his distracted thoughts had just cost him. Generous is what Velena had always been with her many assurances that Tristan would find Gwenhavare upon his return to Oxfordshire, never mind that he'd never had any indication that she'd ever returned his affections, or if she was even alive for him to have the chance to persuade her to such. Giving his horse's flank a gentle pat, he stuffed the book into one of the satchels.

No. For Velena it was ever just *find her and marry her*—what could be simpler? Except, he'd done neither. He'd not even tried. Moving on towards the inn, he allowed himself a deep breath, but started coughing so hard, he had to stand still, allowing the fit to pass. Groaning, he laid his forehead against the horse's shoulder. His lungs felt thick with what he'd just had to spit out.

"Uuugh," he sighed, wiping his mouth with the back of his sleeve. Coming back to full height, he walked on, thinking how overdue it was for Velena to let her dreams for him go—she was the one in front of him now. And though it might not be ideal...or...or what they'd expected—in fact, he fully expected her to laugh in his face—there was no reason to believe they couldn't be both friends...and lovers.

The hilarity of that word in reference to themselves nearly spilled over into audible laughter, tempting him to another coughing fit. He cleared his throat. They'd just have to change their thinking. And how could he expect her to think differently of him if he didn't start doing the same? Determination drew his lips together. Starting now, nothing would deter him from doing so.

"Esquire, is that you?"

Tristan froze at the sound of a woman's voice behind him, even going so far as to scrunch up his face in hopes that it was another esquire being addressed. He didn't want anyone informing Sir Richard of his return before he had a chance to go to him, himself.

"Esquire Tristan," the voice persisted.

Having no recourse but to acknowledge his name, he turned around to find a tall, dark-haired woman staring very pointedly in his direction. He breathed a tentative sigh of relief. He'd only met the lady once but had left that encounter with a strong feeling she was more friend than foe.

Pulling away from her female companion, she approached him. "My word, you're not someone I expected to see in Totnes this day."

He smiled. "Lady Rainydayas, if I remember correctly."

She dipped her head. "You have a good memory."

"I was thinking the same."

"Then we must have something in common—which of course means I have to like you."

"Thank you. I think."

She laughed. "You may very well wonder if you ought to be

offended, but you'd do better to persuade yourself otherwise, for I don't like just anyone. Though in all fairness, I had decided ahead of time to like you should we ever meet again."

A bit taken aback at the forthright nature of this woman, still wholly a stranger to him, he wondered how to proceed. "I'm flattered then. Should I assume Velena had a hand in persuading you to this?"

"Indeed. But there is no need to humble yourself into thinking she's alone in her good opinion of you. There is also the opinion of Sir Richard, Squire Rowan and Baroness LaDawn to consider. All these together, and I was quite persuaded of your good character."

"Baroness LaDawn, you say? I'm not acquainted with that name. I can only assume it was another Tristan she so admired, though I'm quite willing to accept your accolades in his stead. Feel free to continue."

Rainydayas laughed, gesturing back to her companion. "Nonsense. I'm sure you know her, and if by chance you've forgotten, allow me to re-introduce you."

By this time the woman had turned around from the booth she'd been perusing and come to stand by her side.

"Is this not the same esquire you and Lady Velena both acknowledge to knowing?"

Eyes as large as saucers, Gwenhavare appeared to be just as surprised as Tristan, but did more than him in managing a smile. "It is, indeed. I praise God to see you well."

His head reeled, her voice feeling more like a slap to his senses than a greeting. He tried his best not to stammer. "Thank you. Though, I...I have been a bit...a bit ill."

"She means *not dead*," Rainydayas clarified. "The Pestilence and all that."

Tristan raised his eyebrows. Was it possible he'd just been befriended by a woman just as candid as Velena. "Oh. Yes, well thank you then. I'm quite alive—and well-ish." He smiled then, trying his best to appear at ease. "And what of you, Baroness..."

"LaDawn," she finished for him. "My married name. And I'm quite well, thank you."

Another slap. "Oh. You're married?"

"Only for the briefest of moments." She gave a wry smile. "I'm now widowed."

His heart beat faster. "I'm sorry to hear it," he said, doubting the sincerity of his own words.

"With so much in the world to be sorry for, my situation need not be one of them. Furthermore, I abhor the thought of another man's pity, for I'm quite content in my present circumstances, truth be known."

"I promise to keep that in mind," he said, pushing away all questions on the matter for what plagued him most. "So, I have to ask. How is it you've come to be in Totnes, Baroness?"

"My aunt has a home in Oxfordshire," Rainydayas answered for her.

Tristan forced his eyes from Gwenhavare to await further explanation, only to turn back when none came.

Gwenhavare smiled at her friend's brevity. "That's the short story. We met there a few months past, but we got on so well that I'm currently a guest here in her home."

"I see." He didn't. "And how long will you be staying?"

"As long as she likes," Rainydayas interrupted again. "Her visit is quite indefinite as far as I'm concerned."

He could tell from Gwenhavare's expression that she enjoyed the arrangement.

"Oh, my," Gwenhavare exclaimed, as the thought suddenly struck her. "Does Lady Velena know you're back yet?"

He blinked. "You're...um..." He reached up to tug at his hair but forced his hand back down. "You're acquainted with Lady Velena?"

She nodded, a wide grin spreading brightly across her face. "Indeed. Fast friends, I dare say."

Tristan lost his balance as Augustine leaned into his arm. He shoved his head away. "Really? Fast...fast friends." *Already?* He'd only been gone, what? Weeks? "Had you ever met before...um, before..." He wanted to die. "Sorry. What I'm trying to ask is when did you and Velena first meet?"

"We were introduced the day you left, if I'm not mistaken."

His entire insides groaned.

Rainydayas nodded to confirm. "It doesn't take long to get on well with Nenna. I'm sure you could attest to that."

"You call her Nenna? I thought that was something particular to Rowan."

"We all grew up together," Rainydayas explained. "You're not the only one who knows her as well as you think you do."

He was taken aback yet again. "No...of course not...I wouldn't suppose to think so..."

"I think he can suppose whatever he likes," Gwenhavare interrupted. "That you mean the world to her is undeniable. She's missed you greatly. And from the way she talks about you, I'm sure you feel the same."

"Of course, he does," Rainydayas affirmed. "He wouldn't be here if he didn't. So. *Does* she know?"

"That I'm here? "Tristan coughed into his elbow, then rubbed a hand down his hip as if he had an ache worth attending to. "Actually. She doesn't, and I'd…I'd greatly appreciate your silence on the matter. I've not yet made myself known to Sir Richard, and I need to do that first for…personal reasons. Second, I don't want to cause her any grief should others, who wouldn't exactly welcome my presence, find out I've returned."

"Stuart, you mean," Rainydayas said. "We'll not say a word. Only don't keep your whereabouts a secret for too long. The Lord's day is just around the corner."

He looked confused.

"We have a standing invitation at Landerhill to share in the noon meal following mass every Lord's day," she explained. "Something we quite look forward to."

"I see." He still didn't.

Gwenhavare took pity and elaborated. "If you haven't made you presence known by then, it'll be impossible for us to keep it to ourselves. The excitement will be written all over our faces."

"Oh." He chuckled. "I send word today, so you'll be quite in the clear by then."

"If it's Lord Stuart who has you concerned about visiting Landerhill," Gwenhavare said, "you needn't worry. He hasn't been there for days."

"Oh…really. Might I inquire why?"

Exchanging glances with Rainydayas, she muttered something about how the tournament seemed to be keeping the men busy training at home.

He smiled. "While that does set me at ease, I wish to select my words most carefully. And for that, I'll need pen and paper."

The women nodded. "Where do you go now?" Rainydayas asked.

"Kingsbridge Inn."

"Then might we accompany you as far as South Street? We're done with our errands and will be going the same direction.

Tristan bowed. "I'd be delighted of your company." After all the

107

shock of finding Gwenhavare still alive—and in Totnes, no less—he was surprised by the ease with which the three of them fell into conversation. Smiling to himself, he attributed this new *easiness* around women to Velena's influence over him. He was better because of her, and he knew that well.

Walking his horse at Rainydayas' right, he peeked around her to address Gwenhavare. "I still can't help but be amazed that two people I've known from such different times should have come to know each other. I certainly never expected it." Thinking to smile, it suddenly faded. "Makes one question how the mind of God works."

Rainydayas quirked her head at him. "Why would anyone want to do that? My goodness, have we not a difficult enough time dissecting our own thoughts?"

Tristan stuck out his bottom lip. "Why, indeed." Clearing his throat, he had to fight down the urge to cough. "Out of curiosity, Baroness, how long has Velena known of *our*...acquaintanceship?"

"Yours and mine?"

Tristan nodded.

"Honestly, I didn't make the connection until just recently, myself."

"And why would you?" Tristan asked, feeling the ridiculousness of the situation. "Someone you hadn't seen or...*thought* of for years."

Gwenhavare threw out a hand for emphasis. "Exactly."

Tristan smiled, but kicked at the first rock in his way. "How did she react when she found out?"

"She was pleased," she replied simply.

"Not...too surprised?"

She shook her head. "Just happy to have a friend in common, I think. She said it made her feel closer to you."

"Glad to hear it," he said, realizing Velena must not have made the connection between Gwenhavare and Iseult, which made sense, as she'd never allowed him to speak her real name.

Reaching South Street, he made the turn with them, without any of them thinking strangely of it.

Stopping a short way down from her home, Rainydayas studied him without having to look upwards, for she was nearly as tall. "Nenna told us you left to find your brother. If I were any kind of proper, I'd mind my own business, but curiosity has me wondering if your trip home was successful in this regard."

"I did, as matter of fact."

Gwenhavare clasped her hands together. "Glorious news! I'm so happy for you. Truly. I heard about your mother…and sisters. I think often of Ann in particular. She was a sweet friend."

A warming spread through his chest. "Thank you."

"How fares your brother now?" Gwenhavare asked.

He opened his mouth to speak, but a young man descending the steps of Rainydayas' home interrupted and said, "Beggin' your pardon, my lady, but your brother's here. He's been asking for an accounting record of your spending, but I don't know where you keep it."

Rainydayas rolled her eyes. "That's because I *don't* keep one. But tell him I'll be in presently. If he hits you on my account, I'll buy you a new hood."

Grinning, Thomas disappeared back into the house.

"He's my favorite," she said, smiling.

"Will you be alright? Tristan inquired, becoming apprehensive about her going in alone.

"His bark is worse than his bite," she replied, taking the four steps two at a time. Hand on the door, she turned back around to face them. "Feel free to linger. There's no need for the baroness to overhear what foul language I've planned for him. I'm not nearly as pious as she thinks I am."

Gwenhavare leaned into Tristan. "I think no such thing," she confided.

Tristan chuckled…then smiled. He looked away, then laughed again, realizing he had no idea what they'd been talking about before the interruption. He pulled at his hair.

"Is that painful?" she asked.

He lowered his arm. "A nervous habit."

"Do I make you nervous?"

"I'm trying to remember what we were talking about."

She laughed in amusement. "Forgetfulness is for the aged—like me. But not you."

Tristan liked the sound of her laugh. It was light and airy, the kind that invited you to join in. "You consider yourself aged?"

"More aged than you," she teased.

"Surely not."

"I'm the same year as your brother."

Tristan raised his eyebrows in disbelief. "That much?"

Feigning insult, she was soon lavishing on him yet another of her tinkling laughs.

"I didn't mean it like that," he said, appreciating her good humor on the subject. "I only meant…I knew you were older than Ann, but I don't think I knew by how much. What would that be? Philip is two and twenty, so…three years older than me?"

"Surprised?"

She had no idea how much, especially as he realized what little chance he'd actually had with her. *Why not come clean, then?* He reasoned. *Get it over with for Velena's sake.* "It leaves me a bit embarrassed," he answered.

"How so?"

"It's humorous to think of it now, but back in Oxfordshire—after…after that party we both couldn't stand being at…" Again, that lovely laugh. "I fancied myself…quite taken with you, actually."

She raised her eyebrows, failing to suppress her smile. "Did you?"

Losing some of his embarrassment, he grinned in response. "I was fifteen—barely a man. And you…you were already a mature woman. Laughing at my attentions, I'm sure."

"Don't be absurd. I found your company most enjoyable."

"I was awkward."

She giggled. "I suppose you were—but less so now, I dare say."

"We've Velena to thank for that. If nothing else, her friendship has taught me to be at ease with the fairer sex."

"What a pleasant thing to say of her. I've always been under the impression that the majority of men find a woman's influence to be a burden."

"She's been a great many things to me—but never a burden."

"I can tell you've been a good friend to her."

"She's been a better one to me."

Her eyes softened, her voice kind and sincere. "Is she why you're here?"

He held her gaze, perhaps longer than what was prudent. "I don't approve of her marriage," he answered. She nodded, and he knew she felt the same.

"Do you have the means to end it?"

"I'm praying so."

"Would you marry her, yourself?" she asked.

Unprepared, he choked back on his saliva before starting to cough. That she, of all people, should ask him. What sort of twisted state of things had he come back to?

"I'm sorry," she stammered. "Clearly, it's none of my business."

"No…no, not at all. You just…surprised me."

"I hope you do."

"M-marry her?" He was beginning to wonder if it wouldn't be easier to simply stay in a constant state of shock. "Has she...said something—to make you feel this way?"

"No, not at all, actually. I just think a loyal friend is a husband worth having."

He crossed his arms. It was a nice sentiment, but he fully expected their friendship to be one of their greatest hurdles.

"And as her friend, you also ought to know that her situation has changed?"

"In what way?"

"A few days past, Lord Stuart forced himself on her and—"

"What?" His arms dropped as he squared his feet.

"A kiss," she explained quickly.

"But forced?"

"Unwanted, yes." She went on. "Squire Rowan stopped him, thank goodness, but also beat him quite badly. That's the real reason Stuart hasn't been at the manor. Another thing. Velena was injured in her attempt to stop the fight."

Running his hands through his hair, he linked his fingers behind his neck, forcing himself to remain quiet so she could finish.

"I don't know if you've heard, but King Edward is coming to the tourney. Because of all that's happened, her father has said that if she decides she no longer wants to marry Stuart, he'll go to the King and try and have her contract annulled."

"That's wonderful." His shoulders relaxed.

She frowned. "Perhaps. But it also means she'll be given in marriage to someone of the king's choosing. We've been speculating, and Rainy thinks the mostly likely match will be Lord Vitalis."

"He's twice her age."

"And has a mistress, or so we've heard. But his wife and children died with the Plague, and he's in want of a legitimate heir."

"Still, this is speculation. It could be someone else—someone better."

"Or *him*...or someone worse. She's quite torn as to what to do and has asked that we be praying for her. Perhaps your being here is...that answer?"

What could he say?

She reached out to touch his arm.

It was a forward gesture, and his head shot up, the look in her eyes void of anything Velena had ever hoped she'd feel for him. Indeed, all he could see was a love for their friend.

"Her engagement to Stuart has been a disappointment, but marriage to just *anyone* is hardly something better." She pulled back. "If you can do something about it, I pray that you do."

13

disclosure

"Has she made a decision yet?" Britton asked. His legs were stretched out towards the cabinet hearth where he sat side by side with his father.

"Not yet. Has she said anything to you?"

"I've barely seen her. She's hiding, I think."

Sir Richard shook his head. "Not hiding. Praying. And it's good she is." He looked over at his son. "I've kept something from her. Possibly something she has a right to know."

Britton turned his head. "What?"

"Before Tristan left, he came to me—said he had knowledge of Stuart's involvement in a wrongdoing. But I dismissed his concerns because the accusation came without proof." He swallowed. "I was angry with him for interfering and more suspicious of his motives for telling me than of the information, itself."

"And now?" he asked, knowing his father was more interested in talking out his thoughts then disclosing private information. Curious as he was, Britton knew better than to push him.

"I'm beginning to believe the accusation holds merit."

"What's changed?"

"Magnus' response to Rowan." Sir Richard steepled his fingers in front of his lips. "After what he did to Stuart, I expected him to call down hellfire and brimstone on his head. But not a word. This says to me he doesn't want to bring attention to Stuart's actions, lest they bring to light something else…something worse." He reached over to squeeze Britton's arm. "The love you showed your sister in telling me of her unhappiness was an admirable thing to do, and I'm proud of you for it. But it was Magnus' inaction that solidified my resolve to reconsider her engagement. Proof or no, I now feel bound by my conscience."

"And you're wondering if you should tell her."

Sir Richard nodded.

"If it will help her decision, why would you hesitate?"

"The possibility—nay the hope—of it being false. Her estimation of Stuart has already suffered, and I would never forgive myself for slandering an innocent man."

"Let me ask this. Is it easier to believe Stuart didn't do this thing he's accused of...or that Tristan's lied?"

Sir Richard crossed his arms. "He wouldn't lie, but he could have been deceived. If he knew for certain it was true, he would have given me the name of the woman in question."

"He wronged a woman?"

"That he gave none was more proof of Stuart's innocence than guilt," he continued. "I was so certain of this...so certain. Now I doubt."

Silent for a time, Britton could no longer help but ask, "What was the accusation?"

"Ravishment," Sir Richard answered solemnly.

Britton's mouth hung open. "He raped someone? How could you for one moment not consider telling her?"

"Feelings, Britton—hunches—that's all I have. You cannot make life-altering decisions based on hearsay."

"I say you can."

"And I say you'd feel differently if the same allegations were unjustly brought against you. As an impartial judge, this is the position I must assume. At least, this is what I've always done. Only, never before has it involved my own daughter."

Britton turned back to the fire. "I wouldn't even begin to know how to advise you."

Sir Richard gave a helpless smile. "The preferable outcome would be for her not to follow through with her engagement to Stuart. We could then move forward with nothing more to disclose."

"And if she chooses to stay with him? Would you tell her then?"

"If I did, I would also have to stress the lack of proof for the claim. Without it, she may accept it as hearsay. But always, it would fester in the back of her mind as a possible truth. A sad beginning for any marriage, wouldn't you say?"

Britton stared into the flames. "This must have been Tristan's position as well."

Before he could respond, there was a knock at the door. "Father..." Velena's face appeared. "May I come in?"

"Please."

She acknowledged her brother and entered. "I've come to see how best to employ myself."

"Ready to join the living, are we?" Britton teased.

"Ready to walk among them anyway."

Sir Richard gestured her over and settled her sideways upon a knee as if she were still a little girl. She smiled bravely, and he patted her hand. "I told you to take all the time you needed."

"And I thank you for it. Only now, tell me what I can do. It's time to busy my hands so that my thoughts might have a rest."

"Well…" Sir Richard began, "Lady Margarite is in the great hall finishing your wedding garments. Stuart and your uncle are due to join us within the hour for the noon meal, so she would probably welcome the help getting it done before she has to clear out. Plus, she's been asking after you."

"Alright." She stood to leave.

"Do me a favor," he added, "take the opportunity to brush up on your royal etiquette. If it comes to where you'll be needing to stand before the king, she may have one or two valuable tidbits of advice to give."

A chill ran up her spine.

"Afraid?" Britton asked.

"Intimidated."

Sir Richard smiled. "You'll do fine…if it even comes to that. You may not have to speak with him at all."

"I don't know…" Britton drawled. "She has this thing with standing on chairs and—"

"Shut your mouth." She laughed. It caused her pain, so she reached out to kick Britton for his part in it.

Entering the great hall, she found that life had truly gone on without her. Tapestries were being taken down from the walls to have the dust beat out of them while banners bearing the blue, gold, and yellow of the king's coat of arms were hung up for display. Several women, including the one she'd often noticed staring at Makaias, were chatting loudly around the dais where they had heaps of candles and garden cuttings laid out just so to be arranged into extravagant center pieces to be distributed to the lower tables. Old rushes were being taken up and the hearth swept out as several pages worked to pile high two stacks of freshly cut wood.

Velena may not yet have made the decision to engage the king as her future match maker, but it appeared her father was certainly preparing for its potentiality. Amid all this, Lady Margarite was engaged in exactly what her father had said. Seemingly oblivious to the buzz of activity surrounding her, she sat alone at a table, head bent over her work.

Fast to her side, Velena smiled a sincere greeting and joined in on the last of the stitches—never mind that the finished product might end up tucked away in a trunk for longer than originally intended, rather than displayed on her person. Regardless, she took great joy in the time she spent with Auntie, knowing the memories of it would stay with her long after this day.

As was expected, she was questioned about her absence over the earlier course of the week. Taking Auntie into her confidence would grow the circle of people who knew of the choice set before her to six—with the sixth being none other than a blood relative of Stuart's. Still, she knew she could trust her and so spoke the details of her dilemma in hushed tones. Time passed quickly in this way, and otherwise contented to wait for the midday meal where they were, she grew anxious to leave before Stuart arrived and told Auntie as much.

"Come then," Lady Margarite said, folding the wedding tunic and surcoat into a tidy pile. "You have a big decision before you. That is for certain. I shall be praying for you—earnestly, earnestly praying the Lord makes His will obvious and does it sooner rather than later. For my part, if you would be gone from here, I would take you out of doors. It sounds as if you've shut yourself in long enough and a change of scenery might be just the thing to clear the senses and shed light to your path."

Velena followed her around the curtain wall as they walked through the kitchen, first, enveloped almost at once by the balmy heat boiling up from the soups and sauces atop the cook stove, then out through the garden. She breathed it all in, enjoying the savory aroma of fresh cooked bread and spices. So also, the garden seemed to welcome her back into its potent little world, displaying its many varieties of budding flowers and leaves in every shape and shade of green. She plucked lavender, thyme, and mint and rubbed them in turns between her fingers to release the best of their scents. Despite a predominately overcast sky, there were patches of sun breaking through, and she felt a lightness of step return to her as she followed Auntie away from the pleasant smells of garden and on towards the sounds of the practice yard.

There was the crack of wood against wood and the smooth whistle of arrows meeting their targets. Steel on steel rang the loudest as swords clashed and sparked in the hands of the knights practicing for the melees of the tourney. They were grunting and groaning—drenched in sweat—and egging each other on with shouts and jeers very nearing profanity. Velena cringed but continued on, fascinated, if not a little apprehensive about witnessing any violence that should actually lead to injury.

"Nenna!"

Velena and Lady Margarite turned to find Rowan jogging their way. Covered in grime and face flushed red from exertion, he reached their side, a look of poorly disguised concern revealing itself in his eyes.

He bent over to kiss his aunt. "What are you doing here?"

"I came to watch my son beat you lads into shape." There was a twinkle in her eye. "Also, Lady Velena needed a change of scenery. Where is my son, might I inquire?"

Rowan pointed. "That way. Might I delay Nen—the lady—for a moment?" he asked, chuckling to himself as he tripped over his informality.

She smiled up at her nephew, which was quite the distance as he hovered at least a head and a half above her. "I'll be just over there."

Velena waited for him to speak.

"I haven't seen hide nor hair of you for days," he began. "How are you?"

"Sore but otherwise intact."

He shook his head. "I don't mean that. I mean—I do. It's good, of course, that you're feeling better, but...I was talking about the letter—and Stuart." He put his hands on his hips in frustration. "I heard the wedding was to be delayed but can't for the life of me understand why it hasn't been called off altogether. Does your father still expect you to marry Stuart after...you know...I mean, he did let you read it, didn't he?"

"I don't need to read it to prove what I saw happened. I just need to forgive it and move on."

Rowan ground his heel in the dirt, realizing she still didn't know.

118

"He should have let you read it. Did you at least try talking with Daisy?"

She shook her head. "It won't change the decision I have to make. Father told me if I don't want to marry Stuart, he'll approach King Edward about nullifying the engagement contract. That's the reason for the delay." Her gaze was direct. "I have to weigh marrying a man who would be so brazen as to bed my own maid or a stranger of the king's choice who may treat me worse. Do you think this is easy?"

"I do, as a matter of fact. You expected to find some sort of truth in Tristan's letter. Nigh desperate for it, as I recall. I can't believe you still took *no* for an answer. Nenna, you march right back into that manor and demand to see it. If not for yourself, for Daisy. I can't believe you still think she would do this to you."

She wrapped her arms around her middle. "The letter is gone."

"It's missing?"

"No. Gone. My father knew nothing about a letter—at least not that one. And I couldn't press him without incriminating Daisy for having taken it."

"What?"

"*She* was the one I gave it to…to give to him. Do you understand? She must have known that Tristan knew what she was doing and destroyed it. I'm sorry, Rowan. I know you don't want to believe it, but it's true."

Dismayed, his hand dragged down the length of his face as he remembered Daisy putting a letter into her pocket the day he'd approached her outside the church. "Does she have any family she still corresponds with?"

"She is the only one of her family to survive the Pestilence. She has no one."

How could he have been so stupid? He might have put this together long ago, and now it was probably too late. Unless… "I have to go! Make no decisions before we speak again. Promise me."

"Rowan, what are you going—"

"Just promise me!" he called back, sprinting towards the manor.

"…to do?" she finished under her breath. Sensing the shadow of something truly sinister standing above her, she prayed for God's peace to return.

14

be done with it

Lord, if I wanted to keep it a secret...I surely would have burned it. But would she? Rowan bound up the stairs two at a time, heading straight for Velena's solar. He passed a man carrying down a bundle of old trodden down rushes and could smell the fresh scent of new ones as he reached the top. He could hear rustling from the open guest rooms, so he knew they were still in the process of being scattered. He didn't know what he would say should someone see him enter Velena's solar without permission, but he figured if he simply strode in with confidence, he might avoid questioning.

The door was already open, so there was no trouble entering. He stood out of eyesight of the corridor, scanning the room when Daisy stepped out from the bed chamber. Both surprised and confused, her eyes betrayed a glimmer of pleasure, which only made what he had to do worse for him.

"Rowan?"

He liked the way she said his name. It warmed him, and he wondered if she might not just give him the letter if he asked.

"Lady Velena's not here," she said.

"I'm...not here to see Velena."

Her eyes traveled the length of him, taking in everything from his soiled shoes to his disheveled top knot. "Then why are you..." her voice trailed off as she mistook the nature of his expression. She knew very well she could trust him, but that look in his eyes—what did it mean? She tried to dismiss it, but the shadow of an old fear began to cloud her thinking.

He noted the change in her demeanor, the way she white-knuckled the handful of rushes she carried—and hated that he should be the cause of it. *You distance yourself from me already, Daisy? I should not be at your door. Too late.* How should he begin? "I need to ask you a question."

"Then let us meet below stairs."

"Sorry," he said, extending his arm to shut the door, "but we need to talk here." Sensing her panic, he held up his hands. "I'm not here for anything untoward. And had I the time to dwell on it, I should be slightly offended at the fear in your eyes. You should know me better."

"Just tell me why you *are* here."

"I need to ask you somethi—"

"Then ask it," she said, growing impatient.

"I've come to retrieve something that belongs to Sir Richard, and I would be most grateful if you would produce that *something.*"

Her breath came faster. "That wasn't a question."

"The letter I saw you with at the church. It was Tristan's; wasn't it? Will you give it to me willingly or must I conduct a search?"

Her mouth fell open. "What game is this?"

"I would that it was a game, Daisy. Nevertheless, that wasn't the answer I was hoping for. Come now, I would know what you've done with it."

"What would I have done with it but deliver it as instructed?" Daisy scattered the rushes at her feet, willing him to leave.

"Where?"

She crossed her arms.

"Where?" he demanded.

She stepped back. "To his cabinet."

He shook his head.

"Well, I don't know where it is past placing it on his desk." Her hands grew sweaty. "Did he ask you to come to me about it?"

"No."

She shrugged. "Then what business is it of yours?"

Rowan looked her straight in the eyes. "No more lies. Velena deserves to know the truth—and she needs to hear it from Tristan. I'm sorry for what I have to do."

"That your legs would simply carry you elsewhere would be apology enough."

"Please, Daisy. Do you not consider me a friend? I was hoping we'd developed a certain amount of…trust between us by now."

"We're not on intimate terms, if that's what you're suggesting."

"What if I told you…I wanted to be." The look on her face echoed both their surprise. He hadn't planned to say it.

"Get out!" she hissed, shoving him towards the door.

"Daisy, I'm serious."

"Your toying with me to get what you want."

"I'm not talking about bedding you; I'm falling in—"

"Shut your mouth. Shut your mouth! Don't you dare come to me spouting love and calling me a liar in the same breath."

"Wait...just listen to me."

"Leave!"

"No," he said, easily setting her aside. "We can talk about this later, but I won't leave without that letter." The last thing he wanted to do was to set her against him, but he had to finish what he came to do. Turning away from her, he began to examine the perimeter of the room. "If there's yet a chance you've held onto it, I'll find it."

"Rowan, please. If you won't leave, then I will."

"You need not be present for me to conduct a thorough search. If it's here, I'll find it."

Her face blanched as he went to a side table and began rifling through the pages of books, discarding them one by one to the bench in front of the hearth. He lifted the braided rug; he checked the mantel for cracks and the hearth for loose stones. He peaked under the table and benches to see if it'd been secured to their undersides. Finding nothing, he crossed to the window seat, pushing aside the sheets hanging from the ceiling before checking the seat itself for flaws and hidden compartments.

Taking advantage of his focused attention, Daisy edged past him through the door to the sleeping quarters she shared with Velena.

Rowan swore under his breath as his foot got tangled in the sheets. *What is this thing?* Extra blankets were piled on the ground within the prayer closet, and he made a quick sweep with his foot to see if anything lay beneath, but there was only a short stack of papers, all verses of Scripture Tristan had left for Velena. Turning around he realized Daisy was no longer with him. Bolting into the sleeping chamber, he caught her pulling something out from beneath her mattress.

"Don't!" he exclaimed, running to place himself between her and the fireplace, sure it was her next destination. But now there was the problem of the unguarded door going back into the outer room. She moved towards it, but he thwarted her again, hovering just between the two, arms outstretched should she run in either direction. "Please don't," he said, senses alerted to any sudden movements. He took a step towards her, and Daisy backed away, clutching the letter to her breast. "It'll be alright," he tried to reassure her.

"It's not alright!" she spat.

"Then give me the letter and let's just let it be over."

"No. What part of this aids you?"

"Not me, but the ones I serve."

"You've known all this while. You could have told them, yourself. Why need you the letter?"

"I would give them more than hearsay."

"It's all hearsay without Stuart's confession."

"Your testimony still counts for something. Think past your pain and do what's right."

"Is it right that all consideration be given to Velena and not to me?"

Rowan held his breath. Two steps and the letter would be within reach. "Not so," he whispered, holding out his hand to her. "This, I do also for you."

"Making known what I've endured cannot be the only way to free her from her situation. Find another way!"

"This is the surest path. Can you really keep silent while she marries the man who raped you?"

"I can," she sobbed.

"Have faith in Sir Richard's judgment of the matter. What happened to you was not your fault. He'll know that."

"But you have no way to prove it."

"You won't need to prove it to Velena. Tell her what was done to you, and she'll embrace you. If you don't, she'll forever believe you went to him willingly."

"What?"

"She saw Stuart leave the room—and you with the money—and assumes he's been paying you all this time."

"It's what I feared she thought."

"Can you blame her?" He took a step.

She retreated two. "Don't touch me!"

Rowan lowered his hand. "Touching you is the last thing you need worry about from me."

"Because I'm used."

"Because you're not my wife."

"As if the lack of a wife ever stopped you from taking a harlot between the sheets."

"I know less of harlots than you think, but enough to know you're not one of those."

be done with it

Tears spilled from her eyes. "Without proof against him, he'll have me slandered as a mere wanton. Indeed, if there was any proof to be had, it would be that I had been with Bowan that same night."

Rowan felt as though the wind had been knocked out of him. "You gave yourself to him?"

She shook her head. "I offered myself, but he was too honorable for that. Stuart found me in...disarray." Her voice trembled. "But I would have—you see—and Stuart only finished what'd been started. God used him to punish me. I'd be guilty because that's what I am."

"Not so. This secret has left you alone with your thoughts, and they're none to clear." He stepped forward. "You've been in need of comforting—"

She recoiled. "Not by you!"

"Velena would have done the job if you'd been willing to share your burden."

"You don't think it's killed me not to tell her?"

He nodded at that which was still held tightly within her grasp. "We'll tell her together." He put his hand out.

"I forbid you to touch me!"

Rowan frowned. "You know I won't."

"Yes," she said, her eyes pained and glassy, "I do know it. And I thank you." And with those words, she shoved the letter down the front of her tunic even as he reached for her hand. It came up empty.

Clasping her wrist, he swore. "You test me, Daisy."

"You said you wouldn't touch me—it was my only recourse."

"Yes, I said it...but you're not playing fair."

"I'm not playing at all. There's more you don't know."

Rowan saw a new kind of fear in her eyes—fear of discovery, fear of rejection. Tempted to forget all about the letter and take her in his arms, he cupped her face instead. She didn't pull away. "Tell me, then."

"You'll know soon enough."

Her cheeks were wet beneath his thumbs. "Do you love me?" he whispered.

"What?" Her eyelids fluttered.

"I was hoping you loved me."

"I..." her chest rose and fell with every breath. "I..."

"Do you think you could? Because if you give me the letter and your testimony, and things still go badly for you...I'll marry you." His smile turned hopeful. "I'll marry you anyway...if you'll have me."

Hardly believing him, visions of Bowan flashed before her eyes.

124

Three years at the castle, she'd loved him. Could she let that go?

"Daisy?"

Rowan's face came back into focus. "My affection has grown for you."

"I can accept that."

"But could you accept me?" *Tell him,* her heart whispered. "I'm with child," she confessed before she could change her mind.

Unprepared, his hands dropped away, and with them, Daisy's hope that he might mean what he'd said.

Something akin to a sob and a cry erupted from her throat, and he knew he'd done wrong to let her go. In despair, she attempted to escape past him, but he caught her around the waist, pulling her into his body and stilling her escape.

She squirmed against him. "Release me."

"Be still."

"Rowan. Release me..." Panicked, she wanted to fight; she wanted to run, but she could do neither. He was too strong, and it brought her back to a time she could never forget. She heard a buzzing in her ears and began to whimper and at last to beg. "Please...please...please, let me go. Please, please, please..."

"Daisy, listen to me!"

"You're holding too tight."

"Of necessity...to keep you in one place."

She pushed against him. "You didn't mean what you said."

"I'm sorry—I'm so sorry. Just give me time to think—" His voice was lost as the unpredicted thrust of her knee lodged itself between his thighs, crippling him and nearly bringing him to the floor. Groaning low in his throat, his eyes squeezed shut, legs threatening to collapse. He needed a minute to recover—and perhaps several—without letting her escape, so he stumbled into her, pinning her to the wall. But he needn't have worried for she'd stopped fighting him. In shock of her own actions, she now stood quite still.

He could feel her chest heaving against him as air streamed in and out through her nose—felt it against his neck as he rested his forehead on the wall above her, willing the pain to pass more quickly. She kept silent so that he felt, rather than heard, she was back to crying.

"Forgive me..." he rasped. "I meant what I said about marrying you. You just surprised me...is all."

Daisy pressed against his chest, and this time he let her. Praying she wouldn't run, he eased himself down upon the floor, waiting for relief.

Lowering herself beside him, she laid a hand on his arm. "You needn't mean it, and I'd certainly never hold you to it. I'm carrying your cousin's child—*Stuart's* child. See how you cringe at his name. You'll never be able to overlook that."

Rowan closed his eyes, timidly readjusting his position.

"Would you take me to Tristan before I begin to show? No one knows me there. I could have it in secret."

"More secrets. Does Tristan know?"

She shook her head. When he remained quiet, she fidgeted with her dress. "I'm sorry I kicked you," she said at last. "Tristan never gave me so much trouble as you." She attempted a crooked smile, shallow dimples bringing life back to her face.

Exasperated, his eyes rolled to the back of his head. "Perhaps, because you never attempted to stuff something he wanted into your bodice."

She stared into her lap.

Rowan laid a hand to her knee. "Would that he were here, and I was not; the day might have gone easier for you."

She shrugged one shoulder. "I knew you'd change your mind about loving me. Any man would."

Rowan's lids dropped in regret. "I feel more for you than I've felt for any woman. But face to face with this…" he studied her stomach, with new interest, "I find I'm a coward."

"It's alright."

He shook his head. "No, it's not. I need time to think about it, though—think it through. I *will* make good on my pledge."

"When I can't say I love you in return? Why should you burden yourself for such a meager reward as that?"

A week, a day, an hour even—give me some time to pray."

"Do you pray?"

"Not nearly enough."

Daisy smiled, though it felt more like a frown. She turned away and seemed to disappear within her own thoughts. When she spoke, her voice was full of longing. "Do you see those flowers?"

Rowan followed her gaze to a vase on Velena's desk. He nodded.

"Flowers don't make me happy anymore. Though, I can remember that at one time they did. The reality of that frightens me. So, I think, perhaps…I've not known an hour of true happiness for longer than is fitting for a person to be without it."

His brows knitted together. "It's a good realization, Daisy." Then he watched in disbelief as she pulled the letter from her bodice, placed it into his palm, and curled his fingers down over it.

"Here," she said softly. "It's choking the life from me. Stop the wedding and promise to take me to Tristan when it's all over. I don't belong here anymore."

A feeling of helplessness washed over him, and it was all he could do not to give in to it and weep. He pulled Daisy into his arms, cradling her head against his chest, and whispered, "What I do, I do as much for you as for Velena."

A chill ran down her spine, dreading the moments to come.

"I know you have no hope of Stuart coming to justice—"

"He won't."

"He will," he assured her, holding her out in front of him. "His wrong won't go unpunished. If not through the law than by my own sword will it be executed."

"Would you harm your own cousin?"

"I already have," he reminded her.

She nodded, looking weary in body as well as soul. "I would have taken what was done to me to the grave, except the babe won't allow it."

"Did you never think…to be rid of it?"

Daisy might have flinched had she not already considered it a thousand times over. "I have, but I've not the heart for it. Tis none of its own doing how it came to be. Would you ask it of me?"

He couldn't deny the temptation to do so, but he shook his head and remained awkwardly silent.

"You want to ask me something else." She could see it all over his face.

He took a deep breath, not wanting to, but feeling it would eat at him if he didn't. "The money purse…what was it really for?"

"Stuart knows about the child. I was going to leave, and he was paying my way."

"He really *was* helping you?"

She smiled bitterly. "He found his conscience," she admitted, "but too late."

While Rowan took that in, dread was going to beat a hole in her chest if they waited any longer. "Let's we be done with it then."

Nodding, Rowan slipped the letter inside the breast of his jerkin. "I'll not tarry. In all likelihood, Sir Richard will send for you—to hear it confirmed." With care, he hefted himself back onto his feet before reaching down for her.

"Will you stay with me when he does?" she asked, rising up before him, her look far too vulnerable for Rowan to linger beneath. He pulled her hands to his lips and nodded. Denying himself any final words, he walked away with an exaggerated hobble, bringing the last small laugh from Daisy's lips that he'd hear for some time.

15

what a waste

Seated in one of the two armchairs alongside Lord Magnus, Sir Richard laughed so hard it caused a brilliant shade of red to creep up from his beard and into his cheeks as he made no effort to control his merriment. Even Lord Magnus appeared amused as Jaren laughed at his own retelling of one of his mother's more humorous mishaps from her time at the convent.

Sir Richard raised his glass to him as he resettled his muscular frame into his chair. He exhaled with an elongated sigh and stretched his legs out before him, a smile lifting the corners of his mustache. "By my troth, a funny woman, your mother."

Jaren grinned. "My brothers and I used to say that someday we'd come home to an empty house and find she'd run off to become the king's court jester." The corners of his mouth dipped slightly. "Unfortunately, my father favored a more…demur version of her. It was a rare occurrence for us to see her so animated—mostly holidays."

"Which is where such displays belong," Lord Magnus said, bringing a tankard of ale to his lips. "Though diverting at times, a woman's talents are best saved for the bedroom."

"Hmph." Sir Richard turned to Stuart. "I must council against such words. Thinking like that won't bring you any joy in marriage."

Magnus smirked. "I beg to differ."

"Joy for a night pales mightily in comparison to a lifetime of the same. Treat her as a queen, and you'll live as a king. I guarantee it."

Magnus waved him off. "Bah. Rare the woman who can deliver such bliss."

"Your sister brought me such," Sir Richard reminded him.

Magnus laced his fingers over his stomach. "He'll find joy in his sons."

Stuart fingered a splinter of wood coming up from the table. *Would that you had taken joy in your own sons, Father.* He looked up to see Sir Richard staring at him.

"Your mother was a sweet woman, Stuart. As you well know, she was gentle and kind—had a pleasant word for everyone."

Magnus baulked. "Not for me, she didn't."

"If you hold someone under glass, don't be surprised if they run out of air."

Uncomfortable with where the vein of their conversation had gone, Jaren let go an inner sigh of relief when Rowan entered the room.

"My lord," Rowan said, presenting himself to Sir Richard.

"Squire Rowan."

He held out the folded piece of paper. "A letter—from Esquire Tristan."

Sir Richard eyed the parchment, appearing almost hesitant to take it. "The seal is broken," he said, sliding his thumb beneath the top fold. "Can I assume my daughter got to it first?"

"Not so, my lord, but if you will allow a me a private audience, I can better explain."

Sir Richard straightened out the folds of parchment and scanned the first few lines before immediately closing it again. "With me," he instructed Rowan, large strides carrying him hastily from the room.

Rowan obeyed, catching Jaren's eye as he left. As brief as it was, Jaren saw what was coming.

"Prepare yourself," he said to Stuart under his breath.

He looked at him. "For what?"

"I told you Tristan knew something."

Stuart took a drink. "Impossible," he muttered half into his tankard.

"Entirely probable," Jaren corrected.

Stuart looked down at his feet. Nothing to do but wait.

"If not Velena, then who?" Sir Richard questioned, fingering the broken seal again as he took the seat at his desk.

"Daisy. But I beg you not to make judgment until you've read all that it says.

Sir Richard gave him a hard look. "As you have, I take it."

"God help me if I were ever so bold. I only know what Tristan confided in me—and assume it's the same as is written there."

Sir Richard began reading where he'd left off. "Leave me."

Rowan obeyed, exiting the room but not straying far from the door. Standing erect, he waited. Minutes ticked by—a time far too long for his thinking. Then again, he knew Sir Richard. As patient as Rowan thought himself to be, Sir Richard was more so. He never acted rashly. When he opened the door, he would know his mind, and there would be naught that could change it.

A muted commotion from within brought his head around, as though items of considerable weight had suddenly been toppled to the floor. He was on the verge of going in when the door opened. His lord stood before him looking grim, and Rowan glanced over his shoulder to see the contents atop Sir Richards desk strewn across the floor. That he might have swept them away, seemed a fitting response to such news, though somehow still out of place for Sir Richard.

"Geoffrey!" he shouted down the corridor, calling for his valet. "Where's Velena?" he asked Rowan.

"In the practice yard with Auntie. Shall I fetch her for you?"

"No."

"Yes, my lord," the valet answered, hurrying towards him.

"Please put my cabinet back in order. There was an accident with my desk."

"As you wish, my lord."

Wondering what course of action would come first, Rowan waited until Geoffrey skirted past his master before speaking again. "I'm at your service, my lord."

"Am I to assume you've known who it was this whole time?"

"I was aware, my lord, though I was unaware you didn't. And what could I have said that Tristan had not. My promise was only to keep Velena safe in his absence."

Sir Richard took a careful moment to form his thoughts before speaking. "Which is why Tristan asked for me to take you on at Landerhill—which is where all this courtly love nonsense has come from."

Rowan nodded. "I had to keep her close."

Sir Richard crossed his arms. "And incense Stuart whilst doing it."

Rowan smiled for the first time. "A perk, I have to admit."

"You've spoken with Daisy, then."

"I have."

"And you believe this to be true?"

"As sure as I live and breathe. She's confessed to it—though not readily. She was found out quite by accident and then went to great pains to keep it hidden once Tristan was gone."

"By taking the letter."

"Aye, but she was only buying herself time," he said, lowering his voice. "She's with child, my lord."

Sir Richard's eyes fell shut, his face contorting with pity—and a grief he might have felt had she been his own daughter. "Heaven, help her."

"Shall I bring her to you, my lord?"

"Velena first. As Daisy's mistress, she should be present. As the future chatelaine of her own manor, she'll need to learn to address…hard things."

"As you wish, my lord. I'll bring her straight away to your cabinet." Rowan turned to leave, but Sir Richard's hand shot out to halt him.

"Bring her back by way of the kitchen but stay out of sight behind the curtain wall.

"My lord?"

"Hard things, Rowan. It will be hard for her to hear it this way, but she should hear it from him. As there is no proof of the action, I will have to use his own words against him, and I want no room for Velena to doubt." He noted the look of apprehension flitting across Rowan's face but was pleased when he obeyed without question. Watching him go, Sir Richard took a calming breath. It was time to confront Lord Magnus and his son—in a calm and controlled manner if he could at all accomplish it. God help him. What hopes he had for his nephew rising above his father's influence were now shattered. What a waste.

16

sudden notice

Reunited with Lady Margarite, Velena rested her arms atop a stretch of fencing separating one part of the practice yard from another. Behind them, was a generous section of cleared land where a group of knights were running exercises under the direction of Sir Andret. In front, was its duplicate, except for the large ring, fifteen foot in diameter, raked into the ground. In the center of the circle was Sir Makaias, using his sword to wave in the next squire from a lineup of five squires still awaiting their turns.

"First man out of the ring loses," he shouted above the noise. "Winner goes on to fight the next opponent."

Lady Margarite gripped Velena's arm in anticipation. "It's been so long since I've seen him in action. Fills a mother's heart with pride."

Velena responded in surprise. "Does it never frighten you that he might get hurt?"

"Oh, pish posh," Lady Margarite said with a wave of her hand. "He could get hurt tripping over his own shoes if a stone were in the right place to meet with his head. One mustn't worry until one has to," she stated emphatically. "Christ warns us away from such folly. Remember, dear, that—" The first clash of steal brought their eyes back to the ring.

Velena understood the importance of Makaias not allowing his students to best him in combat, but after three opponents, she marveled that he was still fighting as though he'd just begun. Up to several inches shorter than some, who like Rowan, were heads taller than most, it made no difference. His skills were unmatched, and she suddenly had an image of him by her bedside in his wet tunic, pressed flat and outlining the swell of his muscles.

"Impressed?" a male voice asked from her side.

Velena bumped her brother's shoulder in greeting. "I didn't hear you. Your limp is getting quieter," she teased.

Britton put some weight on his bad leg as if to test it. "That it is."

"How's it feeling today?" she asked.

"Well enough to be out there," he said, eyes locked on the fight.

Velena gasped as the fourth squire was forced out of the ring, and none too gracefully. Makaias was breathing hard but managed a grin and a wink at her brother. Noting the exchange, she turned to take a better look at Britton, dismayed to see him in his chain mail, sword buckled at his side. "You're not really going to fight are you?"

"Yes, baby sister, I am."

"You're leg?"

"It's been over a month."

"Are you sure you're ready?"

He gave her a sideways grin. "I certainly hope so."

Velena frowned as Makaias took up swords with the final squire. *At least he'll be tired,* she reasoned.

"You're still recovering," Lady Margarite inserted. "I'm sure he'll go easy on you."

Britton snorted as he looked from the sword play within the ring to the defeated squires still calling out encouragement to the remaining man. Their enthusiastic cries became something of a frenzy as Sir Makaias was suddenly thrown off balance, bringing the back of his heel mere inches from the boundary mark. With a twist and a block and a full turn, he deflected what would have been a crushing blow, regained his balance, and disarmed the other man entirely.

Lady Margarite *whooted* out a very unladylike cheer along with several knights behind her who'd stopped to watch. Velena clapped in earnest until her brother left her side to take his place in the circle. A momentary hush fell over the men as they wondered how their lord's wounded son would fair against the man none of them could put down. Expecting it to be over in seconds, they had to respect him for risking the embarrassment.

Stopping to see what was happening on the other side of the fence, Sir Andret called an end to the exercises and approached with the others.

Velena tensed at what had now become something of a spectacle. "Sir Makaias!" she called out. "Pray, remember he's injured."

"Shhh," Auntie chided, "you embarrass your brother."

Makaias smirked as Britton took a ready stance. "Have you ever tried approaching an injured animal, my lady? Pray for *me.*"

Laughter followed but died away as soon as the first stroke was dealt. Steel against steel, sparks flew as Britton's limp miraculously became non-existent. Nevertheless, he continued to rely on his good leg to pivot, using the strength of his arms and chest to meet Makaias sword both high and low, until both retreated to opposite ends of the circle to catch their breath. Winded, but determined, they came at each other again with dogged determination, faces hard as if they didn't know each other.

Velena winced and had to look away several times as their swords drew dangerously close to meeting their mark. "They'll hurt each other," she fretted. Then as if by prophecy, Britton swept the tip of his blunted sword across Makaias rib cage in a broad stroke that chinked across his chain mail. She caught her breath as the force of it halted his advance, but only for a moment, as Makaias paid it no heed, swinging all the harder until he had Britton balancing on his bad leg for support.

He held his ground for as long as he could, but his leg burned, and his arms trembled with fatigue. One final blow and Britton was on the ground with Makaias standing over him.

"I'm still in the ring," Britton gloated at his feet.

Makaias' answer was a full rotation of his sword. Bringing the hilt above his head, he thrust downward with both hands, dropping to one knee as he sunk his blade into the sand just above Britton's shoulder. "Yes—but you're dead."

Britton's grin stretched from one side of his face to the other. "And as dead men can't fight, neither shall I." Chest heaving, he tossed his arm outside the ring, speaking loud enough for all to hear. "I yield."

The crowd erupted into a mighty cheer as Britton accepted Makaias' proffered hand. Coming to his feet, he turned to his father's knights and squires and bowed low in acceptance of his humble defeat, knowing he'd earned their respect despite it. Taking a step forward, he stumbled, but caught himself on his sword. The fight had taxed his leg, perhaps too much.

Velena flew to his side, clutching him by the face, and kissing his cheeks in thanksgiving. "You were extraordinary!" she cried above the din. "I know now to pray for your enemies and not for you."

Makaias chuckled. "That's the truth of it. You should see him in full form. It's certainly something to behold."

Velena turned her smile to Makaias next when suddenly there came a cry from the crowd. "A kiss for the victor!"

"A kiss from the lady!" sounded another, until it came from all around them.

Taken aback, Velena's eyes searched out Lady Margarite, who'd come around to her son's side. She nodded her approval.

"You've kissed the loser; it only seems fair," she said, laughing at her son's look of disapproval.

"It doesn't look as though the knight would like one," Velena said, suddenly embarrassed, but the eyes he turned to her were tipped in good humor.

"The knight would like his mother not to meddle," he teased, "but would never turn down a kiss from milady."

"Beating me was hard work," Britton insisted.

"It certainly was," Makaias agreed, lowering his cheek and tapping his finger to the spot she should kiss.

"Then I shall," Velena announced to a new set of cheers. "And not for your victory alone, Sir, but for such a *fine* show of humility."

Facing each other, his eyes twinkled in good humor. *Mirth and water*, she thought again. She leaned forward. Lifting onto her toes, she steadied herself with a light hand to his torso, bringing her mouth to his cheek to the applause of all.

His face was overdue for a shave, and it pricked at her lips. But the warmth she felt there, no doubt a result from the exertion of the fight, seemed now to affect her senses in ways most unexpected.

Had she not just kissed her brother in similar fashion? And a peck on the cheek should hardly feel like an intimacy after she'd been kissed by Stuart—and on the mouth. Admittedly this was different, though, for her cousin's kisses were an intimacy she hadn't wanted, and the nearness of this man, not so familiar to her as family, awakened an awareness in her that set her to wondering what it might be like to kiss someone…else.

Unsettled, she prepared to mask her thoughts, lest they become apparent on her face. Tristan had often laughed at her inability to hide what she was thinking. Though, since her engagement to Stuart, she felt certain she had improved. Pushing back from Makaias, he grunted, gingerly pressing his hand to the area of his ribs she'd just vacated.

"Sorry about that," Britton said, taking responsibility for his friend's pain.

Makaias shirked off the apology. "Not sure I believe you."

"What's wrong?" Velena asked, unsure what they were talking about.

Makaias grimaced at his own touch. "Couple of bruised ribs most likely."

"Ohhh." She linked her hands behind her back and smiled. "Could be broken," she said, bringing to remembrance a similar conversation.

He chuckled as Lady Margarite wagged her finger at Britton. "You'd better hope they're only bruised. I saw that swing. He needs to be in top form for the tourney."

"You fret for naught," Britton said with a laugh. "Bones of steal, this one."

"Just the same, let's have a look. Help him with his chain mail," she directed one of the squires.

Velena stood back as Makaias first unbuckled his belt, then bent over at the waist with his arms extended forward. The squire's job was made easier by Makaias' not having worn plated armor over top—which would have required the undoing of a good deal more buckles and ties—but only the elbow-length chain mail, itself. To remove this, the squire had to pull it forward at the arms before it gave enough to be slipped over his head. Beneath was a waist length, padded doublet, which he unbuttoned himself.

Velena's feet shifted position beneath her, and the ground seemed to do the same. It wasn't that the removal of his doublet would expose anything untoward, but that the movement, itself, caused an unwelcome buzzing sensation in her stomach. One at a time, his fingers moved down the row of buttons—and there were many. It was as if she'd suddenly become aware of him—all from a kiss—and not even a proper one.

She looked to his face, but he was looking past her, dismissing the men back to their exercises. He was the same as ever. Still Makaias. Still friend to her brother—too old and much too serious for her liking. Too *intense*, anyway—as evidenced by his recent sword play. It was then that Britton said something to make him laugh, and Velena had to amend her thoughts to *intense only in the things that mattered*. Truth be told, he was rather playful—in his own way.

Shrugging out of his doublet, the lighter weighted tunic worn beneath was soaked through and did little to hide the breadth of his shoulders or swell of his chest. Seemed a bit unfair that even a man should have more than she, she thought, peering down the front of her own surcoat. Holding back a smile, she crossed her arms over her petite chest and against any further wanderings of the mind. Alas, she had not quite the control she hoped for.

Lady Margarite stepped forward to lift the front of his tunic, wanting to inspect the full impact of Britton's sword. The blunted blade had certainly left its mark. Shades of purple, red, and black all mixed together to create a most woeful mosaic across several of his lower ribs.

Curling forward to have a better look for himself, Makaias' stomach contracted into a most pleasant set of ridges, no less firm than a washing bat.

Velena turned aside, fluttering her eyelids at her own ridiculousness. The buzzing was now in her chest.

"It's bruised, only," Makaias remarked.

"I'll be the judge," Lady Margarite said, reaching her hands to her son's side. Then, as if in afterthought, she paused, turning back to Velena. "Do you know how to tell such things, Lady Velena?"

"If ribs are broken? No, Auntie, I'm afraid I haven't the experience."

"Come then," she said, bidding her forwards. "Place your hands just so." And before Velena could deny her, Lady Margarite pulled her hands to Makaias' side.

Taken aback, but admittedly interested in learning the skill, she found herself probing about his lower ribs for she knew not what. The skin beneath her hand was not only warm but slick with sweat, allowing her fingers to slide easily across the bones. "Nothing seems out of place," she said, glancing up to see Makaias peering down at her.

"What next?" he asked, an encouraging ring to his voice.

"Next? Uh, well, I…" Uncomfortable beneath his stare, she shifted her gaze to her brother, but this was a mistake, for he was in full delight of her obvious discomfort. Obvious to him but not to Auntie, who denied her retreat.

"No, no. Keep your hand there." She practically held it down. "Add pressure to the bone."

Velena did as told, remembering now how Makaias had done the same to her in her solar. No doubt he'd been referring to it, expecting her to remember. Feeling foolish, she pushed until he grunted.

Velena jerked away.

"That's a telling sign," Auntie explained. "It'll cause him more pain if it's broken."

"I'm sorry," Velena mouthed.

Makaias shook his head. "It pains in the way of a bruise."

Velena's brow knitted together. "You're sure?"

"Take a deep breath," Auntie directed.

He complied—as did Velena—watching the repeated rise and fall of his chest. She met his gaze expectantly. "Any sharp pains?" she asked, before he could challenge her memory again.

He looked pleased. "Not a one."

"Praise God for that!" Auntie exclaimed. "But for the sake of our lesson, one more test. Pray, twist from side to side."

Makaias did so with arms held aloft, grinning as he thwacked into Britton's chest with his hand. "There, you see? All is well."

Velena wrinkled her nose. "All is not well," she said, as the odor of a hard day's work wafted up from his sweat soaked tunic. "I'd say you're in dire need of a bath."

"Oh, would you?"

A smattering of laughter from those men still in ear shot left her wondering if she should have held her tongue.

He crossed his arms and speared them with a look. "After the walloping I gave you, I suppose the rest of you smell like roses."

Velena giggled. "Apologies, Sir Makaias. I shouldn't have offended."

"There's no offense in the truth," Britton piped in.

Lady Margarite shook her head. "Would that were always the case. At least you've no broken bones. Take a bath, my son. The lady speaks true."

"As you wish," he said and immediately took hold of the fabric of his tunic behind his neck. Peeling it forwards over his head, he exposed all Velena had been working to ignore.

Her mouth gaped.

"It's not that bad," Makaias said, taking note of her shocked expression, looking down again at the discoloration of his ribs.

Britton laughed outright as Velena turned away. He leaned into his friend. "I don't think she's gawking at your bruise," he confessed out the side of his mouth.

"*Brit-ton!*" she scolded, but he laughed all the more.

Makaias' blinked. "Why Velena Ambrose...I'm surprised at you." He lifted his tunic to the front of his chest, looking aghast.

Too late for excuses, Velena flung out her arms, flopping them at her sides. "Would you not also feel flustered if I disrobed in front of you?"

Britton sobered at once. "Velena!"

"What?" she said, exasperated.

"Enough," Lady Margarite chided. "Let us not go back and forth. The lady speaks truly. Modesty is not reserved only for women. So, as for you, my son, I told you to take a bath, not to take a bath *here*. Now, off with you and no more prancing about before young women in all your glory."

"Quite right," Makaias said, kissing his mother a farewell. He then bowed to Velena with the intent to leave, but vanity got the better of him, causing him to rise with arms flexed, curved in at the waist, and chest bulging by degrees. "Ever your humble servant, my lady."

"Have you no fear of your mother?" Lady Margarite exclaimed, slapping at his arm. "I said, go!"

Chuckling at her attempt to hurt him, he trotted off towards the creek without looking back.

Velena's shoulders shook with laughter—and mostly at herself for being so caught up in her own head. His direct attempt at impressing her accomplished exactly the opposite, and she sighed contentedly, pushing aside her attraction. Makaias was, indeed, a beautiful man— but what was that to her? Stuart, too, was handsome. What then was beauty but a mask to hide behind? Her sudden notice of him had been naught but a reflection of her own discontent. And this she must take to the Lord…*again*.

"Will you come?" she heard Sir Andret ask Britton. Exercises over with, he dismissed his knights to follow after Makaias for a badly needed soak.

"I'm going to talk with my sister a while."

"As you like." Sir Andret turned to place a kiss to his mother's temple. "Enjoy the rest of your day, Mother."

"You as well, my love." Lady Margarite smiled, contented as any mother should be. "I'll see you back inside," she said to Velena and moved on, allowing them their privacy.

They followed behind her at a much slower pace and in no hurry to catch up. She frowned at her brother's limp. "I fear you've done too much too quickly."

"The exercise is good for me. And though it appears the worse for my actions, my leg grows stronger day by day. As do I."

Silence. And then a sideways glance, a smile lifting the corners of her mouth. "Not so strong as Sir Makaias."

Britton laughed, and Velena along with him. "Get an eyeful, did you?"

"It would have behooved me to close them."

Mirth dulling into the remains of a grin, he bumped his shoulder against hers, shaking his head. "Not so strong as *Makaias*," he mocked.

"I'll give you *not so strong as Makaias*!" Turning on her quickly, he hefted her up into his arms, cradling her as if she weighed nothing at all.

She squealed, grabbing tightly about his neck as his first step seemed sure to pitch her to the ground. The next a bit steadier but with an obvious hop as he tried to maintain all of his weight on his good leg.

Velena went back and forth between shrieking and laughing as Britton took another three very unsteady steps. She tugged at his chain mail. "You're going to hurt yourself. Put me down."

Unwilling to admit to it, just those few steps alone revealed just how much the sword play had taxed his injury. "Take it back," he said, taking another unsteady hop.

Velena yelped. "I take it back! You are as strong as—"

"As strong?"

"Stronger! And more so for bearing me through pain."

"Better." He laughed, setting her feet to the ground.

"I'll have to remember not to goad you," she said, taking up their walk again.

"Best not to." He placed an affectionate arm about her shoulders. "So. Are you ready to tell Stuart you've become enamored of Makaias?"

Velena gasped. "You're evil." And she pushed his arm from her shoulders.

He ignored her snub and sighed. "Poor Kai. He'll not be able to look you in the eyes again."

"*Me?*"

"Yes. You embarrassed him."

"Hmph. If that be so, it'd be your doing—and he didn't look so embarrassed to me. It was I you embarrassed near to tears."

"There were no tears."

"How would you know? Velena exclaimed. "You were too busy laughing at me to notice."

"Well, it was hard not to…with your mouth hanging open like—"

"Don't finish that."

He chuckled. "Any longer and we could have used you to catch flies."

"You're awful."

"At least I'm not prone to trouble. I'm not saying you are, but one of us is, and it certainly isn't me."

She wrinkled her nose at him. "What do you mean I'm prone to it?"

Britton laughed. "Dangle a carrot in front of a filly, and she's sure to bite."

"I'm serious. What do you mean by it?"

He could feel the angst crossing the distance between them. He scratched behind his ear. "Come on, Velena, you know how you are."

"Pray, tell. How am I?"

"Not so tame as you could be."

She rolled her eyes.

"Actually, it has me worried. Who in all the world is the king going to find worthy enough to tame the heart of my baby sister?"

"Father told you."

"He did."

She sighed, a cynical lilt to her words as she said, "Well, perhaps there's no one. Perhaps, I'll become a nun as Auntie was, content to live out my life as the bride of Christ."

He chuckled. "He'd be the best one up for the job to be certain—God and maybe Kai—except he doesn't want you."

Velena blinked, not only at her brother's thoughtless remark but that such a conversation between them might have ever taken place. "Well, I don't want him either," she quipped.

"Velena, I didn't mean—" he began, but Rowan's voice interrupted his explanation.

"Pardon my intrusion, but I'm under orders to bring Lady Velena back to the manor."

Britton looked confused. "Orders? Has Stuart arrived or something?"

Rowan nodded but didn't elaborate.

Regretful that their conversation should end here, Britton let her go. He shouldn't have said what he did about Makaias not wanting her. It was entirely uncalled for, and as soon as he was able, he planned to pull her aside and apologize. Unfortunately, that might be a while now that company had arrived. Limping along, he wondered how he'd greet his cousin now that he knew what he'd done. The whole thing still seemed quite unfathomable.

Entering the manor through the kitchen door, he expected to find it a working den of activity, as the noon meal was not so far off. Instead, a pot bubbled over while the cook's daughter, Juliana, stood with a wooden spoon hovering above the floor, pudding dripping at her feet. A man stood at the table, dumb, with hands buried in a mound of dough up past his knuckles. Even the cook seemed to have set down his carving knife to listen. It was a room of statues, every person speechless, every eye focused as one on the curtain wall separating the kitchen from the great hall and the tirade of words spewing forth from the other side.

Standing closest to the partition was his sister. Drawing near, he could see her profile. Lips parted, eyes round with disbelief, she stood there with tears sliding down her cheeks. So too, Lady Margarite appeared much pained. Hands clasped at her chest and head bowed in prayer, she was the very picture of a saint.

Hesitant to speak, Britton touched Velena's arm just as another barrage of words hailed from their father.

"What's happening?" he whispered. "Velena?"

"Stuart thinks he's a king."

Britton turned to the voice behind him. It was Rowan. "What do you mean?" he asked, thinking his face was as unreadable as he'd ever seen it.

"Shh!" Lady Margarite slapped the air at them both.

Finding the situation nonsensical, Britton left them all to their vigil. He refused to be caught eavesdropping like a common house servant and stepped around the boundary and into the great hall.

17

from his own mouth

Sir Richard had been stroking his fingers through the gray streaks of his caramel colored beard when he first walked into the room. His posture had been casual—his demeanor, eerily calm.

"So," Lord Magnus said, looking bored, "what news was so important you had to be pulled away from us so abruptly?"

Sir Richard flicked his hand at the manor folk still working to make the room ready, and they left without question. Jaren, too, was dismissed before Sir Richard laid Tristan's open letter atop the table where Stuart was seated. "Do you know what this is?" he asked.

Stuart tried not to look at his father. "Tristan's letter?"

Magnus swirled around the last bit of ale in his tankard and frowned. "I certainly hope that rascal isn't thinking to come back any time soon."

"It's an accusation," Sir Richard stated simply, ignoring remark. He looked from one man to the next, taking note of the muscles twitching in Stuart's jaw. "Were you aware of it?" The question hung in the air like foul smelling meat. "Stuart?"

Magnus shrugged his shoulders. "For crying out loud, Richard. How can he respond? We won't know what it says until you tell us."

Sir Richard looked directly into Magnus' face while Stuart refused to look at anything above his uncle's beard. "Tristan accuses your son of rape. That's what it says. A heinous crime to be sure."

Stuart did his best to look bewildered, releasing his breath in a great huff. "Preposterous. Obviously, he's lying."

"Is he?"

"Of course," Stuart sputtered, "and it's not hard to know why—though I never thought he'd stoop this low."

"Quite right," Magnus added. "Surely, you don't take this seriously." He gestured to the letter as though it were a pesky fly. "He's been against their marriage from the beginning."

"That's very true," Sir Richard conceded, "and it does cause one to be a bit skeptical—at least it did me." He stuck out his lower lip, taking in every nuance of expression and movement. "Still, knowing Tristan as I do…it's hard to believe he'd fabricate such a lie—even for his own gain."

"Then where is the proof of it?" Magnus asked, holding out his arms. "Surely, the word of a jealous man isn't enough to condemn my son."

"He's not the only one," Sir Richard warned.

Magnus scoffed. "You speak of the woman?"

"I would be remiss not to hear her side."

"The word of a woman…" He laughed. "I expect you to be thorough, of course, but who's to say she's not lying?" He drummed his fingers on the side of his chair. "No doubt, they've been plotting this together. Tristan wishes to deny Stuart his due, and she sees an opportunity for profit. I'll bet you a bucket of coin, he's promised to pay her for her troubles. Ladies' maids are notoriously greedy, Richard. Happens all the time."

Stuart's head snapped up.

Sir Richard's jaw flexed. Feigning ignorance, he reached back down for the letter. "Wait. Did I…did I say who it was?"

Stuart could have hanged his father—could have ran him through. His palms grew sweaty—his pulse quickened. Fire and ice, he could hear the blood thrumming in his ears. "I believe you did, Uncle Richard," he said, using every bit of resolve to look him straight in the eye.

Sir Richard looked back with nothing short of sorrow. "You know I didn't."

Too late, Magnus realized his mistake and stood, flailing his arms in emphasis of his point. "This is ridiculous! Of course, you did."

"I didn't," he repeated.

As if his uncle held him by a nose ring, Stuart wanted to retreat, but couldn't.

"Two old men such as us," Magnus continued, "it's impossible to remember what we say half the time. Why quibble over words? What's important here is this woman has lied, and she ought to be punished for bringing such false accusations."

Sir Richard took a moment to refold the letter before sliding it within his jerkin. "She's made no accusation of any kind. Remember, this is Tristan's letter—not hers."

"Then really, Richard." Magnus swore. "What needless stress to lay on the boy before his wedding—slander through and through."

"Except that I believe it."

Stuart stood to his feet. "You can't be serious."

"Richard," Lord Magnus argued again, "this isn't like you at all. To…to…to make judgments before all parties have been heard. Why haven't you spoken to the girl—and where's Tristan? Not here, and that's a fact. He's a coward. Only a coward would leave behind such accusations instead of speaking them himself."

Sir Richard approached Stuart, slowly, until they stood face to face and toe to toe. "Do I need to hear Daisy before hearing the truth from you?"

Stuart's jaw clenched.

"Do I need to send for Tristan to speak on her behalf?"

Still no answer.

"After Velena reads this, will it matter to her if I do either of those things?" Sir Richard paused a moment and then turned to leave. "I don't think it will."

"I didn't mean to," he suddenly blurted.

"Say no more," Magnus barked.

Stuart glared at his father. "You've already said too much. Uncle, please don't tell Velena."

Sir Richard straightened to his full height. He was shorter than Stuart but twice as imposing. "What defense do you give for your actions?"

"I had too much to drink that night. She was with someone else, but he left her alone. What I did…it…it haunts me daily. I'd wish it away if I could, but I cannot. I've not laid a finger on her since—nor shall I. All I can do is beg your forgiveness."

Sir Richard shook his head. "You're not the man I thought you were."

"Even the best of men are besotted by sins, Uncle."

Sir Richard raised his eyebrows. "And do you want to be like *these* men? Besotted? Because, Stuart, in case you haven't yet formed this opinion well enough in your mind, *these* kind of men are not *good* men! They are not *honorable* men! They are not the sort of men that a man of *Christian character* would want to emulate! Unfortunately for you," he glared at Lord Magnus as well as Stuart, "they are now the sort of men with whom you can identify."

"Now, just one minute—" Magnus sputtered.

"And unfortunately for *me*," he continued, "I almost had such a man as a son-in-law—which I can't even fathom because, right now, just having you for a nephew is disappointment enough." Turning on his heel, he left them speechless as he moved to the fireplace. "That I might have handed my daughter over to such a man—it makes me ill!"

Stuart was panicked. "They say even the King, himself, raped the Countess of Salisbury. If you can serve him, can you not forgive me?"

Sir Richard's lips rolled in before making a faint popping sound. "Are you comparing yourself to the King?"

"No, I just meant that—"

"Ah, Stuart, I can see now that the error is mine. It's perfectly understandable," he said, his voice dripping with sarcasm as he paced to and fro before his squirming nephew. "When the king wears a beard, we all wear beards. When the king shaves it off, do we not all do likewise? If it is talked about that the king has raised his tunic by two finger measurements, so too are we tempted to follow suit. We all *so* want to be like the king, do we not?"

"Uncle…"

He held up his hand for silence. "So. You come by this bit of gossip that the king has ravished the Count's good wife. You judge it to be true, and upon reflection, decide that the best course of action for you to take is none other than to be about the king's business, yourself. Is that it?" His voice grew louder until he was shouting. "Ought I to apologize to *you* for questioning your good and reasonable service to *king* and *country* by ravaging my daughter's maid?"

"Of course not!" Stuart raised his voice. "I meant only that all manner of men have fallen into temptation. Uncle, you have to understand that I…" His voice faltered as Britton appeared from behind the partition.

"Say no more," Magnus warned.

Sir Richard gave his son an almost imperceptible nod of admittance, then continued as if no interruption had occurred. "There's nothing he *could* say to assuage me, Magnus. What he did is unpardonable."

Stuart joined him at the hearth. "I wasn't in control of my senses."

"You were weak!"

"I was stuck in the shadows while she allowed herself to be pawed at by some upstart who didn't know his right from his left! It wasn't my intention to seek her out."

"Excuses!"

"Yes! It *is* an excuse," he said raising his voice again, "and a valid one. She'd been willing, and I was drunk! Under any other circumstances, I never would have touched her. Never had it occurred to me to do so. You have to believe me."

"What I believe is that your inability to control your own fleshly lusts has put my daughter at risk of not making it to her marriage bed unmolested. I believe that you are not the man your brother was—"

Stuart seethed. "What has Peter got to do with this?"

"Not the man your brother was," Sir Richard continued, "and I believe that I made a very poor and hasty judgment in letting you take his place."

Stuart stood, stunned. Old embers of jealousy he thought had gone cold now burst once more into flames. Was his brother to thwart him even in death? His voice came slow and deliberate. "Peter cared *nothing* for Velena. I can assure you of that."

"Hold your tongue, Boy," Magnus ordered.

"I *do*," Stuart stated emphatically, ignoring him.

Sir Richard raised his eyebrows. "Do you?"

"I do. You know I do. I love her, Uncle. I've loved only her my whole life."

Sir Richard exhaled through his nose. "You have no idea what that word means. As surely as I stand here, whenever I wanted my wife to know that I loved her, I never once had to rape her maid to do it."

"What I did was deplorable. I don't deny it. But I *do* love Velena," he protested.

"No, *I* love Velena!" Sir Richard bellowed without warning. "And it was *my* job to protect her! It was *my* job to see that she married a good man! And I chose poorly."

Stuart felt the gravity of the moment weighing down on him. His father was wrong. Dissolving the marriage without the legal proof to do so was exactly what Sir Richard was going to do. His throat tightened. His chin began to quiver, and he fought to maintain control. "None of us are good, Uncle. I can only beg of God his mercy. I beg it of you now…"

"There's no need to beg," Magnus reprimanded, "We have a contract."

Stuart paid no heed. "Though it may mean little to you, I *did* go to Daisy. I admitted wrong and compensated her for my actions. I cannot undo what I've done, but I pledge this day, on my soul, to be a better man and do whatever penance you require of me." He knelt at his uncle's feet.

"Get up!" Magnus commanded. "Where's your self-respect?"

"This is your fault," Stuart ground through clenched teeth.

"Brought on by your actions," he reminded him. "But fear not, it'll be I who'll save you from them." He turned to Sir Richard. "This entire conversation is rubbish. What you've gotten him to admit here will never be repeated, so don't even try to bring him to trial. And there will be no breaking our contract. Let's be clear on that! Don't forget we've got money tied up together. This sheep venture is worthless to you without my buyers—buyers loyal to me. I'll give you a day to think on it, Richard. One day!" Lord Magnus brushed past him then, running into his shoulder without apology. "Stuart—we're leaving," he called over his shoulder and sent Jaren, who'd been waiting outside in the corridor, to ready the horses.

Stuart looked only to his uncle, a tremor in his voice. "I'll not leave until you tell me how I can make amends. Command me anything, and I'll do it."

"Stand trial and admit to your crime."

Stuart stood to his feet. "Will you…abide by the contract if I do?"

"If she's willing."

Stuart looked down. Though Velena promised she could forgive him anything…he knew better. What reason would he have to accept punishment if he was to lose her in the bargain?

Sir Richard wasn't surprised by his silence. "I suppose *anything* has its limits."

His head came back up. "I'm not afraid of punishment. A year for my crime is nothing if I thought she'd still have me. But if you won't make her…"

"Go home, Nephew. Repent of your actions and be a better man than your father. Velena isn't the only woman worth having."

But she's the only woman I want. An overwhelming feeling of loss settled over him, so much that it nearly toppled him over.

"Go home…" Sir Richard repeated.

There was naught else he could say. With weighted steps, Stuart took his leave. At the door he stopped. "I can't accept this," he said, turning his head back to face him. "I'll prove myself worthy of her. You'll see." Then, he was gone.

Sir Richard's shoulders sagged. Drained, he locked eyes with his son. "Bring your sister out."

Velena emerged with Lady Margarite, Rowan following behind. Her voice was soft and full of anguish. "Had I heard it from anyone other than his own mouth...I could not have believed it." Her dam broke, "I can't even..."

Sir Richard crossed the room, pulling her into his arms where she wept.

"How did you come by this?" she asked.

Sir Richard led her across the room to a chair beside her brother at the dais. "This."

Accepting the letter handed to her, Velena's vision blurred as she began reading. "Tristan," she mouthed, silently. She wiped her eyes but could not stem the tears from falling.

"I'm sorry, Nenna," Rowan said, coming behind her to lay a hand to her shoulder.

"This is why you attacked Stuart the way you did. Isn't it? You already knew."

"We both did," her father confessed.

"What?" Her eyes were filled with confusion and disbelief. She had a hundred questions, but kept silent, trying to swallow, in detail, all that her father and Rowan began revealing about what they'd known—or hadn't known—and their reasons for keeping it from her. She wanted to accept their motives for doing so, but it was hard to forgive a secret of this proportion—a secret so ugly it never should have remained hidden in the first place.

Guilt consumed her for the things she thought Daisy had done. But that Stuart had been capable of rape had never crossed her mind—not even once. Even now, she had to stop herself from irrationally justifying his actions by allowing him his excuse of drunkenness.

Sir Richard took his daughter by the hands from across the table. "We can go around in circles all day wondering the whys and wherefores, but at the end of the day, it is what it is."

"Surely there are actions we can take," Britton said.

Velena inhaled of the present, realizing her future was about to shift right out from beneath her feet.

"First things first," Sir Richard said, addressing his daughter. "If Stuart agrees to plead guilty at a trial, will you still have him?"

Britton was aghast. "Surely, you wouldn't let her—"

He held up his hand. "I just need to know her answer."

"My answer is *no*," she said without hesitation. "I can't...I couldn't possibly marry him now."

Sir Richard nodded. "Nor would I have you do so."

"Poor Daisy," Lady Margarite said, reminding them of her presence. "She's had so much to bear."

Rowan looked to Sir Richard. "When will she have to give testimony?"

"I don't think she'll have to," he said. "If Stuart doesn't change his mind and make a formal confession, there will be no trial."

"I don't understand. Did we not just witness his confession? There must be a trial."

"It's too risky. Like it or not, Stuart's a man of good standing in Totnes. And those who disagree are too wary of Magnus to say so. It wouldn't be a fair trial. And as Daisy's status is of almost no account, it would be nothing to accuse her of making a false allegation. Found guilty, she'd be facing imprisonment."

Rowan turned away, then back again, his every movement conflicted. "But she's with child," he reasoned, "surely, that's proof of something."

Velena's chair scraped the floor as she sprung to her feet. "What else do you know that I do not?"

Sir Richard gave her an understanding look. "A child could be proof of a lot of things, including a tryst," he answered Rowan, who crossed his arms in displeasure. "I say again, it's not likely a court would side with Daisy. Conception comes with enjoyment. At least, such is the common belief."

Lady Margarite huffed. "Surely, no *woman* would agree."

"Nor any *married* man, if he were honest," Sir Richard said ruefully. "But Magnus would take this before the priory."

"And there are none there who'd know any better," Lady Margarite quipped.

Sir Richard nodded sadly. "It would be proof of a consensual act."

Rowan's shoulders slumped. "All for nothing. Daisy was right to have kept quiet after all."

"Do I not need to know what goes on in my own household?" Sir Richard countered. There was a definite edge to his voice.

"What good is the knowing, if still he goes free?"

Velena stepped around the table and away from the dais, certain if she remained still a moment longer, she'd crawl out of her skin, her mind in such a thick fog, she could have sliced it through with a knife.

How long had she fought to keep hold of the Stuart she'd known from her childhood? Her hands moved to support the back of her neck as she looked up, but there was no answer in the rafters. No answer to why Stuart had betrayed her trust in every way. There could be no more doubt that he was as Tristan had always said. An evil man. An evil man with evil intentions. But still, she did not hate him, and this felt like a betrayal to Rowan and Britton—and Daisy. For this, she hated herself.

Sir Richard watched her. "On the oft-chance Daisy were to be believed, Stuart would spend no more than a year in prison and possibly less. If he were especially fortunate, he'd be fined and forced to pay her the amount of a dowry."

"Marry her?" Rowan nearly choked on the words.

"No," he corrected, "he'd be supplying her a dowry should she be married someday. But as to that," he directed his attention back to Velena, "consider it taken care of. I'll pay whatever dowry she needs should the time come."

"Thank you." Velena's voice fell to a whisper, "But who will marry her now? And…what of the baby?"

Rowan cleared his throat, wishing he could say with certainty that he would—but alas, he was no more certain of his answer now, than he was in the presence of Daisy. "Tristan promised her a place in his household should she ever need it," was his answer.

Velena wanted to slap him for knowing the *why* behind yet another thing she did not. Turning away, she fought for control.

Her reaction didn't go unnoticed, and Sir Richard seemed in no hurry to entertain any more conversation. His eyes shifted from one person to another. "A discussion for another day," he finally said.

"May I go?" Velena asked. "I would wait no longer to see her."

Sir Richard nodded. "Squire Rowan will escort you."

"Father, I don't think I need—"

"Squire Rowan will escort you, and then he will search the grounds to make sure your uncle and cousin have indeed left the manor."

Nodding, reluctantly, Velena made her way from the room, Rowan by her side.

Once gone, there was a collective sigh of all who remained. Sir Richard pulled out a chair from the table and sank into it. He turned to Britton and Lady Margarite, asking, "Have either of you anything else to say?"

"I wouldn't have thought him capable of such a thing," Lady Margarite confessed.

Britton only picked at the green linen tablecloth blanketing the dais.

"I blame myself," Sir Richard confessed.

"Father, no—"

"Yes. I shan't excuse myself of sin simply because it existed in the form of a poor decision. I was warned but would not take heed. I wanted to give Stuart the benefit of the doubt—the chance to prove himself as something better than his father—"

"It's over now," Britton said, uncomfortable with the self-deprecation he was seeing in the man he'd only ever known to be confident in all his doings.

"Not yet," he said, knowing he hadn't even begun to feel the ramifications of crossing his brother-in-law. "In the meantime, I dare not wait for the King to come to Totnes but must go to him before Magnus catches wind of it."

"To have the contract annulled," Britton explained to Auntie, but she seemed to already know.

"And to persuade him towards an agreeable alternative to Stuart. I tell you the truth, Margarite, if I can—"

"Excuse me, my lord," a young voice said, peeking in through the door. "This just came for you."

Receiving the note, he dismissed the lad.

Lady Margarite patted Britton's arm with a reassuring hand and waited for Sir Richard to read.

The beginnings of a smile pushed up the corners of his mustache as he chuckled at the timing of it all. "Tristan is back."

Britton's eyebrows went up as his father continued.

"His brother lives but plans to take orders at a friary. He leaves the full inheritance to Tristan, and..." he laid down the letter in disbelief, and not without a little humor. "He asks that I break Velena's contract and accept his proposal instead."

Britton sat forward in his chair. "As in marriage proposal?"

Sir Richard smiled. "God bless him; I should have expected nothing less."

Britton smirked. "So much for the *without the marriage part...*"

"What?"

"Nothing. It just seems we've underestimated his feelings for her."

"On the contrary, it's that the man's loyalty to her knows no bounds." He left the dais to stick his head into the corridor, giving orders to have Tristan brought to the manor.

"You'll accept him then?" Lady Margarite asked, attempting to mask her disappointment.

"I suppose with that much money and land, the king could hardly be disagreeable to it," Britton said, feeling a disappointment of his own.

"I can't afford to dismiss the possibility of a union between them, Margarite, but he'd not be my first choice."

Perplexed, Britton looked from one to the other, wondering at the familiarity of their conversation. "Why is that?" he asked.

"They fight like siblings," he said, bringing his attention back to his son. "They're equals in each other's eyes, and she has a will that won't easily bend to his—nor could I see him forcing it to, no matter how she might vex him. It would take great effort on her part to submit to him as her lord."

"Have you someone else in mind?"

Sir Richard nodded, feeling rather than seeing, the look of hopefulness exuding from Lady Margarite. The hint of a smile broke through his whiskers. "I do. And tomorrow I'll take my request to Devonshire. It'll take a great deal of *finesse* to get the contract nullified without there being any financial repercussions—and perhaps more than I can manage. I didn't want to worry your sister but breaking the contract will pose me a greater problem than I let on. I was overly confident when I signed it. At best, I stand to lose the entirety of her dowry."

"At worst?" Britton questioned.

"Your uncle wasn't bluffing when he said he could turn the buyers away from me. He has the influence, but his power will lie in his ability to claim that I've wronged him. My purpose, then, is to convince Edward that a husband of his own choosing would far outweigh her current situation with Stuart. He'll have to think it's his own idea. Next—and more importantly—I'll have to convince him that *my* choice…is *his* choice. This done, a new contract will be written with the king's seal, making the one I have with Magnus forfeit. He'll not be able to refute it."

"What if he rejects your choice of husband? Or worse, believes Stuart to be the best choice and orders the contract to stand?"

"It had occurred to me, but this changes all that." He held up Tristan's second letter. "He'll not choose Stuart over Tristan's money. I don't wish to take advantage of his offer this way, but—"

"I wish it were possible for you to consider Makaias," Britton threw out. "I know he has no land or title or money…but you favored him once."

"I still do," he stated, a smile playing at the corners of his mouth. Now, if you'll excuse me, Son, I have a thing or two I need to discuss with this good woman."

Her smile lit the room.

18

a time to mourn

Velena hastened up the stairs ahead of Rowan, but as her hand fell upon the door handle of her solar, her composure wavered.

Rowan squeezed her shoulder. "It's alright."

Velena rested her forehead against the door, "It's not alright. Why did he confide in you and not me?"

"He asked me to look after you."

"That doesn't answer my question."

"His concern was entirely for you."

Velena ignored Rowan's attempt to cast what he'd done in a good light. "Why didn't *you* tell me?"

His shoulders sagged. "I wanted you to hear it from him."

"Well, *he's* not here, is he?" She looked away. "He ought not to have kept it from me."

"He thought it best."

Velena rolled her eyes upward, sending a pool of tears trailing down her cheeks. "It wasn't." She placed her thumb upon the latch.

"Wait, Nenna—here." Rowan pulled a handkerchief out from his sleeve and let her dry her tears, only they wouldn't stop. "Come on," he finally said, leading her by the shoulders across the hall to the very room where she'd spent the last three days in prayer.

"I want to see her," she protested.

"There's time for that," he said, careful to leave the door ajar. "Have your cry first. It'll do you well."

"I don't want to cry, Rowan, I want to scream." She placed a hand to her throat as it constricted. Turning away, she walked the length of the room to an open window looking out over the front of the manor. He followed.

Fighting for control she licked her lips, rolled them inward—the salt from her tears on the tip of her tongue. She used Rowan's handkerchief to wipe the moisture from beneath her nose and took a ragged breath. "How could Stuart do this? How could he do something so...ugly?"

He opened his mouth, but she didn't wait for an answer.

"To take her by force—my own maid. To be so brazen as to take the woman closest to..." her voice broke off, and she cried in earnest, chest caving with each sob as she gasped for air between words. "All those lies...telling me Daisy was no longer herself...and ought to be sent away. He must have thought me...such a fool for...believing him."

Rowan frowned. "Did you really, though?"

She shook her head. "No. But I had nothing else to believe. Daisy's word was no better, and Jaren... Looking back—he knew. Did you know he knew?"

"I suspected."

"Oh Rowan, I'm so ashamed. I would have sooner accused Daisy of poor moral character than I would have ever considered the possibility that Stuart could have done this to her."

"None of us would have wanted to believe it. Not even me."

She slammed her palm down on the sill. "I should have known!"

"You couldn't have. It's not your fault, Velena. If you're going to blame someone, blame Stuart. Hate *him*."

Velena took one deep breath—then another. "How long have I prayed against that very thing? All these past days, I've had to lay my resentments down before the Lord in hopes of never taking them up again. How much heavier would my burden be if I hated him?" She shook her head. "I can't."

"How can you not?"

Velena understood the disgust in his voice; she felt the same but turned to face him. "He must be dead to me now—I know that." Tears continued to gather in her eyes, forming glassy pools in which he could see his reflection. "But it's not for us to hate the dead, but to mourn them. His soul is lost, Rowan. His sins—"

"Are unpardonable."

Velena nodded. "It feels that way."

"It is that way."

"I pray not," she said, grasping hold of his arm. "It would be awful to die...in our sins. To be in torment for always."

"He deserves it."

"We all deserve it. Lest we be saved, our end is the same."

Rowan gave her a crooked smile. "Tristan turned you into a theologian, I see."

She looked away.

"So, you can forgive Stuart for his sins—but not Tristan for keeping them from you? Nor me?"

Velena frowned, struggling with the complexity of her emotions. "Time. I need time for both—and all of it. While I may clearly see my spiritual obligations, my execution of them remains painfully slow."

"So, you're *not* perfect then?"

Velena gave a half-hearted smile. "As if you've ever thought so."

"You don't know the half of what I think."

"A blessed truth."

Rowan turned her back to face him, sliding his thumb over the last of her tears. "Find your smile, Nenna. Daisy's in sore need of one. Are you ready to go to her now?"

"How do you know so much about her? Why did she tell you and not me?"

Rowan pulled her into a tight embrace, her cheek tacky against his jerkin. It'd be a wonder if she ever trusted anyone enough to confide in them again. "I forced the letter from her," he confessed, squeezing her tighter as though he were the one in need of comforting. "She gave it to me, but only because she was at her end. I made promises to her and then took them back. I've done her yet another wrong. She needs you, Velena. Pray forgive her, her deceit."

Pulling away, he forced a weak smile. "When you see her, would you be so good as to let her know I came back? She asked me if I'd stay with her when your father came, but it wasn't my place to make such promises. And I think you'll be better suited for the job."

"She's come to like you a great deal," she said, realizing the full extent of it.

Rowan proffered his arm and led her out. "I hope so."

19

an end to secrets

Prior to Rowan coming to find her, Daisy thought that admitting the truth to Velena would be the hardest thing she'd ever have to do. But now, as her mistress gathered her close, weeping over her as a sister—letting her cry until she was spent—she wished she'd had the courage to do it sooner.

For certain, her own mother would never have been so kind. She would have judged her for her theft of the letter, condemned her for her behavior with Bowan, and exhibited no small amount of shock over her expectant condition. God certainly blessed her the day she came to live at Landerhill.

When Velena finally held her at arm's length, Daisy saw only sympathy and affection.

"Would that you had come to me when it happened," Velena chided, wiping Rowan's handkerchief across Daisy's cheeks, pushing her hair away from her face.

"I should have, but I was too ashamed."

Velena squeezed her hands, then left her on the bed to fetch her a cup of mead from the sitting room.

"What happens now?" Daisy asked, taking the drink into her hands.

"Nothing, and so many things. What shall I tell you first?"

"Will I have to give testimony?"

Velena held her gaze, feeling both disquieted and relieved that Daisy should be spared such a trial. "No. Because it would be your word against his. He could just as easily accuse you of bringing false testimony. It would be worse for you in the end."

"I thought as much. What of you? Are you...would you be free of him?"

"Of course!" Velena snatched up her hand and kissed it. "I could never marry someone who..." she shook her head as if to push it all behind them now. "I just couldn't."

She grew anxious. "Does Stuart know it was me who had the letter?"

"I don't think so," Velena was quick to assure her.

Her eyes closed. "Thank Heaven."

"Everything is going to be alright now."

She looked doubtful. "Perhaps, but I can't imagine him being very keen about losing you. How angry was he?"

Velena's forehead wrinkled as she recalled all she'd overheard. "Not angry. Distraught. Repentant. I couldn't insist upon his sincerity, but for your sake, I hope he was." She crossed her arms about her waist. "He still wants to prove himself worthy of me. But time will show his hopes to be futile."

"You've got to get away from here."

Velena gave her a reassuring smile. "Rowan keeps watch over me—over us both."

Daisy's eyes moved to the door. She had the urge to ask where he was now but knew it would lead to too many questions. Had she really been in his arms only a short while ago? It seemed a world away, and yet...she felt bonded to him now. She had no idea if she'd marry him—or even if he'd ask her again—or if she wanted him to. Suddenly, she was never so happy for things like wooden doors or stones and mortar. They seemed the only things standing between her and a world of uncertainty.

"Daisy?"

Embarrassed, she regained her focus.

"Is there something between you and Rowan?"

She hesitated, "He's shown me greater friendship than I expected of him." It wasn't a lie, but it wasn't all the truth either. And the look of hurt that crossed Velena's face was only too obvious, and it cut her to see it. "You don't believe me." It wasn't a question.

Velena's mouth stretched into a thin line, and she shook her head.

Tears filled Daisy's eyes as she realized how much trust had been lost between them. "I'm so sorry, Velena—so very sorry," she said, dispensing with titles. "I've lied to you, and I shouldn't wonder that it's come between us. If I hadn't been so afraid..." She ran her sleeve beneath her nose. "It was wrong, and it near tore out my insides to do it. Can you ever forgive me?"

"I can. Of course, I can," Velena said, as Daisy leaned into her, searching again for the solace and affirmation of her mistress. When they finally parted, Daisy had a look of peace that had long been missing.

"That Rowan has shown me friendship is the truth," she confessed, "but there is more to tell. Only, let me start from the beginning," she said, coming to her feet, leaving Velena to puzzle over her enigmatic answer. "From now on, I'll tell you everything. We will be not as before—but better. I swear it."

Over the next hour, Daisy opened the door to her darkest places, allowing Velena entrance into the world she kept secret since the day of her undoing. It was painful, but necessary, as though the telling of it allowed her access to the salve she'd been without. With every word, the essence that was Daisy, seemed to slip back into her being. Little by little, she came back to herself—her mannerisms, her temper, her incredulous expressions. She even managed to knock over her cup of mead in a dramatic retelling of the earlier events with Rowan, more than once leaving Velena wide-eyed and agape with surprise.

"You kicked him where?" Velena asked, cringing as she told her. "Poor Rowan. And that was…after he asked you to marry him?"

"Yes. But it was also after he changed his mind."

"Did he actually rescind his proposal…or is he still thinking on it?"

"Does it matter? It's Stuart's child. He'll not take that on."

"And if you're wrong?"

She appeared lost. "I don't know. I've scorned him longer than I've liked him—and I'm still getting used to that—never mind love. Besides, I still think of Bowan sometimes and wonder…" She shook her head. "But I know that's silly. If Rowan finds it so distasteful, surely Bowan will feel the same." She let a long breath escape her. "He wanted a woman with her virtue intact. Wouldn't even take it, himself, not without us being properly wed."

"Surely, he'd understand."

"What if he asked me to do away with the child?"

"Never."

"I can't expect him to think differently than I've thought, myself."

"I hope you don't mean that," Velena whispered.

She turned away in regret. "There's something I need to be rid of."

Velena watched as she went down on her knees to reach beneath her trundle mattress. Once retrieved, she handed the small bundle up to her mistress but didn't wait for Velena to unfold the cloth wrapping before offering her an explanation. "It's the herbs I got from the healer to make the tea...the day Tristan left. She said it would bring on labor—end my worries."

"That horrible woman! Did you...use these already?" Velena asked, concern stretching across her brow.

"I couldn't," she confessed.

"God be praised!"

"But how shall I live with a babe?" she asked, forlorn as ever.

"We'll manage together," Velena said, smiling. "Come what may, you always have a home with me—the babe too." Then, pulling Daisy to her feet, she led her across the room to the bed chamber's narrow window. She pushed it open, crumpled the dried herbs within her fist, and set Daisy's hand over top. "Together."

Daisy reached with her through the opening and felt the pull of the wind curling around their hands. Loosing their fingers, all traces of the would-be death scattered into the wind. Settling closer to Velena, she laid her head to her shoulder.

Velena put an arm about her waist and began murmuring the lines of a childhood poem. "Away, away, gone forevermore..."

The words felt hopeful, and Daisy responded, "Away, away, take me furthermore."

The day was not even half over, yet it seemed fully spent. The women did not come down for the noon meal—nor for the evening toll. Their food was brought up, and they were soon visited by Sir Richard who repeated to Daisy much the same as was discussed in the great hall before Velena left.

No more was said about Velena's broken engagement, nor anything having to do with it. The subject of Velena's unfinished wedding gown, the upcoming tourney, and her future without Stuart was put on a shelf. They were allowed their time, and come morning, the world seemed an entirely different place.

Rolling over in bed as the first rays of light slipped across her face, still groggy, Velena roused to a hand gently pushing back the hair at her forehead. Opening her eyes, she saw her father bent over the head of her bed.

He smiled as he laid a kiss to her temple. "I'm leaving now."

"Already?" Velena whispered, coming up on her elbows, trying not to wake Daisy.

"The sooner the better," he whispered back. "Edward's on his way to Totness, no doubt. I'll have to find him in route, but I want to speak with him before your uncle gets wind of it. Pray for my success."

Success. There was that word again. Velena nodded her understanding and wished her father Godspeed, then watched him walk quietly from the room. Her eyes felt dry, and her head ached with a dull sort of pain that comes from a night of crying. Fighting her desire to close them again, she peered over the side of her bed to the trundle below. Daisy turned her head to face her. She hadn't been asleep, and when their eyes locked, they exchanged the same sad hint of a smile. Sleep had marked an end to the persons they were before, just as this day would work to define them.

Velena reached down for her hand. "I'm going to get up and pray. Will you join me?"

"In the prayer closet?"

"I have somewhere else I've been going."

Daisy nodded. "I'll get you ready." But only ten minutes into lacing up Velena's tunic, Daisy had to run to the chamber pot. No longer in need of hiding her condition, she dry heaved up her discomfort.

Velena held aside Daisy's plait and rubbed a soothing hand across her back until she finished. "I don't think you're in any condition to go."

Daisy shook her head. "It'll pass. I can manage."

"You don't need to manage. Help me with my buttons, then stay and rest." She held out her wrists, cuffs dangling open. "I'll have some broth brought up to you."

"Your hair is a sight," Daisy said, half-way finished with the right cuff.

"I'll take the brush with me."

Daisy went to fetch it. "You needn't make allowances because of the babe. I'm still here to serve you, my lady."

Velena took a moment to really look at her. "I know. And I thank you for it. But you're going to be a mother, Daisy—and this makes you as much above my station as you were once below it. We serve each other now—as equals."

Daisy's eyes welled up with tears. "You give me so much more than I deserve."

"Is that not what the Lord does for us?"

Her smile was doubtful, but she didn't voice it. "Are you sure you don't want me to do your hair?"

Hand on the door, Velena gave her an impish grin. "I don't think the Almighty will mind the mess." She turned to leave but was less than two steps into the hallway before Daisy hailed her back again.

"Velena."

"Yes?"

"Pray for *me*. I don't have your faith."

Velena gave her a knowing look. "I have…and I will. Now, go back to bed," she whispered. The women embraced before parting ways.

Thinking about what Daisy said, Velena crossed the hall to Tristan's door. Laying her hands flat against it, she was convicted by the words of St. Matthew. *Therefore if you are presenting your offering at the altar, and there remember that your brother has something against you, leave your offering there before the alter and go; first be reconciled to your brother, and come and present your offering.*

In this case, it was she who had something against her brother—only he wasn't here for her to reconcile with. Going to his room was the closest she would get, and she knew once she went through that door, she would have to forgive him. She understood why Daisy had kept her secret from her, but with Tristan… It felt a worse betrayal, but still, she missed him.

Entering the room, she caught her breath. The chair was out of position from its place by the desk, a large traveling bag lay open on the floor, and the blankets on the bed mat were strewn aside as if someone had been sleeping there. Backing out, she closed the door. Who was staying here?

20

an unwelcome arrangement

Early morning mist hung feet high in the air. The sun hadn't yet fully risen when the outline of four people could be seen trekking up a set of built-in wooden steps along the hillside leading up to Totnes Castle. No longer the chief residence of its owners, most of its timber buildings were either unusable or in need of extensive repairs. Left in their constable's care, it was open for the public's perusal and remained good only as a place for holding manorial court or as the best spot to view all of Totnes.

"I'm not interested," Makaias was saying, reaching back to help his mother up the next step, his brothers following behind.

"Not at all?" she asked, taking his hand.

"Well, not *never* but certainly not now."

"What that about *not now?*" Andret called ahead.

"She wishes to know if I want to marry," he explained, wondering if their little exertion up to the castle had more to do with cornering her sons about their lack of wives than with the family outing she claimed it to be.

"Well, surely you don't want to remain a virgin forever," Jaren said from his place at the end of the line.

Foot poised to take his next step, Andret turned around, grinning. "Who says he's still a virgin?"

Makaias chuckled, but seeing his mother's disapproval, quickly assured her that he was. "Pay him no mind, Mother. I'm quite chaste."

"I'm happy to hear it, but you needn't stay that way for long," she chided, reaching the top of the hill. "You're a fine man, you ought to be married."

"All in good time."

She would have said more, but Andret and Jaren came to stand beside her. In silence, she stood with her sons, looking out over Totnes as the first rays of light illuminated the sky from behind the cloud covering, bringing color to the gray of morning.

Andret was the first to break away. Turning his back to the view, he walked on past the uninhabited castle walls, Jaren quick to follow. Lady Margarite lingered, desirous of a moment alone with her eldest. As hoped, Makaias stayed by her side.

"Could it be Johanna's unfaithfulness that has you so set against the idea of marriage?"

Makaias gave her a sideways glance, unhappy she was still pushing the issue. "I'm sure it could."

"My heart breaks for you, my son. You cannot judge all women by the sins of one."

Makaias rubbed the backs of his fingers above his top lip where his stubble itched him the most. "If I remain single, I won't have to judge any at all."

She reached over to hook his arm. "Pray, don't let pain taint a happy future. Many a joyful moment can be had in marriage. Remember, 'He who finds a wife finds a good thing and obtains favor from the Lord.' "

He raised an eyebrow. "When I find her, I'll let you know."

"I'm serious, Makaias. It's time you began thinking about your future."

Warily, he looked down at his short mother, her stature being the only thing small about her if one took time to consider her heart, her courage, or her loyalty to her children. He shifted his feet, once and then again. He crossed his arms. "I'll not be rushed, Mother. If you want a herd of grandchildren, you'd do better to get after Andret and Jaren."

"I'm not concerned about grandchildren."

"Then why so sudden the concern for me?"

"From the day you were born until the day I die shall I ever be concerned."

"You know what I mean."

She nodded. "It was seeing you with Lady Velena—the way you looked at her."

"The way I looked at her?" He scoffed.

"When she examined your side."

"She was standing right there, where else could I look?"

"You're six and twenty, Makaias—too old for celibacy. I could see the way she pleased you."

"She's engaged!" His eyes first rounded then rolled back. "And even if she weren't, don't expect me to discuss with *you* what pleases me."

"I was referring to attraction, not availability," she explained, cringing at her own deception. Clearly, kitchen gossip had yet to reach his ears, but by his reaction, she wasn't sure it would matter.

"I'm sorry, but I can't separate the two. I don't allow myself to be attracted to those that aren't available—and quite frankly—I'm surprised that you'd entice me to such. I swear, Mother, you're as bad as Britton."

"Makaias, come look at this," Andret called from within.

Happy for the interruption, he emerged upon a spacious inner bailey, circular in nature, where he received the full view of the dilapidated buildings smattered throughout the area, the majority unfit for even the commonest of functions, save for one finely made stone structure, which served as residence to whomever remained on-site.

Accepting her loss of the moment, Lady Margarite listened to Andret comment on the buildings' present state of disrepair and what a pity it was that the castle was no longer what it used to be. As she looked around, he began pointing out to Makaias and Jaren what improvements would have to be made if ever the de la Zouche family were to bring it back into working order.

Makaias glanced back at his mother and could tell she was only half listening. It wasn't often she asked for such outings, nor often they all could come together at once. He was sorry for snapping at her but knew her concerns over this marriage business had not yet been laid to rest, and he wasn't looking forward to furthering the discussion.

"Let us go to the top," she suggested and led the way into the stairwell that would bring them up some fifteen odd feet to the rampart where the battlement stood facing outward and nothing but a drop into the inner bailey lay behind. Looking out across the town and countryside, the River Dart was clearly visible, swelled from all the rain and making for a truly spectacular view.

"Well, isn't this wonderful—all my boys together? But not boys anymore. Men—all of you." She was beaming, tears glistening in her eyes. "Your father was always so proud of you; God rest his soul. I hope you know that I'm just as proud and always have been. Seems like only yesterday I was holding you in my arms."

"Our turn now," Andret said, lifting her up off her feet from behind, arms wrapped low about her waist. She yelped as Makaias and

Jaren exchanged looks of amusement.

Back on her feet, she flushed with pleasure and had to tuck several silver strands of hair behind her wimple. "Oh, have mercy on your poor mother. When did you outgrow me so?"

Makaias laughed. "I don't believe a one of us has looked up to you since we were twelve."

"For Jaren it was eight," Andret teased.

He smiled. "Not that young. Maybe ten."

"For me, the years have been but a day," she said, "and a day ending all too fast for my liking. Would that you all could experience such happiness for yourselves, for pride in one's children cannot be described in words."

"Heeere it is," Makaias said, folding his arms across his chest.

"Here what is?" Jaren asked.

"Here's the reason she brought us out here. She has three sons and no daughters-in-law. She's already had her try at me; it's your turn, brothers. God, help you."

"Well, I don't know," Andret said, smiling in his quiet way, "It seems only right you're the first to fall in the line of duty. I mean...be married."

"You *are* the oldest," Jaren agreed.

Makaias held out his hands. "Whoa, now, just a minute. Don't tell me this was a joint effort. You're supposed to be on my side."

Lady Margarite threw her hands towards Heaven. "Lord Jesus, what've I done wrong? Am I to take it I've birthed three sons, and none of them willing to marry?"

Andret raised his eyebrows at Makaias. "Look what your stubbornness has done. She's taking the Lord's name in vain."

"I never have and never shall," she said, raising her chin. "What you hear is the good and honest outpouring of a mother's heart. You may not agree with me now," she said, "but I feel certain you'd enjoy the changes a marriage would bring, if only you'd allow yourselves to consider the benefits of such an arrangement."

Andret patted her arm. "We're teasing you, Mother. Makaias is the only one you truly need worry about."

"Traitor," he mumbled.

"If she has a woman she wants to parade in front of me, I won't say no." He winked at Jaren. "Neither would Jaren, I'd wager."

Jaren's face turned a slight shade of pink, but his smile never wavered.

"There now," Makaias said, throwing an arm across Jaren's shoulders. "You have two willing sons already. What do you need me for?"

Lady Margarite sighed at her eldest. "You used to be like them. Were you not excited when first we thought Sir Richard would choose you for his son-in-law instead of Peter?"

"Indeed, I was not."

"How can you say so?"

"There was eight years between us. When I was twenty-one, she was thirteen. It was hardly something to get excited over."

"The engagement was to have lasted two years before—"

"Fifteen is no better."

"It's a common age."

"I don't care what's common. I wasn't about to bed a child."

She opened her mouth, then clamped it shut again, a distraught pull to her lips. "You should have told us how you felt. If I'd known then, I never would have..." She paused, obviously vexed by this new revelation.

"Would have what?"

"Pushed. Hearing this now, I can't understand why you ever agreed to the match in the first place."

"There was no match," he reminded her.

"It was talked about."

Makaias looked to Andret but found only the same curious stare. Groaning, he gave her the explanation she wanted. "When Sir Richard arranged for me to squire with Britton under Sir James, he paid for my horse and armor when you could not. He was a second father to me and has since given me a roof over my head and a position of high esteem among his knights. I owed him much—and still do. I would've done anything for him."

Looking down at her hands, she spoke softly. "I pray you still feel that way."

Growing quiet, he stared. "Why?"

"Because the time has come for you to thank him—and for all the reasons you just pointed out."

"I hope this is you consulting with me before you actually go out and make some sort of arrangement on my behalf. Tell me that's so."

She turned away.

"Mother," Andret spoke firmly, "you could at least have the decency to answer him. Has there been an arrangement?"

"It's Sir Richard's intention to present you with a wife."

"Why would he do that?" Jaren asked.

Taking a full breath, she turned round to face them. "Because I asked him to."

Makaias was dumbfounded. "You did what?"

"We've spoken, and we're both agreed that…that certainly, it would…behoove you to…to begin planning for a…" Her chin came down. This wasn't going as well as she'd hoped.

"For a what?" he prodded.

"A future."

He shook his head, too agitated to hear her. "*Fix* this. Un-speak it. Un-agree to it. Unplan it! *Mother*—"

"I won't." Her eyes begged him to understand. "I've asked him to give what I cannot. Why would I undo that?"

Makaias turned away from her, clutching the parapets, cold and rough beneath his palms. "What have I to offer a wife? I've no money…no land."

"He goes to the king to request land *for* you. You and Britton both. He respects you as he respected your father. He values your service and your loyalty to his family. You brought his son home, Makaias. He would reward you for that."

"Land…me?"

"How better to show your loyalty then through gratitude?" She pulled his chin around to face her. "Allow him to do this for you."

Makaias looked like a floundering child. She longed to draw him into her arms but knew he would resist. "Not every woman is Joanna. I'm certain whoever the king chooses will be faithful and true."

His shoulders sagged. "We'd be strangers. Why should she be?"

"Consider that you may already be acquainted," she suggested. "Likely, he may choose a woman from Totnes. Would not this make it better?"

"This is all too convenient," Jaren interrupted, a bitter twist to his words.

"Explain," Makaias said, noting a new look of unrest in his mother.

"It's convenient that Sir Richard would go to the king to find wives for you and Britton, when he just happens to be in need of a new son-in-law, himself?" He shook his head and began wagging his finger, "No. This is a ruse—conveniently orchestrated to undermine his contract with Uncle Magnus."

Makaias looked at his mother. "A new son-in-law?" This could only mean that Velena had rejected Stuart. "What's happened between yesterday and today?"

"Stuart has become…unsuitable."

Makaias waited for her to explain.

"The situation is delicate," she tried again.

"But not unforgivable," Jaren insisted.

Impatient, Makaias' voice began to rise. "Someone speak plainly. I take time away for one bath and everything has suddenly turned on its head."

Jaren cleared his throat. "Stuart made a mistake."

"To say the least," Andret added, crossing his arms.

"But he seeks to atone for it. He swears he will show himself worthy. He still means to fight for her. Mother, Sir Richard is wrong to do this. Not even a day, and he looks for another to take Stuart's place? When does the king arrive?"

"Not for days yet," she answered, a truthful statement, yet not without its deception.

"Poor Stuart! He's in agony and now to learn his time's already run out."

"Oh, Jaren." Lady Margarite soothed. She'd overlooked her son's loyalty to his cousin and chastised herself for unwittingly revealing Sir Richard's plans in his presence. What folly. She could only hope Jaren's loyalty to her was greater. If she was wrong, he would be their undoing. "I know you share in his grief, but you must allow the consequences of it to play out. Sir Richard does no wrong in turning his eyes from Stuart to another. You must not reveal what I've said this day."

"How can I not?"

"Because I ask it of you," she said firmly. "Only time will reveal God's plans. We must step aside and allow Him to do his work."

Jaren scoffed. "Like you did, when you converged upon Sir Richard in his moment of weakness, tacking on your own advantage so as to gain your son a future?" Jaren was livid. "I would never begrudge Makaias his due—and, Brother, you're deserving of it all—but Sir Richard means not to petition the king as a charitable act on behalf of a poor widow who can do no better, but as a very deliberate means of breaking his word. His benevolence to you and Britton is but a smoke screen to mask his true intentions. And *waiting on God* is but a means to keeping the truth of it all quiet."

"You forget your place," Andret said, voice calm, but eyes hard and unyielding.

"Makaias can speak his mind, but I can't?"

"Spoken like a true youngest born. If you wish to tantrum, I'd be happy to hold you over our mother's knee. You could use a proper thrashing—and perhaps a lecture on what sort of people you ought not to associate with, Stuart being one of them."

"Try it," Jaren said, stepping forward.

"Enough," Makaias growled, grabbing Jaren by the back of his jerkin and forcing him down the stairs ahead of him. "Everyone down before someone falls over the side. Only thing I need less than a wife is a dead brother." Releasing his collar, he shoved him into the bailey where he immediately stalked out through the gate to stand at the top of the hill, arms crossed, legs apart. He was the picture of defiance.

"All will be well," Lady Margarite said, placing a timid hand to Makaias' arm. "Wait and see."

He glanced down but didn't trust himself to speak.

Turning away, Lady Margarite looked to her other son. "Let us go down. It'll be best if Makaias has some time alone. He has much to think on."

Jaren descended the hill before them, but angry as he was, he still reached back to steady his mother's decent. This small act did not go unnoticed, as she was so very aware of the grief that she'd just caused two of her three sons.

Andret moved to follow, but Makaias caught him by the arm. "What happened to make him unsuitable?"

Andret didn't need to ask who he meant, and he didn't mince words. "He raped Daisy. And now she's with child."

Dumbfounded a second time, his mouth hung open. "You're not serious?"

Andret nodded. "Britton knows more. Talk to him."

"I will."

"You know..." he began, hesitant to bring it up. "She didn't exactly say so, but it could be that Mother is hoping Sir Richard will think favorably of you again. For Lady Velena, I mean."

Makaias shook his head. "Sir Richard may not mind a lowly knight for a son-in-law, but the king will choose someone with a title."

"Yes, well, just in case, you might want to tone down your distaste for the lady. She's not fifteen anymore."

Makaias watched Andret as he turned to go, his mother and Jaren more than halfway down. He could not have prepared himself for this day. He breathed deep through the nose. There was something sweet in the air, and he knew it would rain again. A breeze had already picked up and was now dancing through the grass on the hill, rippling along each blade like waves on the ocean. He stood, transfixed.

The last time he felt this way, he'd been in Calais pining for Joanna...and home. Now home, he wished to be gone. Frustrated with his mother's interference, he allowed the memory of Joanna's betrayal to play through his mind over and over and over again. Images he'd purposefully pushed aside, he gave free reign, fueling his anger and distrust. He didn't want to be married—was not ready to face his own jealous nature should it be aroused again.

Would he ever forget the image of his Joanna beneath the attentions of another man? Like an animal, she'd played into his hands with no conscience or thought to Makaias nor to their pledge of marriage. How surprised she'd been to see him standing there. How aghast she'd been when he flung the man from her person, laying fists to his head and body. By God's grace alone, he'd not killed him. And her eyes...he'd never forget. So hard and calloused, no love at all.

A new thought occurred to him. If what Andret told him about Stuart was true, then Velena would be feeling as betrayed as he had. Why in the world would Stuart force himself on her maid, especially on the cusp of his own marriage? He couldn't fathom it. Was this the *bad thing* Velena had known about? And there he was giving her advice to stay with him. He rubbed the back of his neck. Had he known that her situation so closely mirrored his own, he would never have counseled her in that direction. That she'd even considered it made her a nobler person than he. And her harsh words about having to talk herself into Stuart's bed didn't seem quite so harsh anymore. He smiled. My, but she had a willful streak running through her.

He ran his hands through his hair. It'd grown longer over the course of weeks, and he could now pinch it between his fingers as his thoughts continued. By her own admission, Velena didn't love Stuart, which would save her heart some injury, but he knew she'd be aggrieved for Daisy's sake, and he grieved along with her. If she were his natural sister, he might think to offer her some form of physical comfort, such as an affectionate embrace. But feeling brotherly towards her and actually being so, were two entirely different things. He'd leave it to Britton then. But he would talk to him as Andret suggested— about Stuart and about what more he knew of Sir Richard's plans with the king—specifically, those that involved himself.

He groaned all over again, thinking about what his mother had done. Although…if he were honest, he'd have to admit that his mother had been right about him on at least one account. He wasn't exactly enjoying a life of celibacy. And Velena's touch *had* pleased him. Truth be known, he'd been keenly aware of it—though not because it'd come from her. Lonely as he was, he assumed he'd have reacted the same had she been any woman.

It felt like an eternity since he'd been touched with any sort of romantic affection. He turned his face into the wind. Longer, if it meant *sincere* affection. He had the same yearnings as any man—land, children, a wife to keep him warm—though better a wife he could love and who'd love him in return. Now, if Sir Richard's plans carried through, he'd be wedded to a stranger the same as Velena—the exact same fix he'd warned her about. It shouldn't have made him feel better about his own situation, but he had to admit that it did. At least he wasn't the only one being called upon to fulfill his duty to king and country. And if Britton, also, gained a wife, they'd all be in the same boat with naught to do but grin and bear it.

A smile suddenly played at the corners of his lips as thoughts of Britton and Velena brought him back to yesterday. How merciless he could be when teasing his sister, and Makaias couldn't help but wonder how much more she'd received for awarding him his kiss. She'd certainly been hesitant to do it.

But after… After, it was more than embarrassment he'd seen in her eyes. Had she been anyone else, he would have sworn it was attraction. She was fortunate he knew her so well. Eyes like that could confuse a man. Makaias dislodged a descent sized stone and watched it skip down the side of the hill, kicking up bits of debris with every bounce. She certainly had a lot to learn. She was still too bold, speaking her mind without thought, looking men in the eye when she ought not. He wondered how her new husband would take to such behavior and hoped it wouldn't put her in harm's way. Because, all that aside, she really was quite pleasant company.

Smiling, he recalled the way she lost her train of thought when he'd asked her what to do next when checking for broken ribs. She was flustered, no denying it. More so when he removed his tunic. He laughed softly. Admittedly, he'd been a bit of a scamp, taking it off before necessary. Engaged or no, he *had* enjoyed her reaction—her innocence and inability to hide what she was thinking. This, he liked. Boldness, no. Innocence, yes. But as much as her attention stroked his ego, there'd be no repeat performance. He'd been wrong to toy with her, for if there did exist any true attraction on her part, he'd have to be careful not to encourage it in the future—especially now that her engagement was broken.

He rubbed a hand down his face as the first drops of rain began to fall. He looked behind him at the dilapidated state of Totnes Castle and decided against finding shelter there. Besides, there was no telling when the rain would stop. In quick time, he jogged down the wooden steps.

Time to face Sir Richard—and his future.

21

home

Makaias trotted his horse back into Landerhill's bailey just as the rain subsided—and just in time to see Sir Richard making ready to leave. He had Sirs Gilbert and John Staybrook with him, Navarre, two squires, and another he couldn't immediately identify. Dismounting, Makaias nodded as he approached, surprised by the sixth man turning around.

"Sir Makaias," Sir Richard greeted, "thought I was going to miss you." He gestured to the man beside him. "You remember Esquire Tristan, of course."

"Of course," Makaias said reaching out his hand. "Welcome back."

Tristan smiled. "I hardly recognize you. Forgive me, but you're not as I remember. Less hair…"

Makaias ran a hand back and forth across his soft growth, sending a small spray of water across his forehead. "Aye, a batch of lice forced me to it."

Tristan laughed. "That'll do it."

Another moment of small talk and Sir Richard excused Tristan, who bowed before retreating indoors. He seemed nervous to do so.

"So," Sir Richard said, leading Makaias away from the other men, "did you have a good chat with your mother?"

He licked his lips, praying his true feelings wouldn't show. "I did, my lord. Most enlightening."

"And…"

"She spoke of land. She said you were going to petition the king for land on my behalf. If that's true…"

"It is.

"Then I'm truly grateful, my lord. It's more than I could have hoped for. I've dreamt of it, in fact…"

"But?"

"But…as for a wife…" He took a deep breath. "I'm less disposed to the idea of taking a stranger to be my bride."

Sir Richard folded his arms. "This was your mother's chief concern, though I hoped she was in error. I want to reward you for your service—not cause you grief."

"I would never assume the latter."

Sir Richard cleared his throat. "Consider this. The world is half what it used to be. And as much has been left to ruin, I'm optimistic the King will grant you land. And perhaps a title as well. But for these things, he'll want to ensure your loyalty. Marriage to the daughter of one of his vassals will be a way of securing this. The one will not come without the other. Do you understand?"

Swallowing hard, Makaias nodded.

"Do you still want the land, Sir Makaias?"

He squared his shoulders, muscle twitching in his jaw. "I do."

"Then leave the rest to me. If the Lord be merciful, you'll have a wife worth having." Sir Richard smiled, hopeful yet unwilling to suggest who, lest he be unable to deliver."

Makaias' smile came up crooked. "As long as she's older than fifteen, my lord. I don't relish taking a child to wife."

"Good man," Sir Richard said, slapping him firmly on the back with a belated chuckle. "I'll do my best."

Velena had just turned from the stairs when the door at the farthest end of the corridor opened and shut. Sir Makaias was coming in by way of the kitchen, his eyes catching hers almost immediately. She ducked her head in acknowledgment. So did he.

Why was he looking at her that way? Despite being somewhat self-conscious of her disheveled appearance, she advanced at an even pace. He did the same, long even strides bringing him closer with every step until they stopped an arm's length apart in front of her father's cabinet.

"Sir Makaias," she greeted.

"Lady Velena."

Silence, then they both attempted to speak at once. He smiled his apology. "Beg your pardon, my lady. You first."

"No, you go ahead," she said, letting go a small laugh.

"Ladies first. I insist."

"Alright," she conceded, "I was just saying that I was looking for my brother."

Makaias gestured towards the door. "He's in there, I believe. But I was also on my way to see him, so it looks as if we have a slight dilemma."

"Perhaps. But don't you think I ought to go first?" she simpered

His eyes narrowed. "Progeny before paladin is it?"

"Paladin? My, but I didn't think you were that old."

"I age well."

"I would agree," she said, then instantly wished she could take it back. She hadn't really meant anything by it, but after yesterday, he would think she was flirting—and by the glint in his eyes, he did. "Are you laughing at me?"

"That I am," he said, mouth stretched into a broad grin. He all but forgot his promise to himself not to tease her.

She crossed her arms in front of her chest. "Clear your mind, Sir Knight. If you mean to think I was complimenting your appearance, I meant only that you were more pleasing to look at than a five hundred-year-old relic."

"Point taken, but if we're to discuss appearances, don't you think you ought to do something with your hair before presenting yourself to your brother?"

"You know full well he doesn't care, and having unkempt hair is better than leaving a puddle at one's feet. From the look of you, I'd say you were caught in the rain. Pray, dry by the fire, and I'll be done by the time you do."

He looked down at his damp clothing. "The work of a good sprinkle. I was with my mother and brothers up at the castle. Beautiful sunrise."

Velena smiled. "Is she here?"

"Mother? No. Jaren took her home."

Disappointed, she nodded.

"And what about you?" He gave a strand of hair by her ear a small tug and chuckled when she batted him away. "What are you doing up so early?"

"I wanted to pray."

"Do you often go to the chapel this early?"

"I hardly go to the chapel anymore at all," she confessed, wondering at the way he was looking at her. *Curiosity? Compassion?* She wasn't sure, but his gaze never wavered. "Not since your mother helped me put up my prayer closet."

He cocked his head to the side. "Prayer closet? Is that what those sheets were?" He held up his arm. "The ones hanging from your ceiling?"

Curious as to what he might have first thought them to be, she nodded, and his eyes softened into something akin to admiration. It was the first she'd seen of it in regards to her.

"Might I assume you pray often?" he asked, noting the emotion that quickly clouded her face.

"It's all I've been doing these last three days," she confessed, not bothering to explain she hadn't been praying in *her* solar. "I asked the Lord for answers, and He gave them to me." She took a deep breath. "Now, I must ask for the grace to walk in them."

"Stuart?" he asked, making sure to keep his voice low.

Thinking Britton must have told him, her eyes dropped to the floor.

Licking his lips, all humor faded away. "I'm so sorry, Velena. For you—and for Daisy. Tell her for me. I don't know of what use I could possibly be, but if there's anything I can do..."

"That's very kind of you, Makaias," she said, aware they were falling back into using their given names. It was nice—and freeing, given that Stuart would no longer have sway over her tongue. "But I'm sure there's nothing."

"Still. I owe you *something*. If I'd known what he'd done, I never would have counseled you in his direction."

The corners of her mouth rose. "Perhaps...if you would let me go in to see Britton first..." she said, gesturing to the door.

Makaias chuckled. "Well played. I suppose the entire future direction of my life can wait a few more minutes."

"No need for dramatics," she chided and reached for the handle. It swung inward, startling them both into taking a step back. As Tristan emerged rather than Britton, Velena's throat immediately constricted, and she knew if there was ever to be a day without tears, it wouldn't be this one. *Dear Father in Heaven, thank you. With every part of my being—I thank you!*

Makaias watched the array of emotions splayed out across her face and realized she was just as unaware of his return as he'd been.

As the three of them stood there, all in an awkward sort of silence, it was Tristan who spoke first, clearing his voice in a clumsy attempt to regain his composure. "I suspect that one...or...or both of you are here to see Sir Britton. Allow me to clear a path," he said, crossing between them.

Makaias extended his arm. "Lady Velena, I believe you were first." He watched as she tried to smile, but it was wobbly at best.

"I have no more need of him," she answered, unable to take her eyes off Tristan. "I withdraw my request."

Makaias's gaze shifted between them. "Then God be with you." Shutting the door behind him, he caught a glimpse of Velena just as she was throwing herself into Tristan's arms. Masking his features for Britton, who was gesturing for him to sit, Makaias couldn't help but feel sorry for the man who might be matched up with his friend's sister. How long would it take her to realize Stuart wouldn't be the only would-be-husband to protest such a friendship?

"I assume that this land idea was partly your doing," he said, taking his seat across from Britton.

"Not at all, actually. It came about with his plan to annul the contract with Magnus."

Makaias shook his head, eyes sullen. "So, it's true…about Stuart."

"I'm afraid so. And now father is trying to kill two birds with one stone, as it were."

"Or three in our case—you, me, *and* your sister."

Looking away, Britton gave a dull laugh. He knew his father still harbored doubts about his ability to persuade the King towards Makaias as the worthiest option for his daughter. It was the reason he hadn't told him the whole truth of his plan, and the reason he'd asked Britton to remain quiet.

Sir Richard thought it better to bring back the stranger Makaias was expecting than to disappoint him by failing to secure Velena for his wife. What he didn't know was that this would be no disappointment at all, and that Britton was now having his regrets for not telling him so.

22

second choice

Velena hadn't known whether to shout for joy or cry? She did neither, but had, with her heart in her throat, rushed forward, throwing her arms around his neck—despite the pain it caused her side—pressing her face into his shoulder.

His arms came around her—awkward at first—looking to the door as if for Sir Britton's belated permission to embrace his sister. None would be forthcoming, so he tightened his hold of her, squeezing his eyes shut against the ache in his throat.

Wincing, she held her breath, not wanting him to break his hold. "I'm *so* angry with you," she finally whispered, digging her nails into his back.

"Ouch." He pulled away to see tears glistening in her eyes. "I know," he rasped. "Where can we talk?"

Where, indeed? She could take him upstairs, but Daisy was in no shape to be seen. The fire in the great hall would be warm and inviting, but there would be far too many people going in and out. They might have privacy in the chapel, but that could change at any moment as knights were encouraged to begin their day in prayer.

"There," she said, pointing towards the great double doors, flanked on each side with window seats cut three foot wide and just as deep.

With ginger movement, Velena crawled in first, stuffing the lower part of her cotehardie beneath bent legs as she leaned her back against the wall. He followed suit, seating himself opposite to face her.

For several moments they just stared, reacquainting themselves with each other's presence, each with their own set of burdens to unload and feeling as much strangers as friends.

"I didn't think you'd come back," she finally confessed.

He looked down at his hands. "I told you I would."

"So you did." There was an edge to her voice.

"I don't blame you for being angry."

"It wasn't like you to keep things from me."

He nodded. "I'd never had anything I *wanted* to keep from you."

"Then why did you?"

"I hardly know anymore," he confessed, watching a single tear as it slid down her cheek.

"You should have told me."

"I went to your father, but it didn't change anything. Telling you after that...it just seemed cruel. I tried again with the letter. I hadn't told him about her the first time."

"Why not?"

"She swore she'd deny it, and I didn't see any reason to drag her name into it unless she'd accuse him willingly. I begged her. The letter was an act of desperation, and honestly, I was hoping you'd be there when he read it—asking him questions like I felt sure you would—knowing you would still hear the truth from *me*, even if I couldn't be with you. Forgive me," he begged, leaning forward over his knees. "I thought I was doing right. I prayed your father would have a change of heart and come after me. I...I confess to being resentful when he didn't come. It never occurred to me he hadn't read it."

"Daisy had it. You hadn't told me of its importance, so I employed her to deliver it. She gave it up to Rowan only days ago...and here we are."

"Here we are," he repeated, mouth lifting in a half-hearted smile. The air felt chilled between them.

"When did you get here?" she asked.

"Yesterday. I sent word to your father, and he asked me to come."

"This morning, when I saw that someone was staying in your old room, I thought it too good to be true to think it might be you."

"You went to my room?"

"I've been praying there." She looked to her lap, a hesitant smile creeping into place. "It seemed the best way to be near you."

Tristan's lids fluttered, uncertain how she meant that. Taking a chance, he took a small crack at the ice. "Snuggling into my bed were you?"

Chin up, she slapped at his leg. "No."

"Just checking." He smiled in earnest, letting go a deep breath. "How's Daisy?"

Her shoulders sagged. There was only one way to say it. "She's with child."

Tristan's head fell back against the wall, eyes closed.

"That's how we all feel," she said, knowing rightly there were no words to express it any better. "Especially Rowan. He asked her to marry him."

His head came back up.

"Then he took it back," she finished. "I think that the thought of raising Stuart's child is a little too much for even him to bear. I hope he talks with you about it."

"Does she...I mean does she want to marry him?"

"I don't think she knows."

He exhaled through puckered lips. "Wow. I didn't think I'd been gone long enough to warrant this much change. I'm a bit overwhelmed."

"What changes did you find at home? Did you find your brother?"

Tristan smiled. "I did."

"Praise God!" She could feel her anger melt at the news. "And how has he faired?"

"Much like any of us, I suppose. He lost his wife."

"I'm sorry. Is he alright?"

"Actually, yes. And come to think of it, just about now he should be missing a rather circular patch of hair right about here," he said, circling the crown of his head with his finger.

"He's a friar?"

He smiled.

She laughed. "Well, tell me. How did you find him?"

"It's a miracle, actually. He heard I left Oxfordshire after our family died and decided to stay at our mother's castle, hoping I'd return. He was waiting for me."

"I can't believe it."

"I could hardly believe it myself."

"Out of curiosity, why hadn't he taken orders before you got there? Has it not been his long-time ambition? I recall you telling me that if he hadn't married, it's what he'd have wanted to do."

"He wanted to settle the matter of our inheritance with me first, not wanting the church to have it. Once I got there, we signed papers, and he relinquished his portion."

"All of it?"

His smile was in full bloom. "You are now looking at the sole inheritor of Sir Tobias Challener, The Challenger."

"Oh, my word. *Tristan*! I suppose that makes you very rich."

"I was already very rich. This makes me filthy rich," he said leaning towards her.

She laughed, presenting him with the smile he'd been afraid she'd not offer him again. "Well, I'm happy for you," she said, giving his ankle a quick squeeze. "You deserve it."

"So, here you are!" Rowan exclaimed, thrusting himself suddenly upon them. "Were you surprised, Nenna?"

"By Tristan or by you just now?"

"Both."

"Yes, to the first; no, to the second. I saw you coming."

He hung his head dramatically. "Oh, well." He looked up again, this time at Tristan. "Has she forgiven you yet? She forgave *me* days and days ago."

She rolled her eyes. "Not quite so long as that, and what I said was that I needed time."

"You've had enough. And when have you ever been able to stay angry with me so long as he's around to blame?"

Tristan smirked. "I appreciate that, Rowan."

"Think nothing of it."

"I promise not to."

"Fine. I forgive you," she exclaimed, glaring at Rowan. "Now, will you *please* give us some time—alone?"

He scrunched up his face. "Mmmm, I could do that—but your brother wants to see you."

"He's with Makaias."

"Not anymore."

"Very well." Velena patted Tristan's leg, and he turned aside so she could lower herself down. "Don't leave," she said, pointing back at him.

He shook his head. "I'm entirely at your disposal."

Smiling, she moved to step passed Rowan, but spun back around. "Tristan…"

"Yes."

She pulled his face down by his collar, cupping her hand to his ear. "I forgive you too," she whispered.

He smiled after her, watching her go until Rowan pivoted on his heel to look at him through slanted eyes. "You didn't tell her—did you?"

"There's nothing to tell."

Rowan chortled under his breath. "*Oh, I think there is.*"

"I don't think Sir Richard wants her to know yet."

Rowan rolled his eyes. "For certain. But you tell her everything."

"I didn't tell her about Stuart."

"Which you regret. No need to start a trend."

"It's a complete uncertainty. I'm a second choice. There's nothing to tell…until there is."

"Very articulate," Rowan scoffed. "But fancy this. "You might be Sir Richard's second choice, but you won't be his majesty's—not with all your money."

Tristan looked at him sideways. "You're enjoying this, aren't you?"

"Very much." Rowan smiled.

"Well, what of you? Has nothing of interest happened while I was gone? Surely, there's more to talk about than this."

Rowan pulled out a well-gnawed splinter of wood from behind his ear and wedged it between his teeth. "Plenty. Come on *Second Choice*," he said, heading for the doors, "let's go for a walk."

Tristan looked towards Sir Richard's cabinet.

"She's a smart girl, Tristan; she'll find us."

A half hour later, she did, and it was more than enough time for Rowan to get out all he needed to say regarding Daisy, and all Tristan had to say in return. Though, by in large, his predominant contribution to the conversation consisted mainly of head bobs, hair pulls, and elongated groans.

"I knew I shouldn't have taken my eyes off of you," she said, finding them outside the stables.

"Entirely my fault, Nenna."

"At least we both agree."

"What did your brother want?" Tristan asked, stepping towards her.

"To remind me of things I'd rather not think about. Responsibilities I'm to have should the king visit."

"He's coming here?"

"Not for certain, but it's better to be prepared, especially if…" She ducked her chin. "Oh well, it doesn't matter yet. The very idea of it makes me nervous for how I should act in his presence, and I dread the whole thing."

Arms crossed, Rowan stared at her, failing to look as serious as he pretended. "Just don't go standing on any tables, and you'll be fine."

Tristan looked confused.

She raised a hand to cover her smile. "It was a chair," she explained to Tristan at last, "and it was necessary to frighten away a certain Sir Harold."

"Who?"

"Oh, it was awful. He said the worst things to me. He as good as asked me to take part in a tryst—"

"What?"

"I know—and after I'd been so nice to him."

"Aw." Tristan nodded in understanding. "Nice from you can do that."

"Do what?"

"Make a man think you actually want to be…well, *nice.*"

Velena's hands came down on her hips. "That's ridiculous—and I told him as much of the same and in no uncertain terms to leave."

"Did he?"

"*No,*" she exclaimed, as if she couldn't understand it. "He refused—even going so far as to suggest I'd already been wanton…with you."

"Where would he get that idea?"

Rowan laughed with an *I told you so* nod of his head. "I told you that little goodbye of yours was causing gossip."

"Oh, Velena, I'm so sorry."

"You needn't be," Rowan put in, "She handled herself quite *tactfully*, I'd say."

"Is this where the table comes in?"

"Chair," she insisted. "It was the only thing I could think of. I told him I'd embarrass him if he didn't leave, and he practically dared me to try." She continued to explain but could tell she'd suddenly lost his attention as he looked past her, the silliest grin creeping upon his face. Turning around, she saw Rowan climbing the hitching rail behind her.

"Rowan, no. Stop it," she said trying to pull him down."

"Just like this, she climbed atop the table—"

"Chair."

"Then flinging her arms open with a flourish—"

"I did not."

"She called for everyone's attention." He started to laugh, being sure to demonstrate the whole thing. "It was at this point, just as she intended to embarrass *said* knight, that he realized his folly in underestimating our dear Nenna and left, leaving her high and dry with no one to embarrass but herself."

"Everyone was staring at me—father, Stuart, the whole room. I wanted to die."

"What could she do then but call on her hero?" Rowan said, thumping an open palm to his chest.

Velena covered her face, laughing. "Mercy, I don't want to relive it."

"Rowan! Rowan!" he imitated in a high-pitched voice, "Save me, Rowan!" She pushed him off the rail at his shins, but he landed easily on his feet. "My own paraphrase, of course. But I did come to her aid."

"Yes, you did," she conceded. "You are a most excellent watchman and friend—and I thank you."

"The pleasure was mine."

Behind them the crack of wood rang out from the practice yard as Makaias initiated a mock fight with one of the lesser knights of Sir Richard's household. They all three walked across the yard to watch. The men fought with halberds, a skill both admirable and terrifying. One of the many squires on the sidelines signaled Rowan to come over, and he excused himself, leaving Velena and Tristan alone again.

"He's very good," Velena said of Makaias after a while.

Tristan nodded. "Indeed. I look forward to watching him in the tourney."

"Six more days..." she mused, not really thinking about the tourney so much as the man she may find herself bound to upon its arrival. Feeling Tristan's eyes on her, she turned to him. "Do you know where my father is right now?"

He nodded. "I do. He told me last night of his intention to go to King Edward for a new marriage contract...though it wasn't from him I first heard hint of it."

Curious, she waited for him to continue.

He swallowed the sudden lump in his throat, supposing this was as good a time as any to broach the subject of Iseult. "It was from the Baroness LaDawn, actually...upon my arrival."

"You've already seen her?" She looked disappointed. "Selfishly, I wanted to be the one to tell you of her presence. She said she was a friend of one of your sisters."

"Ann's friend—yes."

"I imagine you were surprised to see her in Totnes."

He cleared his throat. "Very. But more so to learn that she's a new acquaintance of yours." Anxious, he felt as if he was treading water, waiting for her to express even the smallest hint that she knew who the woman really was, knowing all the while she'd be shouting it from the roof tops if she did.

Her eyes did no more than brighten. "A dear friend is closer to it. Her being here has been an absolute gift. She's so...she's been...well, I don't know how to say it other than she's been wonderful. Do you know, she and Rainydayas have asked me to read to them from the Scriptures? And together we hung a prayer closet in my solar."

He raised his eyebrows. "A prayer closet...really?"

"Yes," she answered, noticing that he hadn't yet so much as smiled at the mention of her. "You...you don't mind that we're friends do you? Will seeing her remind you too much of Ann?"

He dug his toe into the dirt before lifting his eyes to meet her. "That you would become friends with the baroness is...it's more than I could have hoped for. For your sake, I mean. I'm happy you had someone, like her, to comfort you in my absence."

"Thank you." She smiled. "Having her here—just knowing she knew you—it was like having a piece of you with me."

Pressing his tongue against the back of his teeth, he wondered what game God might be playing with them, yet repented the moment it came, telling himself that her presence was little more than the Lord allowing him to face his past and move on from it.

"But now that you're here for real," she continued, "I feel as if I can finally breathe again."

Tristan's eyes bore deep into hers, remembering well the words of the baroness. *If you can do something to help her, I wish you would.* Gwenhavare didn't love him and never would. Thus realized, he'd not spend wasted moments loving her. "I'm here to stay. And you don't have to be afraid of your future. I promise."

"Oh, I'm not afraid," she said, without reservation. "I'm terrified. I'm absolutely terrified of the king's choice."

"Perhaps he will find no one worthy of you—as I'm sure no one is," he teased, "and release you to marry whomever you wish."

She glanced back towards the fight...and Makaias. He'd just delivered the winning blow and was then helping his opponent to his feet. Chest heaving from the exertion, he shouldered his halberd and smiled. It wasn't meant for her, but for a split second, she held his gaze, and she could imagine it was.

She no longer held his serious ways in disdain but accepted them as interesting, if not, engaging peculiarities, admitting to herself that there was much in his character to be praised and wondered if there were other men like him for the king to choose from. But the hope didn't last. Remembering what her brother had admitted about Makaias' not wanting her, she was forced to acknowledge that although she might, now, think a man such as he better suited to herself, *she* was probably not suited to such a man. She returned her attention to Tristan, smiling soulfully. "And if there's nobody?" she asked.

"I suppose I'll have to do the job then."

Velena laughed—laughed as he knew she would, though thankfully without the ridicule he was most afraid of. Rather, it bubbled up light and pleasant until she said, "Can you imagine the two of us—married? It'd do away with our motto, that's for certain."

He quirked a smile. "Not to mention upset an already nearly perfect friendship."

"And there's still Iseult to think about. *Oh! Iseult...*" She grabbed his arm. "You've told me nothing of her, but surely there is something to say."

Staring into her eyes, so genuinely bright and hopeful of his finding the one woman she believed would bring him all happiness and joy— he felt a bit lost. Always for him and never against, he wanted to embrace her for her love and loyalty. It would break her heart, almost as much as it did his own, to admit that her dreams for him had crumbled the moment he'd come back to Totnes—dreams he'd secretly wanted to cling to.

"Tristan?" she pressed. "Did you find her?"

"I did."

Her eyes rounded to twice their size. "I knew you would. And..." She was now shaking his arm by the sleeve.

"Aaand she is as lovely as ever she was. Charitable. Kind. Selfless." He tried to smile. "And not at all in love with me."

Her entire countenance fell as she released him. "How can that be? She's your Iseult."

"I guess we forgot to tell her that."

"Oh, Tristan, I'm..." She let her head hang. "I'm *so* sorry."

He raised her chin with his finger. "What's this? Are you pitying me?"

Her breath came faster, and her arms crossed over her chest. "No," she said, squaring her shoulders. "I pity her. She has no idea the man she just lost. And I'd say it straight to her face if confronted with her."

"I believe you would."

"Who is she anyway? What's her real name? Because I'll not call her Iseult again. She doesn't deserve the title."

Tristan chuckled.

"I'm serious."

"I know."

"Tell me!"

"Alright," he said raising both his hands and speaking the surname he'd known her by. "Lady Blair."

"Blair?" she questioned, scrunching up her face as though it caused her significant distaste. Tossing back her hair, still loose from that morning, she took up a brisk walk towards the newly finished sheepfold.

Falling into step, Tristan glanced at her sideways.

"Blair." She scoffed. "What is that? Scottish? If you'd told me she had Scottish blood I never would have encouraged you."

He smiled. "You don't mean that."

She gave him a look meant to say she wasn't so sure but remained silent. When they finally reached the wattle, Velena ran a hand along the tightly woven willow branches and circled around until she came to its opening. Stepping through, she pictured it full of little woolly creatures, all munching leisurely at the grass as if it were the only business worth doing. Calmed by such imaginings, she heaved a lengthy sigh. "Away, away, gone forevermore. Away, away…take me furthermore," she murmured.

"What's that?" Tristan asked.

"A poem," she said, tapping her palm lightly atop one of the vertical branches used to anchor the fence. "Or the end of one rather."

"Sounds like the beginning to me."

She turned to look at him.

" 'Take me furthermore.' That's the beginning of a journey right there. Maybe even an adventure."

A wistful smile brushed over her face. "*Furthermore…*" she whispered, letting it fall from her tongue with new meaning. "That's a place I'd like to be. Away from here…and everything."

He leaned into the wattle, feeling he knew exactly how she felt. "Shall I take you there?"

Her smile grew. "I could think of nothing better."

"Remember you said that," he teased.

Giggling at first, she let go a contented sigh. "You know…now that you're back, everything feels a good deal more as it should be and less like it's been."

"For me as well." Chest heavy, he took a ragged breath and, by some miracle, didn't cough, though the urge was there. Always there.

Oblivious, Velena laced her fingers behind her back and sashayed around the inner perimeter of the sheepfold as if performing its final inspection. "I suppose I should humble myself and admit that you were right to mistrust Stuart as you did." She paused to look over at him. "I'm sorry I didn't believe you."

"As you should be," he said, straightening up. "I don't get to be right nearly often enough, you know."

She laughed. "And that's the real reason you came back, isn't it? To be right."

"No," he said, wanting her to know the truth, "you are."

23

blessed are the poor in spirit

The day was still early when Tristan and Velena headed back to the manor house. For Velena, it was an odd feeling to have Tristan back. A blessing—but odd. He looked at her differently, and she wasn't sure why. Arguably, in the month he'd been gone, much had happened to leave her feeling as if she'd become an almost entirely different person. Almost. And perhaps, it had done the same for him as well. A month could be a long time, she supposed, especially one holding as many trials as theirs had. She kept having to remind herself that his being at Landerhill was really real, and she would have been very happy to monopolize him for the rest of the day, except there was still someone he needed to see.

"Daisy?" Velena inquired softly, cracking open her solar door. It creaked upon its hinges as she passed over the threshold and into the sitting room. Movement in the right corner of the room gave evidence of Daisy's presence.

"Yes, my lady." Her voice was small, and her eyes red-rimmed from crying as she stepped out from behind the prayer closet.

"I brought Tr—" Velena began but stopped short, noticing Daisy's state of distress. "What's wrong?" she asked, coming to embrace her, knowing well it could be one of a hundred different things she had every right to be crying over. The previous day had been an overwhelming day for unearthed secrets, confessions, and tears. It was really no surprise that such raw emotions would continue bleeding over into today.

Daisy swiped a hand across her cheek. "I um..." she began but didn't finish as she spoke in surprise. "Tristan?"

Velena turned around, realizing he'd decided to show himself from where he'd been waiting in the corridor.

"Hello, Daisy."

198

"You're back."

"Couldn't stay away," he responded meekly. "Wondering if I'm welcome though."

Daisy sniffed back her tears. "By whom?"

"You…" He took a step forward, shutting the door behind him.

"Before yesterday, I'd not have been so pleased to see you." Daisy produced a laugh of wonder, grateful sounding to her own ears, despite the sob that ended it. "But you came on the right day. Today, I welcome you," she said, tears trickling down from the corners of her eyes. Holding out her arms to him, he met her halfway, pressing the back of her head into his shoulder as they stood in the middle of the room, finding healing in the embrace.

"I prayed for you, Daisy," he whispered.

"You were angry with me. I know."

He nodded, setting her away from him. "You were angry with me, too."

"I was. I was afraid, but you were right. I was selfish. I wasn't thinking of Velena…or anyone else. If I'd been honest, you never would have had to leave. She never would have gotten hurt…"

Tristan looked over Daisy's shoulder at Velena, remembering now what Gwenhavare had said about her having been injured, but she dismissed Daisy's comment with a wag of her head.

"Can you forgive me?" Daisy asked, calling back his attention.

He was fighting back tears of his own. "Of course. Gladly. Happily. Forgive me, also, for being so harsh with you."

Her shoulders rose in a sad little shrug. "Apparently, it was necessary. It took Rowan nearly forcing my hand to get the confession you were all after. Would that I had responded to your kindness instead." Daisy moved to the table, and the three of them sat down, Tristan seated across from them.

"Speaking of Rowan," he began, "I heard he's asked for your hand."

Embarrassed, she tucked her hands between her knees.

"He spoke with me about it."

She looked up, unable to hide her interest. "What did he say?"

"He's, um—"

"Changed his mind," she finished for him.

"No. No," he stated firmly, shaking his head. "He really *does* love you. He's sincere about that."

"But the babe…"

"He only wants for some time. He just...he wants to be sure he can raise the child with a good conscience—without resentment...or regret."

She appeared to understand. "He needn't struggle so. I never said I would marry him nor am I holding him to any promises of the like."

Losing a hand to the thickness of his own hair, Tristan chose his words carefully. "I understand what you're saying. But..." He let out his breath. "If you don't want him, you'd do well to say so. He is invested."

Weighing the truth of his words, she nodded slowly—solemnly—mulling over her own thoughts and feelings in an attempt to make sense of them. "I take what you say to heart, only pray the Lord gives me some peace in the matter, for I'm entirely without it."

Velena laid a hand over Daisy's wrist. "Is Rowan the reason you were crying?"

Daisy looked at her. It should have been a simple question, but having, over time, become oddly accustomed to the habit of lying, she found that telling the truth came now only as a conscious effort. "Not him," she finally confessed. "Stuart."

Taken aback, Velena tightened her hold of her. "He's not going to hurt you."

"Leastwise, we wouldn't let him," Tristan put in.

Velena looked up. "He has no reason to," she said, unwilling to entertain any doubt on the matter. "He's upset with himself, not her."

"Velena."

"It's the truth," she said, laying a hand on the table. "What he did was awful—beyond awful. But he was re...remorseful. Not...not in a Christian way, perhaps, but in the only way he knew how."

Tristan shook his head in disgust.

"I heard him. *You* didn't."

"I wouldn't have believed him if I had."

"Please!" Daisy interrupted. "Please...Tristan. She's right."

Both eyes turned to her.

"The day he brought up the money, he *did* apologize."

"Truly?" It was Velena who asked it, though Tristan was no less surprised then she.

"It was nothing pretty," she said, remembering the way he'd shaken her. "He was angry; we were shouting, but...he did accept responsibility for his actions...in his way," she added for Velena's sake.

"Do you, um...*did* you...believe him?" she asked.

200

Tristan's eyes shifted from one woman to the other.

"I didn't want to," Daisy admitted. "I wanted to be angry, and it was like..." She took a moment to breathe. "It was like he was trying to take that away from me along with everything else. So, I...I refused to forgive him and said the most hateful things." She looked at Velena with pain-filled eyes. "I told him the real reason you wouldn't kiss him was because of the promise you made to Tristan." She looked down at her hands. "I told him you regretted the kiss you'd had, and that just as I was his mistake...he was yours."

Lost for words, Velena looked across the table at Tristan. She could tell he had questions.

"Worse," Daisy continued, "I let him believe I would end the babe's life." Looking up, she saw Tristan's eyes growing round as saucers.

"He didn't want you to?" he asked, not bothering to hide his shock.

She shook her head. "No," she spoke softly. "And if you're confused by this, you are by no means alone. I've puzzled over it all morning. Indeed, the more I reflect on what happened, I don't think he would have come to me and ever said what he did...without some small measure of sincerity. I'd already tried to threaten him with exposure, but it'd come to nothing. He knew I was never going to say anything. He had no more reasons to placate me, and yet he came asking my forgiveness." Her chin quivered. "But I didn't give it."

"And you feel you should?" Velena prompted.

"I feel compelled in a way I wish I didn't. It weighs heavy on my soul, especially after you so readily forgave me. But I..." Her voice broke, and she had to stop to take a breath. "I don't see how I can. But if God wills it, I don't see how I can't. What do I do?" Her voice pleaded with them.

Velena looked helplessly at Tristan, remembering all too well her own struggle to do this very thing. Thankfully, he appeared ready with an answer.

"While I was away, I spent a lot of time reading St. Matthew. Velena told me before I left that I needed to forgive Stuart, no matter how he might hurt her. But this was before she knew what he'd done," he said, turning repentant eyes in her direction. "But I knew. And I felt justified in withholding it." He smiled grimly. "But in my reading of Scripture, I came to a place where Jesus said, 'Blessed are the poor in spirit, for theirs is the kingdom of Heaven. Blessed are those who mourn, for they shall be comforted...' and most profound, 'Blessed are the merciful, for they shall receive mercy.' "

He interlocked his hands upon the table, recognizing Daisy's confusion. " 'Poor in spirit' means we are without—spiritually destitute and lacking the faith we need to know God. 'Those who mourn' are those who mourn over their own sin and repent in order to receive the forgiveness that leads to reconciliation. We must address this—our own depraved nature—in ourselves before we can possibly address it in others. You have been wounded by Stuart's actions. But they were his actions, and he *will* answer for them—if not in this life, then the next. You need only be concerned about the actions *you* must answer for. That is the most important question you could ask. Have you mourned over your own sinful state and repented? Have *you* been forgiven? Have *you* received God's mercy? This accomplished, you can...and will be able to extend it to others. I say this not to hurt you—or to judge you—but to direct you to the peace you're looking for. I pray you understand my motives. And if you would pray, I would pray with you. For I'm convicted by my own words even as I speak them and see now how much bitterness I still possess."

Trembling, Velena waited, feeling the gravity of the moment as the Spirit within them moved to do its greatest work in Daisy. And so it was, with tears in their eyes, that the three of them entered the shroud, with Tristan smiling inwardly at what was to be his first introduction to their meager prayer closet. In the stillness, they humbled themselves. On their knees, they acknowledged their own offensive nature before God and pled His forgiveness for their refusal to grant the same to the man who'd so offended them. Most importantly of all, Daisy repented, believed, and received her first measure of peace.

As it was with Velena, Daisy opened her eyes, hungry to know more about the God who'd forgiven her so fully. When she began to ask questions, Tristan grinned and excused himself in order to fetch his Bible. The noon meal wasn't for hours yet, so hours is what they spent pouring over the Word. Still, Daisy was disappointed when the horn sounded, calling all to eat. Insisting she wasn't hungry, she had it in her mind to ask Tristan to leave the Bible with her, except she wasn't as versed in Latin as either he or Velena. Even so, she asked permission to stay behind, desirous of a quiet moment to herself to sit and meditate upon all that had transpired.

Sensing she needed more, Velena consented but withdrew to retrieve the few pages of Psalms Tristan had transcribed for her before he'd left for Oxford. Thankfully, he'd remembered what Friar Daniel had said about the Scripture needing to be delivered in the common language and penned them all in French. Elated, Daisy began reading immediately, barely aware when they left.

Entering the great hall together, Velena thrilled as Tristan was greeted back to the manor by one and all. He gave several men his attention but never ceased engaging her with his eyes. They'd now spent hours spent in each other's company, and it was still a pleasure to turn and find the other one present. It was with silly grins that they finally broke eye contact, facing Britton as he welcomed Tristan up to the dais. Grateful, he seated himself beside Velena as a trencher was set between them. It was to be their first meal together since his return, and they partook with hearty appetites, lost in conversation as in the old days and perfectly oblivious to all else surrounding them.

24

hesitations

At one of the long tables, Makaias shifted sideways on his bench, pulling his elbows in as a trencher was set down between himself and Rowan. Having spent the majority of the morning at the quintain, leading the other knights in some particularly grueling exercises, he felt himself drained of energy and nigh on ravenous at the sight of the ample cut of meat drowning in gravy. Anxious for that first bite, he unsheathed his dinner knife only to pause with it mid-air as he was abruptly called to attention by Rowan clearing his throat.

He eyed Rowan, whose gaze shifted, re-directing Makaias' attention to the serving-woman still hovering at his shoulder. When he turned to look at her, he found himself eye-level with the upper curves of the cook's daughter, Juliana, the same woman he'd danced with the night of the fight. Lifting his chin, he produced the smallest of tight-lipped grins, hoping to encourage her with no more than a polite regard.

"I prepared it, myself," she simpered.

"You cooked this?" He raised an eyebrow, and she colored.

"Oh. No...I...I dished it up. I saved you a large piece. I've seen how hard you work."

"Ah," he said, glancing down, wondering if she'd actually been out watching him. His stomach rumbled. "It looks...delicious. Thank you." He cut off a tender morsel in anticipation of her moving on.

When she didn't, Rowan began filling his mouth full of bread to keep from laughing.

Was she waiting for him to try it? Makaias stabbed the large chunk of meat and shoved it back between his teeth. "Mmm," he said, employing the same sort of enthusiasm one might exhibit towards a small child. "Delicious."

She puffed up with pleasure, and he found himself feeling twice as awkward beneath her satisfied grin as he had when she was merely gawking.

"I believe the dais is in want of some more wine," Rowan said, and he lifted a finger to point.

She gave him a cold stare before turning back to Makaias, lips once again poised for a smile. "I should...I really should get back to work. But I could come back with some dessert after you've finished...if you'd like?"

Rowan's ears perked, always at the ready for a good fruity tart, but Makaias spoke before he had a chance to beg one for himself.

"Actually, I have no time for dessert. But, thank you."

Disappointment clouded her face, but not her eyes, as she allowed them to linger in such a way as to make his insides squirm. "If you change your mind, I could...bring it to you later."

Rowan did laugh then, very nearly choking on his food. "Subtle," he said, taking up his tankard to wash it all down.

A deep flush crept up her neck and cheeks, until they were stained pink.

"No, thank you," Makaias said, maintaining his composure, "I'll not be wanting dessert...of any kind."

Nodding curtly, she turned her back to them, retreating into the kitchen without so much as pausing at the dais to see if there was any actual need for more ale.

Rowan chuckled. "Shame she was only flirting. I do actually want some dessert."

"I think she *was* the dessert," he said, plopping a gravy-sopped chunk of bread into his mouth.

"No question. And I'd wager you weren't even tempted."

Makaias shook his head. "If it's a warm body she's after, she'll have to look elsewhere."

"I think your rejection probably crushed any more notions of her trying that again. Turned red as a beet, did you see it?"

"That was anger, not embarrassment," he said, using the water bowl to clean the grease off his fingers. "False modesty. If she were truly given to a bashful nature, she wouldn't have approached me in front of you." He took a drink and set down his tankard with a dull thud.

"I suppose I *have* heard a thing or two said of her."

Makaias shook his head. "For her sake, I hope it's naught but idle gossip. Anything else, and I doubt Sir Richard would be tolerant of such behavior should he catch wind of it. Now, especially." He took a breath. "As to this, it was probably my fault for encouraging her."

"The dancing?"

He nodded.

"Hm." A moment went by, and Rowan pulled a leg out over the bench, so he could better face him. Another, and he began tapping the tip of his knife against the table. "Let me ask you something."

Makaias waited.

"It's about Daisy. By now, you must have heard of her situation."

He nodded.

"I find myself in somewhat of a quandary over it."

"In what way?"

Suddenly embarrassed, Rowan took a deep breath, his lips twisting into a crooked grin. "I want to marry her."

Makaias' eyebrows went up.

"But," Rowan continued, "I don't know what to do about this whole child business. It's Stuart's, and I...I don't know if I can reconcile myself to that. He'll need a father, but...what if he looks like him—talks like him—or God forbid, grows up to act like him? I always thought to be proud if I had a son."

"Or daughter," Makaias pointed out.

"Daughter?" Rowan mused. "I hadn't thought about it being a girl. I suppose she might look like Daisy, then."

"Or not."

Rowan groaned as Makaias sat thoughtful, taking his time to chew one last bite of his food.

"You think the child unworthy of love?" he finally asked.

"I'd be horse dung to say that, but I don't know how else to feel. I think I could accept the child if it weren't for the possibility that it might very well share in Stuart's nature—his poor character. That, I can't accept."

Makaias faced him full on. "Our first parents were Adam and Eve, were they not? Are we not, every one of us, born into that selfsame sin nature that first separated them from God? We are all wretched," he stated matter-of-factly, "unworthy of any good—doomed to do all manner of wrong. Let God's work be your example. Do as He does."

"I would never own to being dense but do clarify."

"Grace, Rowan. Show the child grace. Despite our being so unpleasing a thing to God, He, in His mercy, still saves us—loves us—shows us grace."

"How do I do it?"

Makaias studied him with sober eyes. "Might you not have received it yourself to know?"

Rowan smiled in self-derision. "If you're calling me out as an imposter, you'd not be wrong. I admire your faith, Makaias—Tristan's and Velena's. I've wanted it for myself. But no matter how close I think I am to finding it, there always seems to be…a distance…between myself and God."

" 'The Lord is near to all who call upon Him, to all who call upon Him in truth,' " Makaias smiled his encouragement. "Check your motives, Cousin. Are you seeking Him because you want to follow and obey, or are you simply after your own gain?"

"Am I interrupting?" Britton asked, approaching them from behind.

Rowan lifted his chin. "Not at all," he said, sliding his hands up on his thighs. "We're just talking women. Care to join?"

Britton smiled. "You broach a touchy subject with this one. Tread lightly; I caution you."

"You're the only one who need tread lightly," Makaias warned, "but sit with us anyway. I'm in a tolerant mood."

He shook his head. "I'm headed to town. The building starts, today, on the fences and high seats for the tourney, and I would watch, if not lend a hand where I'm able."

"I'll join you," Makaias said, brightening. "Just give me a minute if you don't mind."

"I'll see to the horses," he said, already turning to leave.

Rowan laughed. "You mean you'll see to someone else seeing to the horses."

"Isn't that what I said?"

Smiling, Makaias turned back to Rowan to finish their conversation, but he was already turned-on to another subject.

"What did he mean about women being a touchy subject?"

Makaias' lips pulled to the side as he pushed the trencher away to make room to rest his forearms.

"You know why Sir Richard left?"

"To secure Velena a new husband."

"Add to that wives, for me and Britton."

"Truly?"

"Truly." His tone softened with resignation.

"Aaand...you don't want to marry." It wasn't a question.

"For my own reasons."

"And that bothers him?"

"Not so much as I've never wanted to marry his sister."

"Nenna?" Rowan looked thoughtful, sliding his feet back and forth among the rushes. "Not a bad match actually."

He huffed. "No matter that I disagree with you, the subject need no longer be a point of contention between us. The decision now rests with King Edward, and *he* will be choosing someone of wealth and rank, no doubt. I only hope he's a good man—for her sake."

Rowan chuckled. "I have a feeling he will be."

"You say that like you know."

Leaning onto one elbow, he lowered his voice. "I know that Tristan put in his name. And if it's wealth that's going to turn the king's head, he certainly has enough of it."

"Tristan? Really? I...I don't suppose I should really be surprised, except that Sir Richard's always given the impression he didn't feel that way about her."

"Tristan doesn't know what he feels," Rowan confessed, humor evidenced by his tone. "But he's a good man—devoted to Velena—and unwilling that she should fall to anyone less worthy than she deserves."

"He seeks to save her."

"In a word."

Awed by such selflessness, Makaias gave his attention to the dais, regarding the pair of them just as Velena found humor in something Tristan said. She laughed, he smiled, and Makaias could see them being happy together. Shaking his head, he turned away. "If he doesn't truly love her, he's a better man than I."

"For marrying her?"

"I couldn't do it," he confessed.

Rowan cocked an eyebrow. "And yet you will," he reminded him.

"And yet I will," he echoed, cringing at the reality of it. Stepping out from behind the bench, he wiped clean and sheathed his knife. "I'd better join Britton," he said, eyes focused at his belt. "Exciting work to be done."

"You really are touchy on the subject."

Makaias chuckled, adjusting his belt. "My reservations are my own;

don't let them influence you. If you choose to marry Daisy, God give you joy. Tristan also. I'm happy for them both."

"Well, don't be too happy yet. He's only Sir Richard's second choice."

Makaias looked up. "Who's his first?"

"I don't know." Rowan shrugged, smiling up at him. "But it'd be funny if it were you."

25

a deviation

The first rays of a new day slipped silently through every nook and cranny of the manor, bringing Tristan's room from dark to dim as it teased his eyes awake. Breathing in deep through his nose, he lifted his arms above his head. Muscles taut, he could feel the stretch opening up his chest as it traveled through his body, down past his thighs and calves and finally ending in his toes.

Pleasant for the moment, it ended in a fit of coughing, leaving him bunched up on his side for a worrisome amount of time before he was finally able to catch his breath. Grimacing, he threw back the blankets and walked barefoot over the newly strewn rushes to expectorate what he could into a hastily-made pile he pushed into the corner with his foot. Finished, he could still feel the thickness of it settling back into his chest. It didn't bode well, but he shook off his concern.

Dressing, he left his room quietly, smiling as he passed Velena's door. Despite his physical ailments, he'd awoken with a deeper sense of peace than he'd had in a long…long time. Stuart was no longer in Velena's life nor was the thought of him bringing the same deep-seeded bitterness that had plagued him since Wineford Castle. He was free, and so was she…at least for the time being.

He exited the manor by the back door, breaking into a jog. The chill of morning hit his lungs especially hard with those first few breaths, pleasant as they were, pervaded with fresh earth and herbs. The terrain was hidden in the morning fog, but he continued forward, knowing the way. He made it only as far as the barracks before having to stop, yards feeling like miles as his heart raced, and his pulse thrummed in his ears. He shouldn't be this out of breath.

When the gravel crunched somewhere in front of him, he looked up to see Sir Makaias materializing from out of the mist. Bare-chested, he strode towards him, a thick belt, weighted down with sandbags, secured about his waist. Drawing his attention, he smiled, a gesture Sir Makaias returned in kind.

"You're up early," he said, large puffs of vapor rising with every breath. He was sweaty from his run and paused at a stump to retrieve a towel and tunic he'd left behind. Wiping down first, he unbelted himself, then slipped the tunic over his head to prevent a chill from setting in. "Everything alright?" he asked, noticing the fatigue on Tristan's face.

"Probably not," he answered, shielding a deep-chested cough with the crook of his elbow.

Makaias put a foot on the stump and leaned forward, feeling the stretch in the back of his thigh. He glanced over in concern. "You don't sound well."

"I don't feel well," he conceded, a slight smile on his lips.

Makaias switched legs. "I can ask Britton to send for the healer."

"Thank you but no. I have no faith in physicians. And this one would probably kill me before she could heal me."

Makaias chuckled, remembering the dung-filled concoction she'd wanted to apply to Britton's eyes. "Maybe so."

"Anyway, I'm not concerned," he added. "I'm sure it's nothing time won't heal."

Makaias straightened. "I pray so. In the meanwhile, I assume you're happy to be back."

"Indeed. It's a good feeling…seeing Velena again, especially. Seems right that I came."

"There's been a lot of changes."

"Good ones," Tristan stated without apology.

"If you speak of Stuart, I offer no argument. As family, I do pity him, but not so much as those he inflicted himself upon. He behaved without honor or restraint and deserves what punishment comes to him."

"Which, unfortunately, has been none," Tristan pointed out.

"Perhaps one."

"Lady Velena, you mean."

Nodding, Makaias reached for his running belt, sandbags dangling at his thigh. "It leaves a cruel scar…losing the woman you love."

"If he ever truly loved her."

"He'd say he did. And he *is* suffering for it. As for Velena, I'd be the first to say the outcome is as it should be."

Tristan's lips pressed together at the informality with which he used her name. A thought occurred to him, and he began to wonder just how close the knight had gotten to his friend in the time he'd been away. "Your concern for the lady is admirable. I imagine your history with her family has drawn you close."

Makaias cracked a smile. "Our history is spotty at best and could be summed up in a mere handful of times I was here as Britton's guest. I'm eight years her senior and admit to paying her little attention, so this is really the first I've gotten to know her."

"And what have you discovered?" he asked, curious how this man might see her.

"Ah, well, she's..." Unprepared, Makaias kept his emotions in check, switching hands with his belt as a litany of words flitted to mind. *Immature. Impetuous. Silly. Undisciplined.* Recalling the way in which she'd flung herself over Stuart's head to shield him, incurring injury, he could add *unrestrained.* Albeit *brave...*

"She's..." He tried again, considering the tears he'd observed from his place by the door of her bedchamber. *Weighted down. Sorrowful.* The way she'd stood up to Stuart in the library. *Sometimes sensible,* he admitted as memory forced him to consider her devotion to prayer—memory from which came new thoughts touting new words *Pious. Kind. Honest. Pleasant...*

Looking up, he realized the drift in his thoughts and immediately reordered them. *Loyal. Loyal to family. Loyal to friends. Loyal to Tristan...and probably in love with him.* Then came a polite smile. "I've found her to be honest and pleasant company," he replied, "though my duties often limit our interactions."

"Still you've come to be...friends?"

"I hope she'd allow me the honor of thinking so."

"I have no doubt of it." Tristan gave him a brief but genuine smile. "Let me ask you, though...if I may," he began slowly, not wanting to accuse, so much as pry a little more into the momentary look of appreciation he'd seen pass over the knight's face when first asked to express what he'd discovered in spending more time with Velena. "Has the thought of Sir Richard's finding Velena a new husband...been upsetting to you?"

Confounded, Makaias set the belt down. "Are you asking what I think you're asking?"

Newly aware of the size of the man before him, Tristan rubbed the back of his neck. "I...thought I was. But if you intend to take offense to it, my answer changes to *no.*"

Makaias laughed, genuinely surprised by the man. So…he who despised so much jealousy in Stuart was not to be immune to it, himself. Had Tristan already received some sort of surety that the King would grant him Velena for his wife? His question could suggest it, but as he was unable to affirm or deny this, Makaias settled on one thing. Tristan clearly saw Makaias' newly grown friendship with Velena as a threat to his future with her, and the irony of this was not lost on Makaias. In fact, it amused him a great deal.

Yet, for the sake of peace, he would not withhold that which the young esquire was looking for, simply for his own entertainment. Not when he could dispel his concerns here and now—and would have, had Sir Andret not chosen that moment to emerge from the barracks.

Yawning, he strapped on his belt. "Fine morning," he said upon seeing Tristan with his brother. "What brings you out so early?"

Tristan smiled, increasingly grateful for what removed him from his own line of questioning. "Something ridiculous, else I'd be back in bed. No decent person should be up this early."

Sir Andret chuckled. "Best get back to it then."

"The body is willing, but the mind…far too awake. I wait now for Velena." He glanced back at Makaias.

"Give her my greetings," Sir Andret said, stretching his arms behind his head in a relaxed manner.

"To be sure. And for you as well?" Tristan asked Makaias.

"Please do," he said, smiling as Tristan turned his back and disappeared into the waning mist.

Yawning yet again, Andret reached across his chest to stretch out his back and shoulders. "What was that?"

"Just talk."

Andret eyed his brother in amusement. "About Lady Velena?"

"You were listening?"

He smiled. "Not nearly long enough. What was his concern?"

"Just a little needless jealousy, I think."

Andret chuckled. "Protective, more likely."

"He good as questioned my feelings for her."

"He wants to know she'll be cared for."

"Lord willing, she will be. But I still got the feeling he wanted to make sure I'll not be in the way."

"In the way of him? Doubtful."

Makaias smiled. "Could it be I finally know something you don't?"

"Seems so."

"Tristan's asked for her hand."

Andret frowned. "As have you. Whether you know it or not."

"What?"

"Mother," he stated simply.

"You suspect."

"I know."

Makaias felt the blood leave his face. "No, you don't."

"I do."

"Still do me the favor and say you don't."

Andret shook his head. "I pressed her after we left you at the castle."

He ran a hand over his face. "And?"

"She confirmed what I already suspected."

Makaias groaned. "Was Jaren there when she said so?"

"No. She realizes now she underestimated his ties to Craft Hall. He only knows Sir Richard has it in mind to replace Stuart, but he doesn't suspect it's with you."

"What a mess..." he muttered, releasing a lengthy breath. "I hate this. I'm eight and twenty, not eight and ten. I don't need others making these decisions for me."

"It's not so bad."

"How is it not?"

Andret arched his brows. "Look at who you'll be marrying."

"Don't do that. Don't act like it's for certain. I don't need this from you. I've no land. I'm untitled. Tristan ought to be the King's choice."

"But if not?"

"How can there be an if?"

"It's you Sir Richard wants. If Tristan's in the running, it's to protect her from a poor match. I guarantee it. And he'll not even mention him so long as King Edward's agreeable to you."

"He has no reason to be."

"Calm yourself, Makaias. Lady Velena's a fine woman."

"Absolutely. But that shouldn't have anything to do with me."

"You were bound to marry someone. Why not her? She'd be an agreeable wife to you."

"Then you marry her."

Andret chuckled, and Makaias guessed he wouldn't find it such a bad idea. "Unlike you, I don't look forward to a life of chastity."

"I never said I did."

"But you're willing to endure it."

"I've controlled my urges thus far."

"Come on, Brother, what do you have against her?"

"I've nothing against her! She's as a sister."

Andret rolled his eyes. "She's as a sister to all of us. She has a talent for it—also for evoking a particularly strong sense of affection from those who embrace her as such."

Makaias' mouth ticked at the corners. "Perhaps. But what husband wants a wife so beloved by other men?"

"One who knows the value in having his entire household devoted to its mistress."

"Granted, but I just…" He struggled for words. "I could never see her in that light—especially after seeing the way she fawns over Tristan."

"You're wrong. And I can't believe you'd rather have a stranger than a woman you know and respect."

"A stranger would be better. At least then, she'd know nothing about me. She'd know not whether my love was real or pretense. I'd have the ability to placate her mind with a smile or to exaggerate my devotion through acts of kindness until, Lord willing, it has the opportunity to become real. But with Velena…I'd lose every advantage. She'd know from the start the things I feel—and the things I don't."

"Do you honestly think she expects you to love her right away?" Andret questioned dryly.

"Perhaps not—but if I never do, it'll only make her susceptible to one who will."

"I think she's more worthy of your trust then that. You ought to have confidence in the feelings time can bring."

The muscles in Makaias' jaw twitched. "Time brought feelings to Joanna, but they were not for me." He shook his head. "It'd not be fair to either of us. If ever there was to be a marriage of civility and nothing more…ours would be it. If she doesn't want Tristan now, she'll wish she had him later."

Grieved for his brother, Andret set a hand to his shoulder. "You don't know that."

"Either way, how would I handle their relationship?"

"It may be he'll have to leave again," Andret stated.

"I'd rather he stays. And when Sir Richard sends word," he said, stabbing the air for emphasis, "I hope and pray it names Tristan as her husband!"

"Even if he's not the best option for her?"

"I see him as the only good option," he insisted, then took up his belt and brushed past him.

Velena's first view of Tristan that morning was of him leaning against the wall opposite her solar door. She wasn't as surprised to find him waiting as she was happy to see him, still giddy over the newness of having him home.

Grinning, he pushed off the wall and came near.

"I knew you'd be here," she said.

"I knew you'd know—so I came."

Laughing, she closed the door behind her before starting for the stairs.

He looked behind them. "Where's Daisy?"

"Asleep."

"She no longer attends you?"

She gave him a look. "Does my appearance strike you as being un-attended?"

"No. But letting her go back to bed?" Tristan *tsked*. "You've gone soft."

"Growing a life is hard work."

"Still, I wouldn't think—"

"Then don't, as you know nothing about it."

He laughed. "Neither do you," he said descending the stairs.

"I know it's the way of things."

"Sooo…what will you do?"

"I'm still thinking about it. In the meanwhile, I'm perfectly capable of going about my business unattended…especially now that you're here." It was a coy glance she gave him, anticipating his reaction.

"Oh, I see. I'm to be your newly-awaiting gentlewoman, am I?"

Velena laughed. "You might just pass as such if you don't cut your hair."

He pulled his bangs down to his bottom lip. "It is getting a bit unruly, isn't it?"

"More than a bit."

"Well, you know where the shears are."

"That I do." Silence followed her response as the memory of Tristan chasing her about the house in an attempt to rid her of her own unruly locks tickled their recollections, along with their smiles. Locking eyes, they laughed. It bubbled up, not merely from their throats, but from familiar wells dug three years deep. It echoed through the corridor, sounded off the walls, until without warning it changed.

Turning aside, Tristan coughed. And more than a mere clearing of the throat, it persisted to a terrible racking of his body that, once it took hold of him, refused to let go.

By the time it was over, Velena stood wide-eyed and straight-faced, alerted to the danger of such a sound. "How long have you been like this?"

"It's fine."

Her eyes softened. "How long?"

"It started a couple of days after I arrived home."

"Why didn't you say anything?"

"It's nothing."

"It's something," she stated flatly.

"I'll heal—same as you."

"Me?"

"Yes, you. More than one person has told me you were hurt, and none of them were you. Let's talk about that."

She brushed it off, continuing their course to the chapel. "It was an accident—over and done with before you arrived."

"No pain?"

"Less every day."

"What was done for it?"

"The healer came but offered little beyond affirming what Makaias had already guessed." They stopped at the threshold.

"His guess?"

She peeked into the room. There were no less than ten knights present, all having come for morning prayers. She lowered her voice to a whisper. "A cracked rib. I've been wearing bindings." She laid a hand across her middle. "But not for much longer."

Entering, they shared a back pew. "It's not the worst she could have prescribed," he whispered back.

Threading her fingers, she began to shift in her seat. "Not the healer."

"Sir Makaias?"

"It was he who first assessed me. Now, shh," she reminded, acutely aware that the man they now spoke of had just entered the room.

"As in touched you?" he asked. Was it his imagination or did her color begin to deepen?

"Shhh." She poked him in the leg this time, grateful Makaias had taken a pew at the front. "Do you no longer pray?"

With effort he faced forward and closed his eyes, allowing the silence to settle but not to last. "I think he may be enamored of you," he whispered at her ear.

Startled, she suppressed a laugh that turned into a snort, gaining the attention of more than a few curious heads. Thankfully, none of them were Makaias'. She cleared her throat as if that was the intended purpose for such a sound and stood up, leading Tristan from the room.

He expected her to stop once they'd reached the foyer, but she slowed only for him to open the front doors, exposing him once again to the brightness of day.

Again, he trailed behind. The mist was gone, but it was still chilly, and he found the crunching of gravel beneath their feet an unwanted jolt back to reality. Warming his hands together, he chastised himself for his lack of timing, even as the grating of stones beneath Velena's heel signaled her about-face and the beginning of another awkward conversation.

She began by clasping her hands behind her, followed by an acute stare. "What made you say that?"

A reasonable question. "You talk of him more than before I left."

"Because I know him better now than I did before."

"So too, he's come to know you."

"As a friend."

"It would be a true statement to say it would greatly honor him to hear it, but you ought to be more careful about who you make friends with from now on."

Velena came forward, ensuring their conversation remained between them. "Are *you*, of all people, now trying to tell me who I can be friends with?"

"I care not who you take into your circle so long as their intentions are honorable."

"He is nothing but."

"But you are to be married very soon. And with as many complications as our friendship has gained us, I would not see you add another to your present situation. At least, not until you know who the man is to be. Would you tempt his jealousy as we did Stuart's?"

She looked down.

"I'm merely concerned is all. I had a conversation with Sir Makaias this morning, and call it a feeling, but I thought perhaps he'd grown overly fond of your time together. Would this not be a complication if his feelings tempted you to return them, prematurely."

"Prematurely?"

"I know your father has someone very specific in mind." He took a deep breath. "And if the King is unreceptive to him, a second man."

She blinked.

"He's doing everything he can to ensure you're not given to some abusive old graybeard with a mistress and ten bastards."

"Tristan."

"He is," he insisted. "I can jest, but the danger is real, and until you know who your husband is to be, you should refrain from engaging any further in the company of other men."

Her hands rested on her hips. "Yourself included?"

"If need be. I'll not put you in the same position I did last time."

Her arms dropped. "You just got back. What happened to taking me *furthermore?*"

Looking down, he scuffed his shoe across the rocks. "I may yet." Bringing his head up, he gave her a silly grin.

She returned it. "I understand you but, please, don't pull away before you have to."

"Alright," he promised. "And who knows? Perhaps you'll be married to Sir Makaias, and then all would be well."

She did nothing to hide her surprise. "My father means to look for a man of position. It'll not be him."

Tristan nodded. "Just another reason not to allow any feelings he might have for you divert your attention."

Velena looked away with naught but a fleeting smile as she reflected on her brother's past words in the wake of her budding attraction towards his friend—as misplaced as it was. *Not even Makaias wants you.* Even now the words stung, needling at her pride. "I would only be so fortunate as to have gained the attention of such an honorable man, but believe me when I say, the feeling is *not* mutual. More than once I've fallen beneath his scrutiny, though I can't imagine what he holds against me."

"What has he done to make you think so?"

"Nothing I can name," she said, a wry expression touching her eyes. "Call it a feeling."

Triston nodded, now curious. Certainly, the knight hadn't said anything to confirm her assumptions, though perhaps, this was, in fact, what he'd sensed during the moments in which Makaias had searched for words. *Aw. There it was.* He'd misinterpreted the man's inner criticisms, kindly left unspoken, for hidden attraction.

"I'm sorry to hear it," he said, compassion on his face. "He must be an idiot then. And I'm sorry if he's hurt you."

"No." She linked her hands behind her back and rocked on her heels. "Not really. I have no true feelings for him."

"But attraction?"

She opened her mouth but could not deny it.

"You talk about him more than you used to."

"Pff." She released a puff of air. "I merely share with you of my experiences during your absence."

"Yes, but you tend to get a certain...look on your face whenever you do."

"I do not."

His grin lengthened. "You do."

"What kind of face?"

"The funny kind."

She squinted her eyes. "Funny as yours?"

He squinted back. "Funnier."

"Stop it," she said, giving his shoulder a small shove. "You're making it up."

He smiled. "Am I?"

She rolled her eyes. "If I have, I've never meant to. And anyway, attraction is nothing."

"See. This was my worry. As a man of honor, he should have kept his distance."

"He's done nothing to entice me," she insisted, even as an image of his bare chest came to mind, her fingers probing for unconformities above his skin at the insistence of his mother. "Not on purpose," she added, now picturing his very deliberate show of masculine prowess upon taking his leave. *Maybe a little on purpose.*

Unsettled, she laughed. "Anyway, silly faces or no, set your mind at ease as there exists no love between us that should alter my father's plans. I appreciate you protecting me, but you know I'd never allow myself to be so affected."

He chuckled, not at all blind to her struggle. "Maybe a little affected."

"Doesn't matter," she said, sobering. "You of all people should know I'm still submitted to my father's choice."

"You mean King Edward's choice."

"Either way, it's the Lord's choice, yes?"

He nodded.

"He brought to light Stuart's sin, and I've not forgotten to thank Him for removing me from it. So, in this new situation as in before, I *will* trust Him." She took a deep breath, eyes drifting off towards Totnes Castle. "And be content, though admittedly, it's something easier for me to say today than perhaps tomorrow."

He smiled in understanding. "Tomorrow has its own concerns," he reminded her. "Don't rush them."

"Tomorrow," she mused. "Oh! I almost forgot! Tomorrow is Sunday. We'll not attend church, lest we run into Uncle Magnus and Stuart. Britton thinks this best. But it shall not dampen our spirits, for every Sunday Rainydayas and Gwenhavare come to see me. I didn't think to ask before, but perhaps I should. Will you be uncomfortable sitting amongst three ladies?" she teased.

His insides buzzed. "Only the one," he said, trusting she'd assume him to mean herself, which she must have by the sound of her laughter.

"I promise I'll not embarrass you," she said, though with less conviction then would make any man comfortable, "at least, not so long as I'm allowed to do so today."

He raised a suspicious brow.

"I've had a thought."

"Dare I ask?"

"I think you'll like it." She was growing giddier by the moment.

"No promises."

Grinning, she tucked her fists beneath her chin, dually dreading and anticipating his response. "If you could ever allow yourself to love again…someone other than your Iseult—"

"Never was she mine," he pointed out.

221

She held up her hands. "Either way, if you ever *could*…" Pausing, she gaged his reaction. "I would say that you'd make a very good match for…" She rose up on her toes. "Gwenhavare," she spit out, hands masking her smile, should he be unreceptive.

Stunned, he attempted to keep a straight face, though attempting was the most he could manage. Staring, she stared back, ignorant of what he assumed she didn't know and still waiting for his response. When he took too long to make one, it was a look of mischief that made its mark upon her lips.

"I see your surprise, but all you need do is trust me," she assured, placing a finger to her temple. "I've marked her for you in my mind, and now all that needs doing is for me to plant you in hers."

"No," he nearly blurted, then softer the second time. "No. I'd really…rather you not."

Her smile faltered. "But she's wonderful. She was your sister's friend and marrying her would make you the husband of mine. And as it isn't untoward for me to see her, we'd be able to see each other as well, allowing no cause for jealousy. It'd be me with my husband and you with your wife. It's the perfect arrangement," she reasoned.

"Awww," he said, massaging his fingers along his scalp, wanting to name folly for what it was but unable to think how to do so without ruining the friendship Velena had made with their Iseult, not knowing it was her.

"But it's not just for our sake, I suggest it," she added before he could say more. "I truly see something in her I think you'd come to love. I can't explain it, but she was a familiar soul from the start. I don't know how she compares to your ideal but—"

"Even if she were…my ideal," he interrupted, a touch of sadness burying itself beneath the truth of his words, "such plans would have to wait."

"For what?"

"For your father's letter," he explained, employing as much candor as necessary in order to put this idea to rest.

"What should that have to do with it?"

He exhaled "Let's just say, I'd like to have one uncertainty answered before involving myself in another." Seeing her confusion, he added, "I want to keep my focus in one place at a time, and right now, that's on your well-being. Now, come on." He managed a weak smile. "Back to our prayers, then I'll let you cut my hair."

Nodding, Velena walked beside him. "But then yours," she persisted.

"My what?"

"Your well-being. You've been selfless, and I would see you happily settled."

"Thank you, Velena. I mean that."

She gave him a sidelong glance, her voice taking on a lighter tone of timidity. "You'll let me know when you're ready to speak of it again?"

He smiled, looking straight ahead. "You'll be the first to know."

26

unrest

"What on earth!" Britton exclaimed, startled from his sleep.

Makaias had entered his solar, flinging open his bedchamber door without so much as a knock. "Lazy..." he refrained from cursing. "What are you still doing in bed?" he accused, voice full of reproach.

"Sleeping. What are you doing up?"

"It's morning," he stated, yanking the blankets from Britton's body and flinging them across the room.

"What the h—"

"I have had time both to strengthen my body and pour out my soul—"

"Good for you—"

"Now, I would give you a piece of my mind, but still you sleep."

Shoving him back, Britton sat up, rubbing a hand over his face and hair. "Not anymore, so go ahead and give it."

Grappling for words, Makaias collapsed into a chair, too frustrated to speak once he was asked to.

Britton stared through weighted lids, having taken a sleeping draught the night before. "What's wrong, Kai? Clearly, somethings bothering you."

"I know about Tristan."

"What about him?"

"That he asked for your sister's hand."

Standing to his feet, Britton approached a towel and bowl of water. Splashing water over his face. "Who told you that?"

"Doesn't matter."

"I suppose not," he admitted, drying himself off.

"What does matter is that my mother went to your father, making the same request on my behalf. Only it wasn't truly on my behalf," he stated, voice beginning to shake, "else I'd have known about it before hand. Which, if I had, I would have spoken my mind—which again—I assume is why she kept that bit of information from me in the first place, unable as you all are to accept I'm not ready to be saddled with such a problem."

Throwing down his towel, Britton crossed back to the bed. "Velena is not a *problem.*"

"Not in the most general of terms, I agree. But if it were asked of me to wed her, a problem she would be...for sure and for certain. Tristan ought to be your father's first choice—not me. But according to Andret, that's not how it is. According to him, Tristan's name isn't to be spoken unless King Edward finds me unsuitable. Is this true?"

"Kai—"

"Is it true?" he repeated.

Britton's eyes never wavered. "Yes."

Makaias stood, the pain of betrayal thick in his voice. "And you didn't tell me?"

"Because I knew exactly how you'd take it, and it was by no means for certain, which is why no one was supposed to know. Not Velena. Not Tristan. And, no, not even you. But it was my father who wanted it that way. To him, Velena is a gift, and one he thinks you will cherish, thus he held his tongue, not wanting to disappoint you if he couldn't deliver. If he only knew how you really feel about her."

Rubbing a hand down his tunic, Makaias nodded, regretting his many words on the subject but unable to take them back. "I don't mean to offend you."

"Well, you do—and Velena doesn't deserve to be the reason for it. She's as good a woman as any you'd ever hope to find on your own, and the pickings have grown rather slim. Or haven't you noticed?"

Makaias returned to his seat, shoulders slumped in defeat. "Still, she ought to marry Tristan. It makes more sense in every way. If they wed, their friendship stands. If they don't, who do you think will bear the gossip for having a wife enamored of another man?"

"You're letting Joanna be the ruin of you. Not every woman strays, Makaias. Gossip is only gossip. Not truth. She doesn't love him."

"Nor does she love me." Lowering his voice, he pressed his forearms to his knees. "Even if one such as your sister intends to give herself most faithfully to a husband, if there is no love in it, even the best of intentions can fail."

"How many marriages begin with love?" Britton argued.

"Doesn't matter. Without *love*, I wouldn't risk it. Not with her..."

Saddened by his answer, Britton finally nodded. "I always thought you'd be the best man for her...and still do." He swallowed. "But...I'll not argue with your conscience. I should have listened before," he confessed. "I should have spoken on your behalf and told my father of your true feelings. Forgive me."

Makaias released his breath, grateful yet fully aware that it did nothing to change his present situation.

"I know what you're thinking," Britton said, "but remember what I said. Nothing's for certain. Be patient, and everything may yet fall where you'd have it to."

With nothing left to say, Makaias stood to leave.

"Go talk with your mother," Britton added, grabbing a tunic to shrug into.

"What purpose?"

Britton approached him, earnest that he should listen. "You weren't spared from the Plague for enmity's sake. Make your peace with her and try not to stew about what you can't control."

"Easy for you to say."

"Not so. We're both in the same boat—or don't you remember?" Chuckling, Britton sent him out of the room with a firm slap to his back.

Three days later, Britton sat hunched over his father's desk where he looked up at Makaias and frowned. "Who on earth is Lady Ann?" he exclaimed, rereading the name for the fourth time. What had begun as a moment of anticipation turned quickly to one of dread as the reality of his situation began to wash over him.

"Is she in Totnes?" Makaias asked, mentally going through the list of *Ann's* she could be.

He looked again at his father's letter. "No. Exeter." He breathed deep. "I'm to join Father immediately so as to gain the approval of her family and sign documents."

"And?"

"And...now I know why you wished to stay unmarried. This is nerve-racking. I've not been this terrified since the Plague."

"Death and women." Makaias chuckled. "Two things we can't seem to escape."

Britton nodded, still in a daze.

Makaias squirmed in his seat. Doing as Britton suggested, he'd gone to his mother for what turned out to be one of the most humbling lectures of his life. Upset, his greatest hope had been in keeping a civil tongue. He'd no idea, she'd be waiting with words of her own, having prayed ahead of time for the strength to admonish, chastise, and even reprove him should he succumb to a lack of faith or fail to submit to her leading, never mind his duty.

What surprised him even more was that she addressed him in the selfsame loving and gentle way in which she addressed all things, yet with a firm and unyielding spirit he'd rarely seen. She'd been on her knees for him—and by Heaven, if he wasn't scalded by the realization of not having done the same. He'd not prayed for the strength to receive the Lord's will for his life. Not once. He'd only prayed to escape it. Riding home that night, he was changed, not his opinions of marriage, but in his willingness to submit to it. If loving God was to obey Him, then he would accept the will of the King.

Clearing his throat, he gained Britton's attention. "Alright, you've had your scare—now what of mine? Tell me quickly. I'm about ready to crawl out of my skin."

"Right." Britton scanned down the first of two pages. "You've got your land," he said brightly.

Makaias moistened his lips. He was glad, but rejoicing could wait.

"And a title," he said next, looking up in amazement.

"What?"

"He granted us titles—you and I." He read it again, truly astonished. "We're barons."

Makaias leaned forward. "Be serious."

"I swear to you," he said, laughing. "Makaias Mannering—Baron. Try that on for size."

"Baron Mannering," he murmured, enjoying the sound until a sudden bout of anxiety overtook him.

"Now, tell me if that doesn't make you happy," Britton exclaimed.

"I'll be happy if you tell me there's no mention of a wife."

"There's no mention of a wife," Britton stated before snickering. "On this page."

Makaias groaned.

"But on this page..."

He closed his eyes. "Just read on and get it over with."

Britton looked up. "You feel the same?"

Makaias readied himself, jaw muscles tensed. "I do. Though I'm willing to accept whatever outcome it be."

Filling his lungs, Britton's eyes roved back and forth across the page, lips parting with each word as he read silently. Breathing out, he looked up.

"Tell me it's Tristan," Makaias said, less a demand than a plea.

Conflicted, Britton smiled, answer coming in stilted reply. "It's Tristan."

The flood of relief Makaias felt upon hearing those words couldn't be exaggerated. Closing his eyes, his chest gave a great heave as if the world had just been removed from his shoulders. It was only a moment before he came back to himself, and realized the uncomfortable wedge now come between them. "Britton, I'm sorry. I know you..."

"No." He stopped him. "Don't apologize. It's over. Everything as it should be."

Confident that was true, Makaias still feared to ask the next question. "Still, you've yet to tell me who *is* to be my wife? Or have I not been granted one?"

Britton smirked. "You'd be happy for that little oversight, wouldn't you?"

"I'd being lying to say no."

Giving one last look to his father's words, Britton opened the desk drawer, committing them to lock and key. "It's still being negotiated."

He took a deep breath, realizing he'd be living in the shadow of anxious uncertainty for days yet. "When will you leave?"

"Tomorrow."

"So soon?"

Britton gave a wry grin. "Better to get these things over and done with. I expect you know the feeling."

The moment was charged, filling the gap between them. "Are we...alright?"

"Absolutely. Everything as it should be."

"You said that."

"You want me to say something else?"

"No," Makaias said, coming to his feet. "I'll be in the practice yard should you need me."

"I'll miss watching you in the tournament," Britton confessed before his friend could exit the room.

He turned back, grateful for the sentiment. "Cheer me on from Exeter."

"You know I will," he promised, the corners of his mouth lifting before turning the conversation back to business. "Just so you're aware, Sir Tarek will be in charge in my absence. Regretfully, there's no time to give Rowan a proper knighting ceremony before the tourney with father gone and myself leaving tomorrow, but he can do the job. But I'll let Velena know and maybe she can throw something together for him."

"I've no doubt of it."

"Makaias." Standing, Britton tapped his fingers on the desk, concern etching grooves into his brow. "For Rowan's first order of duty, I'll be giving him charge over Velena's well-being here at the manor. But with Stuart being so upset...and unpredictable, as he's shown himself to be, I'd like it if you'd take charge of her security as a whole. Accompany her outside the manor as much as you're able and assign someone to keep an eye on Stuart's whereabouts. It concerns me what he might do in my father's absence...and now mine. Will you do this for me?"

"Without fail."

"Thank you." His tension seemed to ease. "Also, if you see Tristan, please send him here."

"You're going to tell him?"

"Not definitively. I think it best to let my father do that, but still I would prepare him for the likelihood."

"I'm sure he'll rejoice at the news."

"More than you would have, eh?"

Unable to contradict him, Makaias took his leave. He exited the back door through the kitchen and set off immediately in search of Andret. Despite the imminent possibility of his eventually having to marry *someone*, there was still much to be grateful for, and this, more than anything else, brought a smile to his face as excitement over land and title flooded through him.

27

point of confusion

A small crowd of people formed at the front of Landerhill's main gate. It was a mix of servants and friends—all of them gathered to see their lord's son safely off for the two-day journey that would take him from Totness to the home of his future bride where his father was currently awaiting his arrival. Sir Andret was to accompany him, along with two other squires disappointed to be missing out on the upcoming tournament.

Leaving Daisy beside Rowan and Tristan, Velena approached her brother for one last embrace, asking, "Are you nervous?"

Britton's horse hoofed at the ground beside him, tossing up gravel and bobbing its head up and down as if affirming his answer. He smiled. "Terrified."

She gave him an understanding look. "Can you tell me nothing of the king's answer for *me*?"

Britton grabbed hold of her hands. "If I could tell you with any sort of certainty, I would. Unfortunately, it's still being negotiated," he said, feeling rather sick about the whole thing. He knew Velena could be happy with Tristan, but still it didn't feel right—even more so today than yesterday.

Her breath was shaky.

"Be patient," he beseeched, kissing her cheek. "It will all be sorted out soon."

Nodding, she produced a compliant smile.

"Come now…let's have a real one," Britton teased. "If anyone's going to be nervous, let it first be me."

She laughed lightly. "Tell me most how you want me to pray, and I'll do it."

"Pray she isn't put off by a man with a limp."

He chuckled, but she refused to make light of what she knew he feared in earnest. "You," she stated, poking a finger to his chest, "are a wonderful man. And you'll make a wonderful husband—and protector." Leaning forward, she whispered, "Leg be damned, she'll love you."

"Such language," Makaias said, coming up behind her.

Self-conscious, she faced him. "You weren't meant to hear."

He pulled his lips to the side. "Would it have made it okay if I hadn't?"

"You know, you needn't play the role of my elder brother until he's actually gone."

"Thaaat's enough," Britton said, smiling as he reached around to squeeze her shoulders. "He's teasing you. Now, kiss me farewell. I'm delayed enough as it is."

"God be with you, Brother." She rose on her toes to do as bid. "Come home to us soon."

Assuring her he would, he turned to Makaias, feeling a prick of guilt he wished would go away. "Walk with me," he heard himself say, leading his horse by the reins, instead of mounting with the rest of his party, who he signaled to go ahead.

"You know…" Britton began, "I never did finish telling you about that land you received."

"Something wrong with it?"

"Well, it's got some squatters. Plague killed the lord and his wife, and I think the villein in charge of planting took over when none of the lord's relatives came back to claim it. You'll have to clear them out."

Makaias nodded, showing no more emotion than if he'd just been told it had rained yesterday and would rain again today. "Alright."

"Might help if you read my father's letter for yourself," Britton continued, "to know the boundaries of the land and what not."

"Where is it?"

"In the desk. Velena can get you the key."

He nodded again.

"And Kai…"

"Yes?"

"Um…well…it can be a bit confusing, so if while you're reading you have any questions…or concerns about it, just…" Agitated, Britton stopped and mounted his horse. "I don't see as how we have to cover that much ground today," he said, "so you can always catch up if you have to."

"Catch up?" Perplexed, Makaias chuckled. "Is it that confusing?"

Britton scratched at his temple. "The interpretation of it *is* a bit fuzzy. But, um…if I don't see you again today, I'll assume you understand everything as it is…and are…happy with it."

Now laughing, Makaias swatted his friend's horse. "Get out of here, Brit. You're talking nonsense."

"I'm just trying to help you understand how it is."

"I've got it handled. Now go. And Godspeed, my friend." Still laughing, Makaias watched as Britton broke his horse into a canter to catch up with the others. Shaking his head, he turned around.

His first instinct was to speak with Velena about the key he'd need to unlock the desk, but both she and Daisy seemed to have disappeared with the rest of the dwindling crowd. Tristan and Rowan remained—either one being a good source of information when it came to Velena and her whereabouts—but they appeared to be deep in conversation.

No matter. She couldn't be that hard to find.

Peeking his head through the open door of the library, Makaias located Velena just in time to hear her loud complaint.

"Ugh! What a waste," she grumbled.

"What's wrong?"

She looked up from a small writing desk in the corner. "Just clumsy. I knocked over the ink." As if to prove it, she held up four black-tipped fingers. "I need to clean this up," she said scooting back her chair.

"Shall I fetch Daisy for you?"

"I can clean up my own messes," she responded pertly.

His eyes crinkled at the corners. "You already have her doing something, don't you?"

"And if I do?" she asked, sashaying past him into the hall.

Smiling, he took up a pace beside her, her destination the kitchen and something with which to clean up the spill.

"Actually," she began, becoming a bit more serious, "Daisy no longer answers to me."

"What do you mean?"

Velena stopped to face him, taking care that her voice didn't carry. "Under the present circumstances, I'd sooner have her my equal than my lesser. If her situation was wrought of poor judgment, perhaps I'd think differently, but as it is…it doesn't seem proper to have her fetching candle sticks and…and emptying my chamber pot. Her dignity was taken from her, but I would give it back. She is to be a mother after all."

Makaias grinned. "Why Velena Ambrose, I'm most impressed."

"You needn't tease me."

"Far from it," he insisted. "What is true religion but to care for widows and orphans in their distress."

Velena blinked, not exactly sure how to accept his compliment. "Well, she is an orphan."

"And she *was* in distress," he said, "until now. And she'll have you to thank for it."

"She has the Lord to thank."

"Indeed. But wonderful He's chosen to work through you."

"It's kind of you to say so."

"I mean it," he said as the moment fell quiet between them…and perceptibly more awkward. He laughed for lack of conversation—as did she. "Who will you choose now?" he asked suddenly. "For a maidservant, I mean."

"Actually, that's where my little mishap comes in. I was attempting to write to Sir Rolland at Wineford Castle and ask if the smithy would allow his daughter to come attend me. She ought to be almost twelve now, and I feel she'll be quite capable."

"Is there no one in Totnes to do the job?"

"No one in Totnes who has such a liking for Daisy already in place. You see, at Wineford, she—Kat is the girl's name—and her brother, Jonas, were much taken with Daisy, and eventually, it's Daisy I want Kat to attend. I don't think anyone in Totnes will be as loyal to her as she'll be—nor as sympathetic when gossip begins to circulate. And Daisy will need someone she can trust—especially when it comes time to care for the babe."

"Which again leaves you without a maid for yourself."

Velena shrugged. "I'm not so demanding that I can't go without."

Makaias gave her a rueful look.

"Alright!" She laughed. "Kat may very well find she'll have her hands full between the two of us, but it won't be for long, Lord willing. I plan to choose a relative from my…husband's family." She nearly tripped over the words, still finding it an unnatural subject. "I'm hopeful this will gain me some semblance of approval in their sight."

Makaias had to work to hold back his smile. It seemed a pleasant sort of secret, knowing that she needn't worry anymore—that she would soon be marrying her dearest friend. "You'll be fine, Velena. You'll marry a good man; I know it."

Velena's shoulders rose only slightly. "I appreciate the sentiment, but I'd rather not speak in absolutes when it comes to husbands. Having been engaged twice already—and both times, quite unsuccessfully—I feel it best to lower my expectations."

Makaias chuckled. "A practice I employ myself from time to time. But in all honesty, I have a feeling you won't have to."

"From your mouth to God's ears. Now, if you'll excuse me," she said with a small curtsy, "I have a mess to attend."

"Allow me to help. How about I replace the paper while you fetch soap and water?" he asked, fairly certain the stain would be permanent.

Trading him places, she began to back down the hall. "Thank you for offering, but I wouldn't keep you from completing whatever task happened to bring you indoors and away from your precious exercises."

"Actually, I have business in your father's cabinet but was in need of the key to his desk. Besides, better not to have your first day without a maid be overly burdensome. If you can humble yourself, so can I."

Velena giggled. "How spoilt we are. The parchment is in the center drawer—and the key beneath the bust on the bookcase."

Grinning, Makaias turned away into Sir Richard's cabinet. When he had the key in hand, he settled himself behind the desk and set to work gathering what he needed. Unsure how many pieces of parchment Velena needed, he separated out three sheets to be on the safe side and retrieved Sir Richard's letter, found tucked just beneath the stack. Perfect.

Everything back in order, he arrived in the library before she did. And as it was as comfortable a place to sit and read a letter as any, he settled into a chair, intending to begin without delay. Yet, he found himself staring at the seal, unable to open it. His entire future was laid out in ink before him, and he could almost feel the weight of responsibility in his hand. It said he had land in Devonshire, but he knew not where. It said he would soon have a wife, but he knew not whom.

"Whhhh…" He let go a deep breath to steady his nerves and began reading until he found the place that concerned him. *I hereby bequeath Sir Makaias Mannering the title of Baron…*

Makaias stopped to run a thumb over the carefully scripted word. *Baron* certainly had a fine ring to it. Smiling, he read on. *And do grant him residence and land in Devonshire, which borders are as follows...* Here it was. His eyes brightened. He knew this land. This was good land—better than good—and quite extensive. And if memory served, it also included a small parish. Reading over the information twice, he began to wonder what Britton might have been talking about. Sir Richard's details of the demesne were brief...but thorough—and not at all *complicated.* Sliding the top page aside, he scanned the next, rubbing a hand across his stubble in confusion. He was just about to close it up when all brightness faded from his eyes. He blinked and read it again, his mouth going dry.

Furthermore, it is the express wish of the King...

"Makaias?" Velena's voice startled him to his feet as she entered the room without warning. "I didn't expect you'd still be here. I hope you haven't been waiting on my account. They're making the most delicious strawberry jam in the kitchen, and I may or may not have gotten the teensiest bit distracted sampling it."

She was all smiles until she noticed the cold look of shock still set upon his face. "What's wrong?" she asked, growing concerned.

"Uh...um...." His brain was having to work far too hard to interpret the sounds coming past her lips. And with the blood thrumming so loudly in his ears, it was no wonder he couldn't. "I have...I have to go. Excuse me." He stalked past her open look of confusion, bent on a quick escape until her voice compelled him to do an about face shy of breaching the door.

"Is that my father's letter?"

Nodding, Makaias looked down at the two sheets of parchment still in his hand, Sir Richard's seal exposed on one edge.

A clear line of worry creased her brow, and she immediately came forward, hand extended. "If something's the matter, I want to know."

"No!"

Affronted, she drew back in surprise. "If that's his letter, I most certainly have a right to see it."

Shaking his head, he made a greater effort to smile. "Forgive me. I only meant..." He took a breath, fighting for words. "Of course, you have a right to see it. But I beg your indulgence in this as it's something that pertains to me."

Her shoulders relaxed, though her concern remained. "I pray nothing is amiss."

Chin down, his eyes flickered upward to meet her.

"There is something wrong."

"There's a point of...*confusion* I need to clear up."

"That's all?"

"That's all," he echoed, ignoring her pointed question. "It's just something unexpected. I didn't mean to frighten you."

"Aw," she said, a faint smile reappearing on her face. "News of your wife, perhaps? Disconcerting is it not?"

He puffed up a laugh.

"Well...can you name her or is she to be a secret?"

"Apparently the latter," he said, stuffing the letter deep within his jerkin, eyes trailing the length of her without forethought.

Disconcerted, she hugged her arms across her waist. "It sounds as if you disapprove of the woman."

"Forgive me if I've given that impression. Like you, it appears my future is still in negotiations."

"Maybe so, but you can't fool me, Makaias. Whoever this woman is, it's unsettled you as I've never seen you before." Her eyes softened. "Rest assured; you'll continue in my prayers."

Lifting a hand, he palmed the cool, metaled knob that began the hilt of his dagger as if grasping for something old and familiar whilst wrestling the new. "You've been praying for me?"

"After you shared with me about...Joanna," she confessed, "I've prayed the Lord would help you forgive her...and grant you someone with whom you can one day be at peace with."

Struck with the knowledge of such a kind and genuine act, he nearly turned away at his own selfishness. Filled with remorse, his countenance fell and with it a layer of resistance to this new course of his life. "Velena I..." He meant to express his gratitude but was unable to puzzle together his thoughts well-enough to deliver. Thus, he gave greater thanks for the sound of footsteps coming from behind him.

"Here you are," Tristan said, inching past him into the room.

Makaias watched as she brightened.

Tristan glanced between woman and knight, "I hope I'm not interrupting, but there's something I, uh... I need to talk with you about. Are you...occupied?"

Raising her shoulders, she looked around. "Well, I was planning to be, but I can put it off. Except for this mess, which is now decidedly a disaster. But!" She flung her hands to her sides. "Help me *pretend* to clean it up, and we can sit and talk about whatever you'd like."

"How about I *actually* help you clean it up, and then we take a stroll to the orchards?"

Her smile doubled. "Even better."

Makaias cleared his throat as carefully suppressed emotions rose to create a distinct distaste in his mouth. "If you'll excuse me then," he said, eyes averted, lest they betray the true depth of his conflict, "I have something to attend to."

"Makaias?"

He paused, reluctant as she eyed the spot on his jerkin where the letter rested safely beneath.

Stepping toward him she said, "I'll be praying that your...*point of confusion* turns out not to be so bleak as you're expecting."

Pressing his lips together into a tight smile, he left.

28

furthermore

Having made the final judgement to remedy the ink stain with a well-placed vase, Tristan now ambled alongside Velena for the orchards, thankful for their moment of privacy. Lord knew they'd need it if he was to tell her what he'd come to say. But content for the moment, he dropped back a step, considering the scene before him.

Headrail aflutter, sashay back in place, Velena made a pretty picture as they came upon the first row of trees, thick with green leaves and mature red apples. *So we won't be parted after all,* he thought, quickening his step as she turned to look at him.

Finding Gwenhavare alive had been a shock. Learning she'd never loved him—along with his now having to see her in Totnes as Velena's friend—seemed both an unfairness and a chore. Yet, he would not complain. Every step away from the fantasy that was Iseult was a step towards Velena—a step both necessary and good. And what was fantasy anyway but a work of fiction? And with that in mind, who was Iseult but a character in Velena's book? Never was she real.

His dear friend was his future now—and why shouldn't she be? Their friendship was both a Godsend and a joy, so there wasn't any reason to believe their union would be any less bright. This in mind, he smiled at all the twists and turns that had brought them to this point. Much had changed, as Makaias had said, and was still about to.

"Didn't you say you had something you wanted to talk about?" Velena asked, plucking a ripe apple from a branch Tristan pulled down for her to reach.

"As a matter of fact, I do."

Rubbing at the fruit with her hands, she raised it to her lips. "Good or bad?"

"You'll have to tell me."

She paused. "You're not leaving again, are you?"

"No, no…I'm not going anywhere."

Taking a modest bite, she smiled. "Then if not that, it must be something good, for I submit all else is good by comparison."

His finger twitched. "That depends on what you do after I tell you."

"Then get on with it," she said, taking another bite, "or must I beg?"

"I'll tell you, but I need your full attention."

Interest wholly piqued, she relinquished the apple to her pocket. "You have it."

Satisfied, he opened his mouth. Nothing came out.

"Are you alright?" she asked, growing more concerned over the sudden changes of mood taking hold of the men in the manor.

"Perhaps not," he mumbled, grabbing at his hair. "I may need another minute."

"I thought you had *good* news. Yet your delay brings a worrisome amount of clouds with it."

"I never said it was good or bad," he corrected.

"Then while you decide, shall I see what shapes I can make of them?" she asked, then flopped down upon the grass.

He lowered himself to join her, his movements stiff and awkward as he rubbed his hands together, finding it harder than he thought to tell her. Actually, it was exactly as hard as he thought. Either way, he'd have to get on with it. "If you were…stranded on a deserted island and could have only one person with you…who would it be?"

"A shipwright," she answered without hesitation.

"Well—alright then," he said, protruding his lower lip. "I hadn't thought of that as an answer, but a good one it is."

Smiling, she picked some grass and tossed it at him. He tossed some back and for a moment they said nothing more.

"Let me present you with some different options," he tried again. "Friend or family?"

"Friend or family what?"

"On the island."

Velena cocked her head. "Oh…are we still talking about this?"

"We are."

"And this is…what you *wanted* to talk about?"

"I'm getting to it."

Rolling her eyes, she took a deep breath, exhaling loudly through her nose before propping back upon her arms. "Then friend," she answered, voice confident.

"Man or woman?"

"Tristan."

"What?"

She giggled. "Tristan—as in *you*. That's my answer."

"Me?"

"Of course. I can imagine life on a deserted island to be a tad boring."

"Just a little."

"And I am happiest when I'm with you."

"Naturally," he said, mouth playfully ticking up at the corners.

"Sooo...I can only assume we'd both entertain each other and drive each other mad in just the right proportions as to make our lives both tolerable and pleasant."

His grin was now firmly in place. "I'm flattered you can imagine spending the rest of your life with me."

Velena giggled. "Is that what I just said?"

"Decidedly."

Her eyes narrowed. "So, on this island...is there any hope of rescue?"

"No."

"None at all?"

"Marooned until one of us dies."

"Just one? Now, I'm really confused. If you're not going anywhere, are you trying to tell me that I am?"

"Where would *you* go?"

She quirked a smile. "An island, perhaps."

He laughed. "No. No one is sending you away."

"Then why, pray tell, are you asking me all these silly questions?"

"Because I still need to tell you something...only I'm finding it too difficult to say. In fact, I could really use your opinion on how to go about it, except it's about you—so I can't."

Her brows went up. "Sounds important."

He groaned. "It really is."

"Alright, then. I'll just have to help you as best I can. Ah-hem." She cleared her throat, rocking side to side on her backside while folding her legs beneath the layers of material. "I'll count to three, and then you'll just say it."

"It's not that easy."

"One," she began, despite his groan of protest.

He pointed a finger. "Promise not to laugh if you don't like what I have to say?"

She shook her head. "Two."

He swallowed. "You're not actually helping me."

Smiling, she waved three fingers in front of his face. "Threeee…"

"Your father sent a letter back to Britton stating your engagement to Stuart is officially ended and very soon you'll be engaged to me," he blurted in a rush of words so fast he could tell she thought she'd heard wrong.

Mouth ajar, she leaned forward. "Say that again."

"Your father's sent word back from—"

"Not that part."

"Your engagement to Stuart is now officially dissolved."

"The other part."

"The king's found you a new husband?"

She slapped her knees in frustration. "*Tristan!*"

"His name *is* Tristan, yes."

"He…as in *you?*"

He gave a tentative smile. "As in me."

Velena stood to her feet. "Are you being serious?"

"Well…more serious than certain, but I had to tell you anyway." He looked up at her. "If only to allow you time to get used to the idea."

"I don't understand. Are you telling me we're engaged or not?"

He exhaled. "When I spoke with your brother, he said it was still being negotiated, but that it was the…most likely outcome."

Velena flung her arms to her sides. "Well, this is just ridiculous."

"Nicely put." He picked up a stick and tossed it aside. "And to think I was worried about you laughing at me."

She huffed. "What humor can you find in ruining other people's lives?"

He stood to face her. "I didn't know that's what I'd be doing?"

"Not you." She blinked in confusion. "The king! He makes decisions for others as if…as if…well, he doesn't even know us."

"He doesn't have to know us."

She shook her head, eyes large and unsettled. "My father must have named you as someone he deemed acceptable, but I can't imagine what he was thinking. He knows we don't—"

"Velena…"

"Oh, Lord," she folded her hands as if in prayer. "Tristan, I'm so, so...so sorry. I'll get you out of this; I promise."

Understanding dawned as he began crumpling some dead leaves with the toe of his shoe, now more touched than offended by the truth of her concern. "It wasn't your father's idea," he said, lifting his head to look her. "It was mine."

"I don't believe that for a—"

"It's true."

"But..." Her voice dropped. "You don't love me."

His smile was weak, the effort looking more lopsided than whole. "Don't I?" he asked but saw he'd only added more confusion than clarity.

"You feel...for *me* what you feel for...Iseult?" she questioned.

"No. I can't...I can't say that. But what I felt for her, it wasn't real, you see. What you dreamed up for me, it only exists in bard songs...and stories of a Tristan who can't act apart from some silly love spell. I suffer no such affliction. When I saw her again, it...well it...it was a jolt back to reality. I know what's real now, and I'm not tied to her as you think I am."

"That doesn't mean you ought to be tied to me. What about our motto? The *I love you except for the marriage part?* We agreed that—"

"I know. I know! We agreed—and I was honest about it then and now. I've not gone about harboring feelings for you I've failed to express. I love you as ever I always have. But when your situation became...precarious, it demanded quick attention." He swallowed. "I knew you were to be given to *someone*—and I couldn't help thinking of what if that someone mistreated you or...or took you far from home so that you were alone? What if he was old?" He attempted a weak smile. "I'm unattached and can take care of you. How could I just stand by and await the outcome when I could do something about it?"

"You do this...for me?"

Nodding, he lips twisted to one side. "Bad idea?"

She looked away but glanced back with a smile. "A ridiculous idea."

"Once again, eloquently put."

"Sorry." She hooked her hand around her opposite elbow, appearing more apologetic than not.

Coughing, he felt the tightness taking hold of his chest, but managed to recover quickly. "Don't be," he said, wiping his hand across his mouth. "It's my fault. The whole thing sounded better in my head. Though I promise you, I did pray about it. I prayed over this a great deal, actually."

"I've no doubt," she stated plainly, turning towards the rustling of leaves from where they hummed softly from the branches. "I've no doubt…" she said again, recognizing the Lord's hand in all things.

Tristan came up beside her, eyeing her profile and waiting for her to speak. "Are you upset with me?" he finally asked.

"No." She twisted her hands behind her back.

Accepting her answer, he followed her line of vision up into the branches. "I suppose you'd rather marry a rich, old man than me."

Bumping him with her shoulder, she huffed. "You know I wouldn't." The breeze dipped down, fluttering her headrail across her face. She held it back. "You've done me a great service, and I can think of few men more noble than you."

Smiling, he didn't have to look at her to know she meant it. Indeed, it seemed good just to stand shoulder to shoulder beneath so beautiful a canopy of trees, silently weighing their own hearts against the unknowns beyond them. "You know, our marrying shouldn't make our lives so much different. We'll all still be together. You and me…and Daisy."

"And the babe?" she questioned.

He nodded. "They'll always have a home with us."

Eyes brightening, her neck swiveled so that she was staring at him. Whether examining the truth of his words or drifting far into thought, he didn't know, but it seemed the kind of look one could pin their hopes on…until she turned away again and laughed.

"Can you imagine it? Us. Married."

Here it comes, he thought, letting go a deep breath. "I'm baring my soul to you, Velena. The least you could do is not laugh."

"Baring your soul…?" Her shoulders shook. "I'm not laughing at your soul. I like your soul a great deal. Furthermore—"

"I don't want your *furthermores*," he interrupted, flopping back down to the grass.

"Well, I want yours," she said, landing in front of him, pulling his attention back to her face. "And I'm not making fun. It'll only take a bit of time to get used to."

He remained skeptical. "Are you saying you're keen to the idea?"

"Ever since the Pestilence and Peter's death—since Stuart and Britton's return home—nothing has ever been so peaceful as when I'm with you." Smiling as his face softened, she continued, "I only wonder if our friendship will be enough to keep the peace between us when times get difficult."

"Times have already been difficult," he reminded her.

"So they have." The breeze circled around them, chilling noses and staining their cheeks pink. "Still…I feel as if I'll be doing you a disservice. Your mother gave you the gift of choice so that you would marry for love. And I never wanted to keep you from that."

Shaking his head, Tristan reached for her hand, allowing himself to do what dreams had not allowed. "It may be that we'll have to walk in faith a while before we find our hearts changed in that regard. But I have hope for it. We have more than most already."

Velena looked down at their hands. How seldom they touched— and how foreign it felt despite so much familiarity between them. On a whim she brought his palm to her cheek, and he froze, silent while she held it there, wondering if she could see something of the future he could not. Then smiling—a little too bravely, he thought—she released it.

"So great is my gratitude," she began, face solemn, "that if you never come to love me more than you do right now, it will be more than I deserve."

"For me as well," he whispered.

Velena stared at her lap, allowing several minutes to pass. "How certain was my brother that we should wed?"

"He said it was 'most likely' and wanted to know if I was still willing. Which could mean…there's still a chance this whole conversation was for naught, I suppose." When she laughed dryly, he asked, "Would you rather I have waited until your father returned and could tell you for sure?"

"No," she added quickly, laughing with more humor this time. "I most definitely would not. This was better."

"I was hoping so."

She smiled. "So…that first day you got back—when you asked me if I wanted you to take me furthermore…?"

His grin was almost shy. "I meant it."

Looking up, she smiled and shook her head. "You're much too full of secrets these days."

He chuckled. "They all come out eventually."

"Well no more," she said, driving her finger into his thigh.

Grabbing it, he hung on until she pulled it away and stood up. "Not even one?"

"You're only saying that because it's me," he said, brushing off his back side as he rose to join her. He picked an apple from a branch above him and took a hardy bite, reminding Velena of the one she still held in her pocket.

She pulled it out as they started back for the manor. "What do you mean *because it's you?*"

He smiled wryly, still chewing. "Tell me you don't allow other people to keep *their* secrets. And in case you want to deny you know what I'm talking about, I'm speaking of you and Makaias."

"That wasn't a secret. I told you what he said."

"Yes, but you didn't make him tell you what he wanted to keep to himself, now did you?"

She glared at him over her next bite of apple. "It was a *sensitive* subject that didn't concern me—"

"How do *you* know?"

"And what I told *you*," she said, pointing a finger, "I told in confidence, knowing you'd keep it to yourself."

"Which I will," he affirmed, taking her outstretched arm through his own in yet another uncharacteristic show of affection.

"Good..." she said, nearly losing her train of thought.

"Good," he repeated, smile off balance.

Taking the same deep breath between them, they walked on, each trying in their own way to see the other in a less apprehensive light— preferably one that didn't bring up a bubble of nervous laughter at every touch. When they came into view of the stables and practice yard, they stopped to wave to Rowan, who was shouldering a load of practice gear for the tourney off the field. Acknowledging them from afar off, his step faltered as he caught sight of them standing arm in arm, so that several of the pages he had in toe, carrying armfuls of their own, nearly collided into him.

"Did you tell Rowan about...us?" Velena asked.

"Yes."

She took a deep breath.

"But he's the only one left here who knows," he assured her.

"Perhaps..." Velena turned to him with apology, "we should keep it that way. In case."

"Agreed," he said without hesitation, releasing her arm as his attention was diverted to the movement of a horse and rider outside the stables. "Is that Sir Makaias?" he asked, just as the knight spurred his horse hard and fast towards the front gate.

Turning to look, Velena felt a small flutter in the pit of her stomach. Planting her hand there to stop it, she released her breath. She might not know what love was, but she certainly knew attraction. Fortunately, she also knew better than to weigh anything by it. Clearing her head with a small shake, she worked to put away the butterflies, having to admit that their unwanted presence was one thing she wouldn't mind keeping a secret.

Pivoting her neck, she locked eyes with Tristan. Handsome in his own right, she knew it was only a matter of time before she felt such things for him. But until then… "I suppose you deserve to have one or two secrets," she said, producing an indulgent slip of a smile. "So long as you keep them for the good of others and don't give hint that you have one. Because we both know I'll not be able to stand it if you do."

"I suppose this comes from wanting a few of your own?" Laughing as she visibly flushed, he guessed right away the reason for her sudden change of mind yet happily possessed no inclination to fault her for it. With Gwenhavare coming immediately to mind, he'd be a hypocrite if he did.

"Tristan, I—"

"So where do you think Sir Makaias was off to so fast?" he asked, not really meaning for her to have to explain herself.

"I don't know…" Eyes drifting in the direction he left by, she again wondered at the name of the woman who was causing him so much turmoil. Thankful for her own newly found peace of mind, she prayed for him then and there.

"Away, away, gone forevermore," he quoted playfully, walking on towards the manor.

Lost in thought but a moment more, she caught up to him, smiling. "Away, away…may he find his *own furthermore*."

Furthermore. Desperate to be alone—to make sense of what he'd read—Makaias ascended the stairs two steps at a time. *Furthermore*—the word thrummed in his ears without pause. Withal. In addition to. Besides. Moreover. *Furthermore, it is the express wish of the King…*

Makaias burst into Britton's empty solar. *Enough!* he nearly shouted, falling to his knees, eyes lifted to the ceiling. *God, why? Why did he do it?*

Clenching his teeth, he addressed his absent friend aloud. "What were you thinking? Of all the half-witted, pig-headed, self-serving, meddling…"

Feeling the sudden prick from the Spirit, he dared not finish. Not when those selfsame words could apply to him. *And certainly did,* he admitted, groaning as he dropped his forehead to the stone, cold floor and began to pray. Soul flayed open, he exposed himself in a way he'd not done since before Joanna. The pain of her unfaithfulness had been something he wanted to forget, and the sin that had placed her beneath another man, something he'd not been able to truly forgive. And in not forgiving, he'd distanced himself from God. For despite all his prayers, self-righteous advice, and preaching, he'd grown numb, having chosen to go His own way, rather than asking God the way to go. His mother had seen this and tried to tell him—as did Britton, as did Andret…as did Velena.

Shamed by the extent of his hypocrisy, Makaias confessed to the Lord his every failure to trust Him for his future, until he felt spent to his core. It seemed an eternity, but when he finally lifted his head, it was with having experienced a renewed state of communion with his Lord. Humbled, he quoted aloud a portion from the Psalms. " 'Rest in the Lord and wait patiently for Him; do not fret because of him….' " Or in his case, *her,* he thought. " 'who prospers in his way, because of the man who carries out wicked schemes.' " Joanna's schemes had put a fear in him that was both sinful and unfounded. But the Lord said, "do not fret," so no longer would he do so. Furthermore…

Like a splash of cold water, that one word brought him back to why he'd come to pray in the first place. *Furthermore, it is the express wish of the King…*

Realizing there was still time to catch up to Britton, Makaias rose quickly to his feet, making rapid strides for the stables. In his haste to get underway, he brushed aside the help of a page in order to saddle his own horse, doubting his resolve only once upon seeing Velena and Tristan at a distance, arm in arm. Closing his eyes, he prayed he wasn't too late to accept the honor that was supposed to be his.

…that Barron Makaias Mannering take to wife…

Digging in his spurs, he raced past the manor.

…one Lady Velena Ambrose, daughter of Sir Richard Ambrose, Baron of Landerhill.

acknowledgements

Words are inadequate to express just how happy I am to place *Take Me Furthermore* into your keeping. There were times that the wants and needs of my characters stumped me for months at a time, and yet I have loved writing this book from start to finish. The revelation of Daisy's secret was especially important, and I so wanted to give it the due attention it deserved. Stuart has been the kind of villain everyone loves to hate, and his fall from grace was more than a little anticipated...as well as the return of Tristan, I hope.

But just because he and Velena are back together again, doesn't mean the next book will be all sunshine and roses, as was made clear from the last chapter. And so I must beg your forgiveness for yet another cliffhanger, but I promise it will be my last. Keep a lookout for *The Lines Have Fallen*, the fifth and final addition, which will bring everything into its proper place.

The voices of Tristan and Velena—as well as Makaias, Gwenhavare, Daisy, and Rowan—are already loud in my head, waiting to express themselves on paper. And I can't wait!

Thank you to all my beta readers. I could not edit this book without you. Thank you to my family, who allows me the time to slip away into another world full of people. Thank you to Selah Press for putting your stamp of approval on my work and to Kayla for your continued help and support. Thank you to Christine for the beautiful cover and to Alisa for your talented artwork on the verse. I could not do this alone, nor would I want to.

Most of all, I am grateful to the Lord for the chance to do what I love...and for His giving me the desire to do it in the first place.

connect with venessa

To connect with Venessa through comment or question, visit her at Facebook.com/Venessaknizley where you can receive updates on her next book or email her at venessa.knizley.com. She's also active on YouTube, creating content full of book reviews, writing helps, and author interviews. Please show your support by liking and subscribing. And of course, watching.

As always, if you enjoyed this book, let her know by leaving a review on Amazon and Goodreads. She looks forward to your feedback.

www.ingramcontent.com/pod-product-compliance
Lightning Source LLC
Chambersburg PA
CBHW071140170626

46809CB00002B/705